"Do you have a man in your life, Sweet Cheeks?"

A man? She shook her head and swallowed hard, past the clog in her chest. She fought an urge to turn her face into his hand and kiss his warm palm. "I don't date," she managed.

"That's what I thought."

He smelled good. Like the last time she'd been this close. Like mountain air and man. Whoa. Wait. What? How did he know she didn't date? Did she look like a loner?

He dropped his hand and moved closer. Closer until the tips of her breasts touched the front of his shirt. "You look like a woman who needs to date." *What did that look like?* She stood completely still as he told her, "You look like a woman who needs to date and with a man who knows how." He lowered his gaze to her mouth. He wasn't touching her, but it felt like it. "You look like you need a man to date you all night long."

By Rachel Gibson

WHAT I LOVE ABOUT YOU
BLUE BY YOU
RUN TO YOU
CRAZY ON YOU
RESCUE ME
ANY MAN OF MINE
NOTHING BUT TROUBLE
TRUE LOVE AND OTHER DISASTERS
NOT ANOTHER BAD DATE
TANGLED UP IN YOU
I'M IN NO MOOD FOR LOVE
SEX, LIES, AND ONLINE DATING
THE TROUBLE WITH VALENTINE'S DAY
DAISY'S BACK IN TOWN
SEE JANE SCORE
LOLA CARLYLE REVEALS ALL
TRUE CONFESSIONS
IT MUST BE LOVE
TRULY MADLY YOURS
SIMPLY IRRESISTIBLE

Coming Soon

I DO!

RACHEL GIBSON

WHAT I LOVE ABOUT YOU

AVON

An Imprint of HarperCollinsPublishers

AVON BOOKS
An Imprint of HarperCollins*Publishers*
195 Broadway
New York, New York 10007

Copyright © 2014 by Rachel Gibson
Excerpt from *I Do!* copyright © 2014 by Rachel Gibson
ISBN 978-0-06-224739-1
www.avonromance.com

First Avon Books mass market printing: September 2014

Avon Trademark Reg. U.S. Pat. Off. and in Other Countries, Marca Registrada, Hecho en U.S.A.
HarperCollins® is a registered trademark of HarperCollins Publishers.

Printed in the U.S.A.

10 9 8 7 6 5 4 3 2 1

To the real Bow Tie.
I love you bigger than the mountains.

Chapter One

It's just us. Grab me by the neck and swallow me whole.

Blake Junger wrapped his hands around the thick arms of the Adirondack chair and pushed farther against the back. Desire twisted his stomach, and his muscles hardened. He let out a slow, ragged breath and turned his gaze to the smooth lake. Spiky pine and ponderosa threw jagged shade across his lawn, the wet sandy beach, and the wooden dock floating on the emerald lake. The tops of the trees swayed in an unusually warm October breeze, and the scent of pine forest filled his nose, so strong he could almost taste it. "You're living in God's country now," his realtor had told him when he'd moved into the house in Truly, Idaho, a little over a week ago. The home was four thousand square feet of beautifully crafted wood, its floor-to-ceiling windows reflecting the emerald lake, the deeper green forest, and the brilliant blue sky. It sat on the edge of a small development of homes and had five acres of dense forest on the undeveloped side.

He'd needed a place. A lair. A place to invest a pile of money with good tax benefits. He'd seen this multimillion-dollar property on a Realtor's site, and he'd called and made an offer from his mother's pool deck in Tampa.

He'd trained for high-altitude winter warfare in some of the most frozen and rugged places in the country, one of his favorites being the Idaho Sawtooth mountain range. Blake could live anywhere in the county, but he'd chosen this property on the edge of the wilderness for two reasons: (1) the tax write-offs, and (2) the solitude. The fact that it had a lake in the backyard had sealed the deal.

His parents thought he'd been impulsive. His brother understood. If Truly didn't prove to be an anchor, he would untether and move on.

What I Love About You

You want me.

Want and need. Love and hate clogged his chest and dry throat, and he swallowed past the urge to give in. To just say fuck it and give up. He might be living in God's country, but God wasn't paying much attention to Blake Junger these days.

No one will know.

Less than a handful of people even knew where he lived, and he liked it that way. From his time spent on rooftops in Iraq, he'd once lived with a fifty-thousand-dollar bounty placed on his head by Al-Qaeda. Blake was certain the bounty had expired years ago, but even if it hadn't, he wasn't worried about terrorists in Idaho. Hell, a lot of U.S. citizens thought Idaho was in the Midwest next to Iowa anyway. He was much more worried that his well-intentioned family would pop up and camp out in his living room. Watching to make sure he didn't fuck up and end up on his face somewhere.

I'll warm you up. Make you feel good.

Blake returned his gaze to a bottle sitting on the wood cable spool a few feet from his left foot. Sunlight touched the neck and shone through the amber liquid inside. Johnnie Walker. His best friend. The constant that never changed. The one thing in the world he could count on. The hot splash in his mouth. The kick and punch to his throat and stomach. The warmth spreading across his flesh and the buzz in his head. He loved it. Loved it more than friends and family. More than his job and latest mission. More than women and sex. He'd given up a lot for Johnnie. Then Johnnie had gone and turned on him. Johnnie was a big lie.

I'm not the enemy.

Blake had faced enemies before. In Iraq, Afghanistan, Africa, and too many shithole countries to count. He'd faced and conquered those enemies. He had a footlocker full of medals and commendations. He'd been shot twice, had screws in his knee, and had fractured his feet and ankles more times than he could recall. He'd served his country without regret or remorse. When he retired from the battlefield, he thought he'd left the enemy behind. Thought he was done fighting, but he was wrong. This enemy was deeper and darker than any he had faced before.

You can stop after one drink.

4

What I Love About You

It whispered lies and plagued his waking hours. It lived in his soul. It had a bounty on his life. A bounty he couldn't ignore. There was no getting away from it. No leave. No passes. No stand-down time. No hiding in the dark as it passed him by. No dialing in his scope to take it out. Like the enemies he'd faced on the battle-field, if he did not defeat it, he would die. No doubt about it, but the problem was, he craved the taste of this particular death in his mouth.

You don't have a problem.

Out of all the things that had been hammered into his head at the fancy rehab his brother had forced him into, one of the things he did believe was that if he did not stop, he would lose his life. He'd been through too much to be taken out by a bottle of Johnnie. Too much to let his addiction win.

The craving rolled through him and he set his jaw against it. His addiction doctors and coun-selors had preached avoidance, but that wasn't Blake's way. He didn't avoid demons. He faced them head-on. He didn't need a twelve-step program or daily meetings. He was not power-less over his addiction. He was Special Warfare

Operator First Class Blake Junger. Retired from SEAL Team Six, and one of the deadliest snipers in the history of warfare. That wasn't a brag, just a fact. To admit he was powerless would be admitting defeat. There was no quit, no giving up. Those words were not in a Junger's vocabulary. Not in his or his twin brother, Beau's. They'd been raised to win. To push themselves and each other. To be the best at everything. To follow in the famous footsteps of their father, Captain William T. Junger, a legend in the SEAL teams. The old man had earned a tough reputation in Vietnam and Grenada and countless other clandestine engagements. He was a tough warrior, loyal to the teams and his country, and he expected his sons to follow. Blake had done what had been expected of him while Beau had signed with the Marine Corps just to spite the old man.

At the time, Blake had been pissed at his brother. All their lives they'd talked about serving in the teams together, but Beau had stormed off and joined the jarheads. In hindsight, it was a blessing that they'd served in different branches.

They were monozygotic twins, had split from the same egg, and were so alike they could pass one for the other. They were not different sides of the same coin. They were identical sides, and it was no surprise that each had signed up for sniper school in their respective branches. No surprise that each earned a reputation for his accuracy and lethal shots, but when it came to numbers, Blake had more confirmed kills.

The brothers had always been competitive. Their mother claimed that even in the womb they'd fought each other for more room. At the age of five, Beau had been the faster swimmer, had won blue ribbons while Blake had won red. Second place spurred Blake on to work harder, and the next year the two traded places on the winner's podium. In high school, if Blake won more wrestling matches one season, his brother worked to win more the next, and because they were identical twins, people compared the two in more than looks. Beau was the smart one. Blake was the strong one. Beau ran faster. Blake was the charming one. A day later, the script would flip and Blake would be smarter and faster. But no matter how many times the comparisons spun in opposite directions, Blake had always been the more charming twin. Even Beau conceded that win.

If they'd both been SEALs, people would have just naturally compared their service. They would have compared numbers and missions and ranks. While the brothers were extremely proud of their service, and the American lives they'd saved with their deadly shots, a man's death, even that of an insurgent hell-bent on killing Americans, just wasn't something they felt the need to compete over. Neither had crouched in the shadows of a shithole hut or rocky crag, alternately sweating like whores in church or freezing his nuts off, thinking he needed to compete. Both knew that numbers were more a matter of opportunity than skill, although neither would ever confess that out loud.

Since Beau's retirement from the Marines, he'd started a personal security company. Beau was the successful one. The settled one. The one getting married. Beau was the one who'd used his skills to create opportunity for fellow retired military personnel.

And Blake was the drunk. Since his retirement from the Navy a year ago, he was the one who'd used his skills to make money as a hired gun. He worked for a private military security firm, and he was the one who'd hopped from hot spot to hostage situation. From country to open seas, living a seemly unsettled life.

And Blake was the one who'd needed rehab to face his biggest demon. Like all enemies, he'd faced it head-on, only to discover that the consequence of sobriety was that at any moment, a flash or smell or sound could spin his clear and sober head around. That a flash in sunlight, or the smell of dust and sweat, or a high-pitched whistle could crawl up his spine and stop him in his tracks. Could make him drop and look for something that wasn't there. The flashbacks didn't happen often and didn't last more than a few seconds, but they always left him disoriented and edgy. Angry at his loss of control.

He looked at the bottle of Johnnie. At the blue and gold label and sun filtering through the rare scotch whisky. He'd paid three hundred dollars for the bottle of booze, and he craved it in the pit of his stomach. It tugged and pulled at his insides, and the sharp edge of need cut across his skin.

One drink. Calm the craving. Dull the sharp edges.

Blake's knuckle popped as he tightened his grasp on the chair.

Just one more. You can stop tomorrow.

The craving grew stronger, pinching his skull. Wasn't day sixty-two supposed to be easier than day one? His stomach rolled and his ears buzzed in his head. He picked up the camera by his hip and stood. He wrapped the black and yellow strap around his forearm and pointed his Nikon SLR at Johnnie. Six months ago, he'd stared down the scope of a bolt-action TAC–338 in Mexico City with two corrupt Mexican police officers sharing his crosshairs. These days, he shot his enemy with a camera. He looked through the viewfinder and dialed up the bottle. His hands shook and he tightened his grasp.

"What are you doing?"

Blake spun around and almost dropped the camera. "Holy fuck!" A little girl in a pink shirt and long blond ponytail stood behind his chair. "Where in the hell did you come from?" He'd lost his touch if a little kid could sneak up on him.

With her thumb she pointed next door. "You said two bad words."

He scrubbed his face with one hand and lowered the camera by the strap to his chair. She'd scared the shit out of him, and that wasn't easy to do. "And you're trespassing."

She scrunched up her nose. "What's that mean?"

He'd never been around kids and couldn't even guess her age. She was about as tall as his navel and had big blue eyes. "Trespass?"

"Yeah."

"It means you're in my yard."

"I know it's your yard." She actually rolled those blue eyes at him. "I saw you move in."

A five-foot stretch of pine and underbrush separated the two properties, and he glanced at the neighboring yard through the trees. The woman living there was working in the flower garden that she had managed to scratch out of the forest. Ass-up in pink and purple flowers, her shorts rode up just high enough to show the naked curve of her butt. He'd noticed her before today. He might be a drunk, white-knuckling sixty-two days' sobriety, but he was still a man. A man who appreciated a nice ass pointed his way. He'd never seen the woman's face. Just the back of her blond head and her sweet butt cheeks.

"What's your name?"

He turned his attention back toward the child and wondered if he should feel guilty for having sexual thoughts about the kid's mama. "Blake." He didn't feel guilty. He just wondered if he *should* feel guilty. "Is that your mom?"

"Yeah. She's not at the store today."

He couldn't recall hearing a man's voice coming from next door as he'd studied the mom's butt. "Where's your dad?"

"He doesn't live with us." She swung her arms from side to side. "I don't like bees."

He frowned down at the little squid in front of him. He didn't know what bees had to do with anything, but after sixty-two days, nausea rolled through him like it was the first. He felt like he might puke and dropped his shaking hands to his hips.

"You're weally weally big."

He was a little over six foot and weighed two-twenty. In the past few months he'd dropped twenty pounds. One of the last times he'd seen his twin, his brother had called Blake "a pudgy fucker." They'd been slugging it out at the time. Arguing over who was the better shot and the toughest superhero, Batman or Superman. Beau had been wrong about Superman but right about the fat. After Blake had retired from the teams, he'd had time to kill between security jobs. He'd stopped working out as much and started drinking more. "How old are you, kid?"

"Five." Her arms fell to her side and she tossed her head. "I'm not a kid."

Behind him Johnnie whispered, *I'm still here. Waiting*. Blake ignored the whisper. He needed to jog or swim. He needed to wear himself out, but that didn't mean he'd quit and let Johnnie win. No, a warrior knew when to withdraw and come back hard.

"I'm a hoss."

Blake moved his head from side to side as the pain in his skull thumped his brain. "What the hell's a hoss?"

She rolled her eyes again like he was a bit slow. "A hhhooooosssss."

Blake spoke perfect English, broken Arabic, and fluent split-fucking-infinitive. He'd never heard of a hoss.

"My name is Bow Tie."

"Bow Tie?" What the hell kind of name was that?

"I have yellow hair with white spots." She tossed her head again and stomped one foot. "I have a white mane and tail. I'm fancy."

"Are you saying 'horse'?" Jesus. She was turning the ache in his head to a stabbing pain. "You're a horse?"

"Yes, and I'm weally fast. Do you want to see me race?"

He'd never been around kids. He didn't even know if he liked kids. He was fairly sure he didn't like this kid. She thought she was a "hoss," couldn't say some of her R's, and looked at him like *he* was slow in the head. "Negative. You should go home now."

"No. I can stay."

"You've been here long enough now. Your mother is probably wondering where you are."

"My mom won't mind." She stomped the ground with one sandaled foot, then took off. She ran in a big circle around Blake. She actually galloped around and around. And God help him, with her head bobbing and her ponytail flying behind her, she kind of resembled a little pony.

Around and around she ran, stopping a few times to paw at the air and neigh. "Hey kid," he called to her, but she just tossed her head and kept going. The pull of Johnnie rode him hard and irritation broke out across his skin. He had better things to do than stand there as a weird little girl acted like a horse. Better things, like go for a jog or swim or poke himself in the eye with a stick. "Time to go home." She pretended not to hear him. What did she call herself? "Stop, Bow Tie!"

"Say whoa, girl," she managed between rapid breaths.

He didn't take orders from children. He was an adult. He wanted to tear out his hair. Christ almighty. "Shit."

Around she ran, her pale cheeks turning pink. "That was a bad word."

Blake frowned. "Whoa, girl."

She finally stopped directly in front of him and blew out a breath. "I went weally fast."

"You need to run home."

"That's okay. I can play for . . ." She paused before adding, "Five moe minutes."

He'd lived in a dirt hole and crawled through swamps. He'd eaten bugs and pissed in Gatorade bottles. For twenty years, his life had consisted of hard, rough edges. When he'd retired from the teams, he'd had to make a deliberate effort to keep the F-word out of every sentence and his hand off his nuts. He'd had to remember that in civilian life, creative swearing wasn't a competitive sport and that ball scratching wasn't a public event. He had to remember the manners his mother had pounded into his and Beau's heads. Nice, polite behavior toward everyone from little kids to little old ladies. Today he wanted this kid gone before he ripped his skin off, and he chose not to remember those nice manners. He purposely narrowed his eyes and gave the kid the hard steel gaze that he'd used to make terrorists cower.

"What's wrong with your eyes?"

She didn't seem at all afraid. She was definitely a little slow in the head. Another time he might have taken that into consideration. "Get your ass in your own yard."

She gasped. "You said a bad word."

"Go home, little girl."

She pointed at the cat on the front of her T-shirt. "I'm a big girl!"

Another day, another time, he might have admired the kid's guts. He leaned forward and towered over her like his father used to do to him and Beau. "I *shit* bigger than you," he said, just like his old man.

The kid sucked in a scandalized breath but wasn't intimidated at all. She wasn't shaking in her little shoes. Was there something wrong with the kid, besides her thinking she was a horse, or was he losing his touch?

"Charlotte?"

Blake and the kid spun toward the sound of a woman's voice. She stood a few feet away, wearing a little yellow T-shirt and those shorts he'd had the privilege of seeing from behind. The shadow of a big straw hat hid her face and rested just above the bow of her full lips. Pretty mouth, nice legs, great ass. Probably something wrong with her eyes.

"Mama!" The kid ran to her mother and threw herself on the woman's waist.

"You know you aren't supposed to leave the yard, Charlotte Elizabeth." The shade of her hat slid down her throat and T-shirt to her breasts as she looked down at her child. "You're in big trouble."

Nice-size breasts, smooth curve in her waist. Yeah, probably had funky eyes.

"That man is weally mean," the kid wailed. "He said bad words at me."

The sudden sobbing was so suspect he might have laughed if he was in a laughing mood. Behind him, Johnnie whispered his name, and in front, the shade of a straw hat rested on the top of a nice pair of breasts. The shadow dipped into her smooth cleavage, and lust plunged straight down Blake's pants. He went from irritation to desire to a combination of both in the blink of an eye.

The brim of the hat rose to the bow of her lip again. "I heard him." The corners of her mouth dipped in a disapproving frown.

His frown matched hers. He'd always avoided women like her. Women with children. Women with children were looking for daddies, and he'd never wanted kids. His or anyone else's.

"Please don't swear at my child."

"Please keep your child out of my yard." Women with children wanted men who wanted relationships. He wasn't a relationship kind of guy. Out of all the SEAL teams, Team Six had the highest divorce rate for a reason. It was filled with men who loved to throw themselves out of airplanes and get shot out of torpedo tubes. Filled with good men who weren't any good at relationships. Men like him, and until recently, like his brother. Men like his father, whose wives divorced them after twenty years of serial cheating.

"Fine." Her lips pursed like she was going to hit him or kiss him. Off the top of his head, he'd guess the former. "But what kind of man talks like that to a child?"

The kind who was white-knuckling his sixty-second day of sobriety. The kind who wanted to pour some Johnnie down his throat, say fuck it, and dive face-first into soft cleavage. "What kind of mother lets her child roam around unsupervised?"

She gasped. "She was supervised."

"Uh-huh." He'd made her mad. Good. Now maybe she'd leave. Leave him to his fight with Johnnie and himself.

"Charlotte knows better than to leave our yard."

He pointed out the obvious. "This isn't your yard."

"She's never run off before."

He couldn't see her eyes, but he could feel her angry gaze. All hot and fiery. He liked hot and fiery. He liked it riding him like a banshee. Wild, screaming his name, and . . . Christ. His lust for Johnnie and this nameless woman made him dizzy. "Only takes once for her to get hit by a truck," he heard himself say between clenched teeth. "I had a dog that only got out once. Bucky ended up as axle grease for a Chevy Silverado." He shook his head. God, he'd loved that poodle. "He'd been a damn good dog, too."

Her pink mouth opened and closed like she was speechless. Then she waved a hand at the bottle of Johnnie and obviously found her voice. "Are you drunk?"

"No. Haven't had a drop." He wished he could blame his erection on Johnnie.

"Then you don't have an excuse. You're just a . . . a . . ." She paused to cover the girl's ears with her palms. "A raging asshole."

She'd get no argument from him.

"I heard that," the kid said into her mother's stomach.

"Come on, Charlotte." She grabbed the kid's hand and stormed off. He could practically see the steam shooting out of her ears.

So much for being the charming twin.

He shrugged, and his gaze fell to her nice butt.

Fuck it. Charming was for nice guys, and he hadn't felt nice for a very long time.

Chapter Two

Natalie Cooper had been raised to believe that a woman was more than a pretty face. More than good hair and a flair for picking out shoes. Her mother and grandmother had preached the need for a good head beneath that hair and the importance of having her feet planted in reality. Above all, the two divorced women had pounded the pulpit about the importance of a woman having her own money. Too make it and stash it for when that no-good bastard of a husband ran off with a younger version.

Too bad Natalie hadn't listened. She'd loved glitter crowns and pink boas. Her hair rolled on big curlers for bounce and body, and her feet in high heels or jeweled sandals. She'd loved everything girly, but most of all, she'd loved Michael Cooper.

He and his family had moved to Truly when he'd been in the sixth grade, and he'd sat at the desk in front of her. She'd loved the cut of his dark hair across the back of his neck and his shoulders in his plaid shirts. He was the cutest boy she'd ever seen, and his dark brown eyes had melted her young heart.

If he noticed, he never let on until the tenth grade when he finally asked her out. He'd taken her to see *Titanic*, and she'd paid more attention to his arm next to hers than to the sinking ship. They spent the next day together and most every day after. He'd been the quarterback of the football team and she the head cheerleader. They'd been on the student council, heads of the debate team, and members of every royal court from tenth to twelfth grade. The coup de grâce came the winter of their senior year when they'd been chosen king and queen of the Truly Winter Festival.

The festival drew tourists from as far as five states away and was famous for such contests as tube racing, snowmobile jumping, ice sculpting, and the Truly Bachelor Auction.

Every year, a parade down Main Street kicked off the festival, and Natalie and Michael had sat atop their snowy thrones, waving to the crowd. She'd worn a white fur cape over a royal-blue velvet gown that perfectly matched her eyes. A big rhinestone crown sat within a mass of blond curls on her head. Michael had worn white, too, looking like a dark-haired Prince Charming.

After graduation that spring, she and Michael had married against her mother and grandmother's wishes. They'd had a beautiful ceremony in his parents' backyard, overlooking Angel Beach and Lake Mary.

She'd followed him to Boise and worked at a camera store in the mall to put him through Boise State University. They'd lived in a tiny student apartment and driven an old Volkswagen. There'd never been much money, but Natalie had never minded. She'd been raised by two women on limited incomes and was used to making her own fun and making do, but it had bothered Michael.

He didn't like "making do" and had always

promised that after he got his business degree, he'd work and put her through school. It took him six years to get his master's of finance degree, and by that time, Natalie was no longer interested in school.

Michael got a job at Langtree Capital, and he started out managing individual 401(k)s and smaller stock portfolios. Friends of his parents invested with their small-town-boy-done-good, and Michael quickly rose to higher-profile clients.

As Michael made more money, they bought a house and new cars and went on fabulous vacations. She loved her husband and he loved her. They had a nice home and great friends and a bright future. They had a wonderful life, but the one thing they didn't have was a family. They'd been married for seven years, together for nine. Natalie wanted children.

On the ninth anniversary of their first date to see *Titanic*, Natalie stopped taking her birth control pills. She expected to get pregnant immediately. When that didn't happen right away, she wasn't worried. She and Michael were young and healthy, but after a year and half of trying, she was referred to an infertility specialist. To her utter shock and dismay, she discovered that she had a hormone imbalance that kept her from ovulating. Other than light periods, she'd never had symptoms that anything was wrong.

For the next several years, she made it her mission to conceive. She took clomiphene, then graduated to Repronex. She took her temperature and ovulation tests, and Michael did his part. Always up for the task, so to speak, and every month that it didn't happen, she fell in to a dark funk that lasted several days.

Then, on Michael's twenty-eighth birthday, she took him to dinner at his favorite restaurant and surprised him with the news that she was six weeks' pregnant.

"I took four tests," she said, all wrapped up in the thrill and excitement and rattling on about baby names and nursery colors. It was really going to happen. Their dream was finally coming true, and it took her several moments to realize Michael hadn't said a word. He drank his Maker's Mark and flipped through messages on his BlackBerry.

"Is something wrong?"

He pressed a few more buttons on the phone and sipped his bourbon. "I didn't think it would happen."

"Me either!" She reached across the table and grabbed his hand. "I'd almost given up hope."

He looked up. "I'm happy for you."

Her heart paused and she slid her hand to her lap. "Don't you mean us?"

He smiled, but it didn't quite reach the brown eyes she'd loved for so many years. "Of course." She tried to tell herself that Michael didn't always show his feelings. Not like her. During the infertility roller coaster of the past few years, she'd been an emotional Ping-Pong ball and he'd been her rock. It was one of the things she loved about him.

That night they made love to each other for no other reason than that they were two people in love. Not because a pee stick indicated ovulation.

The next morning when she woke, Michael had already left for work, and she lounged around the house in a euphoric bubble. Her life was perfect, a warm, soft haven of two people in love and the miracle they'd created.

She stood in the middle of the guest bedroom

closest to the master, envisioning all the different ideas she had for a nursery, lambs and bunnies, or perhaps Winnie-the-Pooh. She called her mother and grandmother and Michael's parents. They'd all waited so long for the happy news and were as excited as Natalie. While she busied herself with laundry, she called her best friend since first grade, Delilah. Lilah didn't have children, claimed she never wanted any, but had been waiting for Natalie to make her a godmother.

"If it's a girl, I want to name her Charlotte after my great-grandmother."

"You always said you wanted to name your little girl Jerrica."

Natalie had laughed, not at all surprised that her friend remembered the old cartoon. "From Jem and the Holograms? We were ten." The doorbell rang as she set the laundry basket on the couch. She got off the phone and opened the door to stare into the dark glasses and badges of the Boise Police Department. They were looking for Michael, and her first thought was that something horrible had happened to her husband. That he'd been in an accident. But they had a warrant and searched her house. They asked her questions about money and Michael and accused her husband, the man she'd known for most of her life, the boy who'd sat in front of her in sixth grade, of embezzlement. Of underreporting profits and skimming money. They wanted to know about a trip she'd taken with Michael to the Cayman Islands. She told them about white sand and pale blue water. Turtles and iguanas and scuba diving. But they wanted to know about accounts in Cayman National Securities.

She tried to call Michael, so he could clear up the misunderstanding, but his phone was shut off. She couldn't get ahold of him that day or the next. She was interviewed and reinterviewed. She was interrogated and passed a lie detector test. Michael's disappearance made local then national news, with his picture and hers splashed across the television. A cameraman caught her walking into her doctor's appointment, her face pale while dark circles shadowed her eyes. She looked ready to jump out of her skin, exhausted and on edge and so terrified her husband was dead somewhere, and all anyone could talk about was money he'd supposedly embezzled.

Michael wouldn't do that. He wouldn't steal

people's money. Two of those people happened to be his own parents, and he would never leave Natalie to face it all alone. That wasn't Michael, but the only other souls on the planet who seemed to agree with her were his parents.

Ron and Carla Cooper came to stay with her that first week and the second. In the past, Natalie and Carla had butted heads sometimes. Carla Cooper was a woman who wanted things a certain way, and the older Natalie got, the more she resisted Carla's "suggestions." But in believing in Michael's innocence, they were united.

Natalie's mother and grandmother came down to Boise the third week, but Natalie did little but stand in her and Michael's closet, touching his clothes and smelling his old BSU hoodie. At night, she wore one of his T-shirts and slept on his pillow.

The government seized all banking and investment accounts. It wasn't until she learned from them that the accounts had been emptied the day before Michael's disappearance that she got the first pang of apprehension. As soon as she felt the twinge in the pit of her stomach, she dismissed it. She was exhausted and confused and scared. Michael had been missing for over two weeks now and her life had become one hellacious moment after another. She feared for him, and she feared that the stress would harm the tiny baby she'd fought to conceive.

For a solid month, she and Michael's parents heard nothing. Tortured by the silence and what-ifs, until the morning she sat at the kitchen table, trying to keep down a slice of toast. The lawyer the Coopers had hired called to inform her that Michael had been found in an El Paso hotel. Very much alive. For two beats her heart swelled in her chest. Michael was alive.

In the next two heartbeats her chest caved. Her whole life fell apart as the breaking news continued. He'd been found with several fake passports and driver's licenses. All under assumed names. How did a person even get one fake passport, let alone three? Worse, at least for her, he also had a twenty-year-old girlfriend, Tiffany.

Natalie would not have believed it if she hadn't seen him on the national news, cuffed and doing the perp walk into the El Paso County Jail, his dark hair longer than usual and a dark beard and mustache covering the lower half of his face.

Over and over she watched her handsome husband, head down, as he hurried past the cameras.

She found out over the next few days and weeks that he and Tiffany were waiting to slip into Mexico and then head for Switzerland. He'd planned it all out. The theft. The bank accounts. The new identities. The new twenty-year-old version of Natalie. He'd planned all that and she'd never known.

Years later, she could still recall that day he'd been apprehended. She recalled the half-eaten toast in her hand. The images on the television screen and the floor rushing up toward her. Sitting for hours and watching the news footage, chewing up her heart and spitting it out and unable to look away.

The summer after she and Michael got married, they'd left Truly. The football star and the cheerleader—off to live a golden life. The town had practically thrown a parade at their parting.

Ten years later, Natalie returned home alone and pregnant, her soon-to-be-former husband facing seven years in a federal prison. The government took everything. Her house. Her car. Her jewelry. Her life. She returned heartbroken, humiliated, and penniless. She had nothing but a suitcase in one hand and a camera in the other. In her head she had a whole notebook of questions.

Questions like when had her life gone so wrong? Had she been so wrapped up in creating a miracle baby that she hadn't noticed the changes in her husband? Had the changes started with little things? Like his preference for bourbon rather than beer. When had the small-town boy turned into a man who would steal from corporations and old people without discrimination or conscience? When had he become a liar and a cheater? When had he stopped loving her?

The answers came in a phone call a year after Michael had been sentenced. It had been the first time she'd heard his voice since the trial.

"You're boring," he'd said.

At the time, those two words had crushed her. Now at the age of thirty-three she was older and wiser and wished for some boredom in her life. She was a single mother of her miracle child. The owner of Glamour Snaps and Prints, a photography studio and digital photo print shop. Her life was very busy. Her life was good, but late at night, when the house was quiet and Charlotte was in bed, she sometimes wondered if she'd ever really known Michael at all.

"I told her she was too mature for the smoky eye."

Natalie placed her elbows on the front counter and her face in her hands. She frowned at the prints of eighty-year-old Mabel Vaughn. "She looks like someone punched her," she told her best friend, Lilah Markham. The two women stood in Glamour Snaps and Prints, located on Main and Second streets, wearing identical scowls, but that was where any similarities ended. Natalie was five-feet-seven. Lilah, five-one. Natalie wore black pants and ballet flats and a white blouse with the name of her business embroidered on the breast pocket. Her blond ponytail was held at the back of her head with a simple black band. She wore mascara and coral lip gloss, and a single silver ring circled the middle finger of her right hand.

Currently, Lilah wore a short leather dress and leather boots with five-inch heels. Perfectly applied gray and purple shadowed her brown eyes. Her red hair was buzzed on the sides and she had white spiky bangs. Anyone else might run the risk of looking ridiculous, but only someone with Lilah's style could pull off the dominatrix-iguana look in conservative Truly.

"She kept shaking her bony finger and yelling, 'More smoky eye.'" Lilah was a talented cosmetologist who worked at the Cutting Edge salon across the street and moonlighted as a makeup artist. When Natalie booked a glamour shot, she always sent the customer to Lilah first. Not only because Lilah was her best friend, but because Lilah had worked for several Hollywood stylists with long lists of celebrity clients. She'd worked in Los Angeles for the rich and famous for over ten years, and if not for an unfortunate incident involving a starlet, a strapless Alexander McQueen gown, and a pair of scissors, Lilah would no doubt still be in Hollywood with her own celebrity list. "She wouldn't listen to me," Lilah added.

Natalie knew what her friend meant. Working with Mabel and all her demands had been a test of her patience, but at least she'd talked the woman out of posing completely naked on top of her floor-length mink coat.

"Fred's going to take one look at these and stroke out."

"Maybe that's the idea. It's the perfect crime." Natalie had known Mabel most of her life. Mabel had been friends with Natalie's grandmother Joan, until Joan's death two years ago. Grandmother Richards had always said Mabel was a character, which meant she was opinionated and bossy and the best snoop in Valley County. As a kid, Natalie had hid behind her grandmother's sofa and listened to such juicy gossip as the questionable paternity of the Porters' latest grandbaby or who in town was drinking like a lake trout.

A dull ache stabbed between Natalie's eyes as she gazed at the boudoir shots Mabel had taken for her ninety-year-old husband, Fred. "I hope she's happy with these." If not, Natalie would have to reshoot them, but the thought of Mabel dressing up in corsets and kitten heels again caused the stab in her head to sink further into her brain. It wasn't just that Mabel was a difficult woman and customer, she had bad taste. And a customer's bad taste reflected poorly on Natalie's business.

"What's she wearing on her feet?" Lilah asked as she scrunched up her pretty face.

"My fifty-dollar kitten heels that I had to cut

up and tape back together so they'd fit her. She said she was retaining water, but that woman has the biggest feet I've ever seen."

Lilah leaned in for a closer look. "They look like Nutty Professor feet."

Natalie carefully gathered up the photographs and slid them into a photo envelope. "When I was pregnant, I had Nutty Professor feet." Behind her, the commercial printer cranked out pictures and fed them into slots. The hum and whirr was money to Natalie's ears.

"When you were pregnant, you had the Nutty Professor everything."

And it had taken a year to get back to her normal one hundred and twenty pounds. Okay, one hundred and twenty-five. Most of the time. "I had water weight."

"You gained Reese's Peanut Butter Cup weight."

"And macaroons." She picked up the photo envelope and moved to her office a few feet away. Two years ago, she'd taken out a loan for the used digital printer. Just as with brick and mortar stores like Walgreens or CVS, or online photo sites like Shutterfly or Snapfish, anyone with Internet access could upload photos to the Glamour Snaps and

Prints Web site. Customers could order regular prints or special order their pictures on anything from birthday cards and magazines to catalogues and canvas panels. "One hour or it's free" was her slogan for residents of Truly.

She charged ten cents a print for four-by-six pictures and more for larger sizes. Between her digital print business and her own photography, she made a fairly good living. She wasn't rich, but she supported herself and Charlotte.

She tossed Mabel's photos on her desk and turned to Lilah, who'd followed. "The Olson triplets are coming in tomorrow. Their mother wants harvest-themed photos." Natalie had a pumpkin patch and weathered barn backdrop that would work, but she'd have to drag in a bale of hay and some leaves to stage the studio in back. "I'm thinking it would be better to meet them in Shaw Park instead of shooting studio photos here." The Olson boys were five and notorious for naughty behavior. Rather than try to control her hyper sons, Shanna Olson had given up and given in years ago.

Lilah shook her head. "Shanna took fertility drugs like you. Think about it."

She had, and every time she was in a grocery

store and heard a case of soda hit the floor and Shanna's tired voice say, "Peter, Paul, Patrick. Get down from there," she thanked God she hadn't conceived triplets.

Lilah leaned one shoulder into the door frame. "What's come in lately?"

Natalie didn't have to ask what her friend was talking about. "It's unethical for me to discuss a customer's personal photos that I may or may not have inspected for quality assurance."

"Save it for your customers who inexplicably send you their private pictures and just as inexplicably believe that you don't look at them." Lilah held up one hand and motioned for Natalie to bring it on. "Spill it."

"I shouldn't." She bit the corner of her lower lip.

"Don't pretend you can keep a secret."

"I can!"

"No you can't." Lilah tilted her head to one side. "You tell everyone what their present is before you give it to them."

"I haven't done that in a long time." She could keep a secret. No problem. No sweat. Not a big deal. "Frankie Cornell has a massive penis," she said really fast and perhaps a little loud as if it burst uncontrollably from her lips.

"Seriously? The Frankie we went to school with?"

She nodded and put a hand on her chest. "Scary huge." God strike her down, but she felt better now that it was out. Like a pressure cooker after it let out a little steam.

"The short little guy who ate a tuna fish sandwich every day?"

"Yeah. When he picked up his prints yesterday, I couldn't look him in the eyes but I was afraid to look down." She dropped her hand and let out a breath. "It was a problem."

"What did it look like?"

"Ugly." She shuddered. "Like an angry mutant."

Lilah laughed. "There must have been something in that tuna his mom packed in his lunch. Probably chromium."

"I doubt chromium gave him monster junk, Erin Brockovich."

"Did you make copies?"

"That's illegal and unethical." She moved past her friend toward the digital printer. "And believe me, I never want to see that enormous penis again." Just the thought made her cringe. "I'm still traumatized."

The bell sitting on the front counter rang once, and Natalie spun around as Lilah stuck her head out of the office. Both women froze as they stared at the man on the other side of the counter. A black short-sleeve shirt clung to his big biceps and bigger shoulders and the defined muscles of his chest. It was the kind of shirt that joggers wore when they ran twenty miles, then stopped to lift a few cars. The kind only a supremely confident man would dare wear in public.

She raised her gaze up his thick neck and square chin. Past the fine definition of his lips and nose to his eyes. Gray. Steel. Stormy. Everything that was hard and cold. Just like she remembered from yesterday, and if he wasn't the biggest a-hole on the planet, she might think he was handsome. With his short blond hair and strong chin and jaw, he could pass for an action hero in a Hollywood blockbuster. Thor. G.I. Joe. Captain America. Magic Mike. And yes, she knew that Magic Mike wasn't an action hero movie, but it had the kind of action that reminded her of this man. The hot and sweaty, bump and grinding kind of action that turned a sensible woman senseless.

Heat flushed her chest and she turned her

attention to Lilah, who looked like she'd been turned to salt for staring at Sodom. When it came to good-looking men, Lilah wasn't sensible and was prone to sins of biblical proportions, and ever since Lilah read *Fifty Shades of Grey*, she overshared the details of her kinky sex life.

Natalie turned her attention to her neighbor and his hard eyes staring into hers. She had bigger concerns right now than Lilah and her Ben Wa balls. More pressing questions, like why her neighbor was in her place of business after yesterday's unpleasant encounter. And more importantly, just how much of her and Lilah's conversation had he overheard?

She licked her dry lips and pushed up the corners into her best business smile. "Can I help you?"

"I need to pick up my prints." He glanced up at the red and pink banner tacked to the ceiling above his head. "This is Glamour Snaps and Prints?" He returned his gaze to hers. Cold. Stony. No humor or hint that he might have overheard her and Lilah's discussion of Frankie's mammoth wiener.

"Yes." She moved to the front counter and looked across at him. "Your name?"

"Blake Junger."

He'd lived next to her for over a week now, but she hadn't met him until yesterday. Hadn't known his name, neither first nor last, but neither suited her image of him. Both sounded a little too nice for a guy who swore at little girls. Too soft for a guy so hard. She pulled open the big drawer beneath the counter and searched the Y file folder. This guy looked more suited to a name like Rock Stone. Or Buck Knife. Or Raging Asshole.

"J," he said. "Junger with a J."

She glanced up as she shut the drawer and moved a few feet to her right. *Junger with a J.* She remembered prints from Junger with a J. He'd ordered them online last night and Natalie had placed them in a print wallet and order envelope this morning. She wondered why she hadn't noticed the address. She opened another drawer and flipped past Jackson, Jensen, and Jones to Junger. She pulled out the envelope with her logo printed on the front and reached inside for the paper photo wallet. He'd paid with a Visa and given a local P.O. box as his mailing address. That's why she hadn't connected him to his photos.

"Please look these over carefully before you take them." Thinking about it now though, she should have recognized his bottle of Johnnie Walker.

He opened the paper flap and quickly fanned through his pictures.

Usually she tried to sell frames, photo books, and other services. Or at the very least, a greeting card from the row behind him. The longer she could get a customer to stay in her shop, the more money he was likely to spend. Not this time. Not with this man. She hated to admit it, but he rattled her nerves. Everything about him was just . . . too. He was too big. Too handsome. His presence was too dominant to ignore. He was too big a jerk, too.

He closed the flap. "They look fine."

"Great." She reached into a drawer beneath the cash register and pulled out a customer loyalty card. "Every fifth order is half price and every tenth is free." She punched a hole in the first square and handed it to him. His knuckles brushed hers, predictably rough, surprisingly warm. She looked up into his cold gray eyes staring back at her, and she pulled her hand away first. "Thanks for your business, Mr. Junger."

This time, she slid the order envelope and receipt across the counter toward him.

"It's Blake." He flashed such a perfect white smile, she could practically see a silver glint on his perfect incisor. "Your raging asshole neighbor."

Natalie raised a brow. "Yes. I remember you."

"No one's ever called me a raging asshole."

"Maybe not to your face."

He chuckled, a warm sound deep in his chest, and Natalie was saved from a response by Lilah, who had apparently recovered from getting turned into a salt statue. "Delilah Markham." She shoved her hand toward the neighbor. "Everyone calls me Lilah."

"It's a pleasure, Lilah. Everyone calls me Blake." He shook her hand and glanced at Natalie. "Well, almost everyone." One corner of his perfect smile lifted a little higher. "I like your hair." Natalie could practically feel Lilah melt into a puddle at her feet, and she wondered what was up with the Mr. Nice Guy act. "And leather. I appreciate a woman in leather."

"Thank you."

He took his hand back and shoved his photos

and punch card into the order envelope. "Good day, ladies."

"See you around, Blake."

Hope I don't see you around. "Mr. Junger."

The two women watched him leave, the back of his wide shoulders tapering to his waist and the zippered back pockets of his black running pants.

"Oh. My. God," Lilah managed as soon as the door shut behind Blake. "Pinch me. That man is gorgeous."

"Do you think he heard us talking about Frankie's junk?"

"Who cares?" Lilah pointed toward the door. "Did you *see* him?"

"I care. I'm a business owner." Natalie put a hand on the front of her white blouse. "Discussing a customer's private photos with another customer is unethical."

Lilah waved her concern away. "Did you see his chest? Like someone painted him with edible chocolate fondue. All dark and yummy and I just wanted a bite."

"Edible chocolate fondue?" She didn't even want to know what Lilah did with edible fondue.

"Please"—she grabbed Natalie's arm—"please tell me that man took pictures of his junk and that you made copies!"

"Sorry." Natalie chuckled. "No junk photos."

Lilah looked like she might cry and dropped her hand. "What were his pictures of?"

"Mostly Johnnie Walker and a few snapshots of some wildflowers." And lots of the lake. Even though it killed her to admit it, his photos were pretty good. Nice color and lighting. Even the shots of his whisky bottle had interesting depth.

"That's it?"

"Yeah."

"Flowers and booze? Is he a drinker or gay?" A frown creased her perfectly plucked brows. "Or is he a big gay drinker?"

Natalie shrugged and moved to the cabinet a few feet from the big digital printer. "I really doubt he's gay," she said as she pulled out a large canvas bag. Big drinker? Maybe, but he didn't look like either.

"No. I didn't get the gay vibe from him, and I can always tell. Gay guys love me."

"Drag queens love you."

"I bet Blake Junger wouldn't mind if I painted him with chocolate fondue."

What I Love About You

Natalie had dated a few times when she'd first moved back to Truly. She'd even had a short relationship with Imanol Allegrezza, a handsome Basque man from a large Basque family in the area, but it hadn't worked out. She'd been a single mom working hard to support herself and her toddler. Manny had been a cheater. Cheating men seemed to be the story of her life.

"Or hot wax dripped on his privates," Lilah continued to dream.

"Ouch." Natalie cringed as she turned on the printer and clicked on a few icons.

"You're such a prude."

"No. I'm boring." She chuckled.

"You're not boring. Michael's an asshole." Lilah looked at her and frowned. "You just need to loosen up and get laid. If you don't use it, you'll lose it."

"Quit reading *Cosmo*."

"I don't need to read *Cosmo* to know that you have sexual shame and old-fashioned guilt. You can't let yourself have sex outside the societal views of a monogamous relationship."

"I don't have sexual shame." Probably a healthy dose of Baptist guilt though. "I can't run around with men. I'm a mom."

"Charlotte wouldn't know."

The one thing she missed about a relationship was the sex. She missed that a lot. "She probably wouldn't know if I stole a candy bar from Paul's Market, either, but I can't tell her not to steal if I do."

Lilah rolled her eyes. That's where Charlotte had learned it. "Blake Junger is probably married," she said on a sigh.

"I've never seen anyone over there." Natalie held the bag up and picked off a few strings.

"Where?"

"The neighbors." She picked off a few more threads. "Blake Junger lives in the Allegrezzas' old house next door."

"What?" Lilah grabbed the bag from her hands and turned Natalie to face her. "And you didn't tell me until right now?"

"I just met him yesterday, and I didn't even know his name until today." Natalie grabbed the bag back and held it clamped in a fist on her hip as she told Lilah about the meeting.

"He actually said his dog was turned into axle grease?" Lilah was a dog lover so that didn't go over well.

"Yes." Though that wasn't his biggest crime.

"Maybe you didn't hear me. He told Charlotte he shit bigger than her and made her cry." Lilah was Charlotte's godmother. Her very protective godmother. Sometimes a little too eager to rush into battle for Charlotte. This time Natalie wouldn't hold her back. "And he implied that I am a bad mother."

"That wasn't very nice. Really horrible." Lilah tapped a finger to her lips. "Maybe he was having a bad day."

"Maybe he's just a jerk." She turned to the printer and fit the canvas perfectly on the plate. "If he was ugly or had a handlebar mustache you wouldn't make an excuse for him."

Lilah's stepfather had once had a handlebar mustache, and that was reason enough to hate them. "I'm not making an excuse for the guy, but maybe he's lonely in that big house. I'm sure he needs a friend."

Natalie looked over her shoulder at Lilah. "He needs something." She frowned. "He needs a shovel to the side of his head."

Chapter Three

He needed to get laid.

Blake pulled his truck into the parking lot of Paul's Market and stopped in an empty space in the second row. In the pocket of his hooded jacket he had a short list of other things he needed. Regular things like soap and shaving cream, potatoes and apples. Those were some of the things he'd written down, but the list in his head had only one thing on it.

Get laid.

He needed to feel hot, naked skin against his. His hand on a warm, soft female. His mouth on her neck and belly and thighs. He needed intimacy in his bed. He needed to make love in the shower. He needed to fuck against the wall.

What I Love About You

Damn. He shut the door of his red Ford F–150 and moved across the lot. He passed a Jeep and a Suburban, and walked into the grocery store. What he needed was to stop thinking about his neighbor in his bed and his shower and against the wall.

The docs and counselors in rehab had preached abstinence, but Blake wasn't the kind of guy who went without. He didn't believe in abstinence for a man his age. He was thirty-nine and had only gone without sex when he'd been down range. He didn't like to go without. It made him itchy and antsy and preoccupied with the outline of a white bra beneath a white blouse, holding full breasts as nice as her perky ass.

It had been five days now since he'd walked into that print shop and seen Sweet Cheeks standing behind the counter. Five days since he'd seen all of her up close and personal, and all of Sweet Cheeks up close and personal was something worth seeing. She was beautiful. The kind of beautiful that turned heads and gave a man thoughts of undressing her for a better look. And there was nothing funky about her dark blue eyes.

It had been five days since he'd seen those big blue eyes wide and her pink mouth open as if he'd caught her at something. Something like discussing the picture of a guy's big dick. Maybe that was why he couldn't get her out of his head. If she wanted to see a big dick, he'd be happy to show her one in person.

A few of the locals stared as he yanked out a cart and headed for the produce aisle. To take his one-track mind off the neighbor and her soft mouth, he studied the area around him. On first glance, Paul's Market needed new weather mats, updated vinyl flooring, and a fresh coat of paint. Last summer, before his brother had hijacked him into rehab, Blake had spent most of June helping out his good friend and retired SEAL Vince restore an old convenience store in Texas. Vince had done a hell of a job on the demo, but he'd needed Blake's help with the restoration.

For the past fifteen years, Blake had been partners with his cousin Dale, flipping houses in Virginia Beach. It was something that he'd started as an investment and a hobby. When he wasn't on deployment, he'd enjoyed working with Dale, and by the time he retired from the teams, he had three Silver Stars and six Bronze with Valor, the Navy Cross, commendations and achievement medals from the Marines and Navy, and a contractor's license from the commonwealth of Virginia.

Blake grabbed a sack of oranges and set it in his cart. Compared to BUD/S or SERE or sniper school, the contractor's exam hadn't been difficult. Not like abstinence from alcohol. Or sex.

His brother Beau had gone without sex for eight months. On purpose. His twin said he wanted to wait until it meant something. Wanted to wait until sex was more than getting off with a faceless woman. Blake could respect that, but the brothers hadn't been virgins since they'd been fifteen. There was no putting that horse back in the barn, especially when that horse liked playing in the field.

He grabbed a sack of potatoes and dropped it in his cart. There'd been a time when he and his twin had grabbed a few weeks together between deployments or met up at bases in Bahrain or Okinawa or Italy or half a dozen other joint installations around the world. Anywhere there were beautiful women and bottles of liquor, the Junger boys were up for some drunken debauchery. There was even a rumor about the two of them picking up identical twins in a Hong Kong bar and spending three booze-fueled days swapping tail before hopping flights back to their platoons in Camp Fallujah and Kandahar, silent professionals returning to the job.

Blake tore a cellophane baggie off the spool and reached for a couple of deep red apples. They'd met the twins in Taiwan, and the only thing he and his brother had ever swapped were bicycles as kids. Their days of drunken debauchery were behind them now. Beau was engagement ring shopping for his little girlfriend and Blake was fresh out of rehab. Even Blake's hell-raising buddy Vince was getting married. That left Blake the odd man out. The last man standing. On his own to hook up with beautiful women. Not that he minded. He'd never needed a wingman, but bars were the easiest places to meet women who wanted the same thing he wanted. Problem was, he no longer hung out in bars and he'd moved to a small town.

He picked up several more apples and put them in his bag. In his thirty-nine years, he'd lived in fifteen different states, been stationed on every continent, and taken his leave in just about every country, and the one thing he knew for certain, there were always women who liked to get wild. Women in small towns were no different. He just needed to get out of his house and look around at what Truly had to offer.

"The Granny Smith are better than the Red Delicious."

Blake glanced over his right shoulder, and his gaze landed on a pile of gray puff. "Excuse me?"

"This time of year, the Granny Smith apples are better than the Red Delicious."

He turned and looked down into a pair of brown eyes creased with age and lined in black. She wore a green and brown plaid wool jacket and a bright yellow scarf. This wasn't exactly the wild woman he'd been thinking about, and he smiled at the irony.

"Are you an apple expert, ma'am?"

"I'm a member of Buy Idaho." She had a black walker with brakes on the grips and a basket hooked to the front. Her hand shook from age as she picked up a yellow apple and handed it to Blake. "These are grown in Emmett. The Red Delicious are shipped in from Washington. Local is always better." She looked into his cart. "I see you have Idaho potatoes in your cart."

"Of course," he said as if he'd actually paid attention.

"Good boy." She turned her attention to him and he almost laughed at being called a "boy." Red lipstick creased the lines in her lips and pink circles colored her sagging cheeks. "I'm Mabel Vaughn." She stuck out her hand. "You're the new fella in town."

"Blake Junger." Her thin skin was cool against his touch. "It's my pleasure to meet you, Ms. Vaughn."

"Call me Mabel." She might have blushed. He couldn't tell for the pink circles. "Roy Baldridge says you bought the Allegrezza house on Red Fox Road."

Roy had been Blake's Realtor. "Yes. It's beautiful out there."

She nodded as if to say, *Of course.* "Nick Allegrezza had to build a bigger house out at Angel Beach on account of having six kids. Five girls and one boy."

He didn't know what to say to that so he whistled like six kids was a lot.

"Roy says you're single. A big fella like you needs a woman to boss him around."

"Yes, ma'am." Who knew Roy gossiped like

an old lady in a knitting circle? "That's what my mother tells me every time I talk to her." His mother had become obsessed with Facebook and was stalking his old girlfriends in a desperate quest for grandkids. After he'd left rehab, he'd spent three weeks with her in Tampa. He loved his mom. She was the single most important female in his life, but he'd had to get away from the worry in her eyes when she looked at him, and the pressure to settle down like his brother.

Blake put his apples in the seat of the cart and reached for a bag of oranges. Fresh fruit was one of the things he'd missed most when he was deployed.

"You're neighbors with Natalie Cooper and her little girl." She followed beside Blake as he moved down the row, and he adjusted his stride to accommodate her. "That little Charlotte is a cute one."

Her name was Natalie Cooper. He liked Sweet Cheeks better.

"Poor Natalie." Mabel held a hand up to one side of her face as if she were about to impart a secret. "That husband of hers is getting out on parole soon."

He hooked a left down the personal goods aisle. Sweet Cheeks was married? To a guy in prison? If he was in a sewing circle like Roy, he'd ask a few questions, but that would mean he was interested. He wasn't. Curious maybe, but not enough to pry. He stopped the cart in front of the antiperspirants. It looked like he had three choices and he reached for the Old Spice Fresh Scent.

"Embezzlement and a passel of other charges," Mabel provided. "Even stole from his own parents' retirement."

He paused in the act of pulling the top off the antiperspirant, but didn't respond. He wondered if Natalie was involved and had testified against her husband to save her own sweet ass. Not that it was his business, but if he wanted information about the neighbor he could get it. Just because he was retired from the teams didn't mean he'd forgotten how to plug a name or two into a computer and get first account information.

"Everyone was so shocked." She continued to follow, and Blake paused to pick up some soap, shaving cream, and a pack of refills for his Gillette Fusion. "I remember when they were young. Folks in town thought they were perfect. Then Michael let all that high finance go to his head." She frowned. "The big city just corrupted him."

"New York?" He tossed the razors in his cart.

"Boise."

Boise? He chuckled and coughed in his fist. Boise was a nice-size town, but could never be mistaken for a big city.

She put a hand on his cart. "I forgot my grabber. Could you get me some of that pine tar soap? Fred loves pine tar soap."

Blake reached on the top shelf and handed it to her. "This one?"

"Yes. Thank you." She put it in the basket on her walker. "There were some people in town who took some satisfaction in Michael heading for the Mexican border and leaving Natalie behind to deal with everything." She paused and pointed to the toothpaste. "Can you get that Polident for me?"

He reached for the closest green box.

"No. The one with forty in it. It's cheaper."

Blake traded it for a different box and had the sneaking suspicion that Mabel had singled him out for more than gossip. The next few minutes confirmed his suspicions when she asked him for a four-pack of toilet paper.

"I'll pay extra for fluffy and absorbent," she told her "grabber."

Most men might have cringed at the knowledge that Mabel liked extra fluffy butt wipe, but after twenty deployments in Iraq and Afghanistan, and dozens of clandestine missions, Blake also appreciated extra fluffy and absorbent. It sure beat the hell out of a round hole in the ground and any kind of paper he carried in his chest gear.

In the cooking aisle, he tossed some coarse ground pepper in his cart and she brought up his neighbor once more. "Natalie comes from a long line of Richards women who've had bad luck with men. It's really unfortunate. Betty's husband left her for a waitress down in Homedale and Joan's ran off with that gal who drove the water truck for the firefighters back in '84, but no one figured Michael would ever run out on Natalie, especially when she was pregnant."

Blake moved down the aisle and tossed a bag of ground Starbucks into his cart. He reached inside the pocket of his hoodie and pulled out his list. He didn't suppose Mabel's gossip was just the random rambling of an old woman. Like choosing him for her human grabber, he was sure she had an ulterior motive.

"Can you hand me that nondairy creamer? Fred is lactose-intolerant."

"Regular or hazelnut?"

"Oh. Hazelnut is too fancy. Fred has to have regular." She took the creamer from Blake and put it in her basket. "Joan was a real good friend of mine before she passed. I could count on her for anything. She was smart, too, but she wasn't a looker, sorry to say. Betty neither," she continued. "That's why everyone was surprised when Natalie came out so pretty. Never went through an ugly spell, that girl. She was head cheerleader, prom queen, queen of the Winter Festival, too. Just gorgeous, and Michael ran out on her and broke her heart." She tsked and shook her head. "But she didn't let that ruin her life. She started that photo studio on Main and made a real success of herself. She took my portrait a few weeks ago and did a real good job. Fred loved my smoky eye."

Sweet Cheeks was a cheerleader? Blake smiled. Growing up, he'd had a ton of cheerleader fantasies. They'd been his favorite.

"A few years back, Betty retired from the Forest Service and moved up north with her sister Gloria and Jed. Now the three of them travel around the country in that fifth wheel. I don't think anything funny is goin' on. Not since Jed busted his hip, but Natalie doesn't have her mama around anymore. It's just her and Charlotte." Mabel sighed. "A woman like that needs a good man."

Blake lifted a brow. "Are you playing matchmaker?"

"Me? Heck no." Her eyes widened like she was innocent. "I was just talking to pass the time."

Sure.

"But I can't stand around and gab all day. I have other things to do, you know." Mabel looked into her basket. "I got everything I came for."

"You sure I can't grab you anything else?"

"I'm sure." She patted Blake on the arm. "I hope to see you around, big fella."

"See ya, Mabel." He chuckled as the matchmaker pushed her walker toward the front. He tossed a few more groceries into his cart and headed to the checkout. He casually chatted with a clerk named Jan who wore a rhinestone bolo tie around the neck of her red Paul's Market dress shirt. Jan put his groceries in four plastic bags and he hooked them in his finger and carried them to his truck. The crisp October air brushed his face and he breathed in that deep scent of earth and pine. The last time he'd spent any time in the mountains during fall and winter, he'd been training in Colorado for the harsh elements of Tora Bora and the Hindu Kush.

He slung the groceries in the back of his pickup and something let out a yelp. He looked into the bed and into the black eyes of a puppy. A small black puppy with white paws sat on a bag of Purina Puppy Chow.

"What the fuck?"

"Yip."

He glanced around but he didn't see anyone. "How did you get in there?" He looked back at the dog as if it had an answer. The puppy let out another yip and Blake reached into the bed of the truck and lifted the dog. An older couple wearing matching red sweatshirts walked to a car a row down, and Blake moved toward them. "Did you lose a puppy?"

They looked at him and shook their heads. "No," the woman answered. "But it's cute."

"It's not mine."

The gentleman laughed. "It looks like it is now."

"No." He looked down into the black eyes staring back up at him. "Someone put it in the wrong truck." He raised the puppy above his head for a closer look at its belly. "*Him* in the wrong truck."

The two just shook their heads again and got in their car. With a frown, Blake walked across the parking lot and into the store. The automatic doors whooshed open and shut and he moved to the closest checkout. "Someone lost their puppy."

Jan looked up. "Poor little guy. Was he just wandering around out there?"

"Somehow he ended up in the back of my truck."

The male clerk in the next register laughed. "You got puppy bombed."

Blake wasn't amused and his gaze slid to the short man's name tag pinned to his red shirt. Frank Cornell. There couldn't be two with that name in the small town. "What's that?" he asked although he had a bad feeling he knew.

"Folks who don't want to take their animals to the pound dump them on people's doorsteps or in unlocked cars," the man answered.

What I Love About You

A girl putting groceries on Jan's conveyer belt asked, "What are you going to call it?"

"It's not mine."

"You could name it Midnight," suggested monster cock Frankie.

"I'm not naming it." They just looked at him and he added, "I don't want a dog."

"Too bad," Jan said, and ran a box of Corn Chex under the scanner. She shook her head as if *he'd* done something wrong. "Take him to the pound, I guess. He's cute. Someone might adopt him. Of course, pound closes at three due to budget cuts."

Blake lifted his free arm and looked at his Luminex dive watch. It was ten after.

"It's closed on Sunday, too."

He wasn't going to keep this dog for two days.

"You can always puppy bomb someone else."

Exactly. "Thanks." He turned and walked back out of the store. With the dog under one arm, he looked around for an unlocked vehicle or truck. In a town full of trucks, there wasn't one in the lot, and all the cars were locked. Apparently, everyone in town knew about the puppy bombing and took evasive action.

With a deep scowl furrowing his brow, he set

the puppy on the passenger seat of his truck. "You better not take a leak on my leather seat," he warned. As he walked to the driver's side, he glanced around the parking lot one last time for the puppy bomber. He'd been trained to spot bad guys and evildoers. Through his sniper's eyes, he observed and perceived things close and at a distance. He saw a black bird and a broken tree branch, but nothing that looked out of place.

As he pulled out of the lot, he glanced over at the dog sitting on the seat like an invited guest. "Don't get comfortable."

"Yip!" The dog panted and its little pink tongue hung out the side of its mouth.

"Cute doesn't cut it with me, squid." The dumb dog took that as an invitation and scrambled across the center console. It jumped in his lap and practically climbed his chest as it assaulted his face and chin with its tongue. Puppy breath filled the air, and Blake had to wrestle the squirming dog off him and into the passenger seat. "Sit," he commanded, using the voice he'd mastered for enemy combatants.

"Yip." The dog circled twice but complied. Until they turned onto Blake's street and the puppy jumped to look out the window. It wagged its tail like it knew the way home and licked the passenger side window.

"I just cleaned that," Blake pointed out, but the dog kept licking. He pulled into the garage and the door closed behind him. Once he'd scooped the dog up and set it on the concrete floor, it sniffed the furnace and water heater before moving on to the tool cabinet. Blake thought about keeping it locked up in the garage until he could take it to the animal shelter Monday morning, and that's when it squatted and peed next to his gun safe.

"No." He rushed toward the dog. "Stop. Don't piss on my floor." Before he could stop it, the dog was done. It sort of shook its black fur and trotted toward the back door leading outside, leaving wet paw prints on the way. "A little late." He opened the door and followed the puppy out into the backyard. A cool breeze stole down the collar of his sweatshirt and ruffled the surface of the lake. He didn't suppose he could just leave the dog outside until Monday. "Do your business," he ordered as the dog sniffed the trees between his and Sweet Cheeks's yard.

"Is that your puppy?"

"Jesus." She'd snuck up on his again. Sniper scouts had nothing on Charlotte Cooper. "No."

"Whose dog is she?"

"It's a boy."

She glanced behind her and took a few steps from beneath her trees. Unlike the last time he'd seen her, she wore a jacket and jeans tucked into furry boots. "Ohhh. He's so cute. What's his name?"

"He doesn't have one."

She gazed up at him and smiled. Obviously she didn't hold grudges like her mother. "Can I pet him?"

"Sure."

The kid dropped to her knees and put her hand on the puppy's back. "He's soft." She looked up, then back down. The cool breeze picked up the ends of her ponytail and made her cheeks pink. "Can I hold him?" she asked, but didn't wait for an answer. She scooped the dog into her lap and buried her face in its fur.

"Sure." Blake smiled. "He likes you." The puppy obliged by licking her face. She laughed, and Blake almost felt bad for what he was about to do. Almost. "He likes you more than me."

She nodded. "That's because you are gwumpy. My mom calls you Mr. Gwumpy Pants."

Actually, her mom called him Raging Asshole, and he was just about to prove her right. Again. The little dog's tail whapped the girl's arm and its whole back end shook with excitement. She held the puppy tight as the dog tried to climb up her chest. It licked the hell out of her face, and she giggled. "Look how much he loves you."

"A whole lot!"

"Do you want him to be your dog? I think he'd be happier with you."

Her little face lit up. "I can have him?"

Blake nodded. "He loves you and wants to live with you. I can tell."

With her arms around the puppy's belly, she stood. "I have to ask my mom."

And just like the Grinch who stole Christmas, he smiled and patted the top of her head. "You should just take him home and let your mom see how much he loves you."

"My mom's not home from her work yet. Tilda watches me on Saturdays."

Even better. "Surprise your mom. Everyone loves a surprise."

Charlotte's shoulders sank. "She'll probably say no."

"Not if she sees how much you love him. She can't say no once she sees the two of you together."

"Mommy won't even let me have a cat." She bit her lip as if she worried. "She'll be mad." Her big blue eyes looked up and she asked, "What should I do?"

"Cry." God, he almost felt bad again. "She'll let you keep him if you cry."

"Weally?"

"Yes." The kid was probably going to get into trouble. "I'll bring you over his dog food."

"Okay!" With the dog squirming in her arms, she turned and carried it into her yard.

Kids loved dogs, he told himself. He watched her as he moved into his garage. The puppy was much better off with a little kid than a guy like him. She was right. He was grumpy. Dogs needed happy owners.

He cleaned the puddle off the concrete floor, then grabbed his groceries out of the back of his truck and moved inside. He walked through the mudroom and past the open door to the wine cellar. He'd never been a wine drinker, preferring a cold beer or a shot of whiskey. The room opened into the kitchen, dominated by granite counters and carved wood cabinets. A big chopping block island took up the middle and was surrounded by appliances fit for a gourmet chief. Blake liked to eat gourmet meals, he just didn't like to cook them. He preferred to throw things in a Crock-Pot and eat it for a couple of days.

He tossed the grocery bags on the island and moved past the empty dining room into the living room. This and his bedroom upstairs were his favorite rooms in the house. He loved the big fireplace surrounded by river rock and the floor-to-ceiling windows both upstairs and down that looked out onto the lake and dense forest beyond. A sixty-inch TV sat in his entertainment center in front of a leather couch and two matching chairs. The rest of the room contained various pieces of exercise equipment and boxes filled with Blake's life. Pitiful few, actually, when he looked at them. Most were filled with remnants of his military life. Books and documents. The helmet that had saved his life on numerous occasions and the plate that had stopped a bullet from entering his heart. His chest ribbons and dress blues and old dusty tech boots.

His boots echoed as he moved to the window. He glanced down at the front of his hooded sweatshirt now covered in black puppy fur. It had a suspicious wet spot on the pocket, and he reached one hand behind his head and grabbed a fistful of sweatshirt. He pulled it over his head and tossed the shirt on a workout bench. He didn't particularly want his house filled with dog hair, let alone pee, and figured he'd dodged a bullet. It wouldn't be the first time, and he scratched the small round scar on his shoulder just below the SEAL trident tattoo on the ball of his shoulder. That scar wasn't the only reminder of his service. He had a four-inch scar on the side of his knee from a hard helo landing, and a permanent crease on his side from an AK–47 round. He had the trident on his shoulder and Hosea 8:7 on his belly just below his navel. He loved the whole wrath-of-God and reap-the-whirlwind prophecies of the Old Testament. He didn't believe that God had chosen him for divine retribution, but he did believe he'd saved the lives of civilians and soldiers. When he looked down the crosshairs of his scope, he liked to believe he'd been inserted in a hostile environment to make sure some evil motherfuckers reaped the whirlwind.

Now what? he asked himself as he looked out at the lake and the sun inching toward the tops of the mountains. What was he going to do with himself? The doctors and addiction counselors in rehab had advised him against returning to work so soon. It was their opinion that his job was one of his biggest triggers. It juiced him up on adrenaline, and knocking back alcohol afterward was not only a social requirement, but a way to relieve stress.

Reaching for the bottle was a habit that had started after BUD/S, hanging out in dive bars with buddies talking shop and drinking his weight in beer. That was a habit he needed to break, but he didn't believe he had to change his job, any more than he believed he was powerless over addiction.

A fish jumped a few feet from his dock and sent a ripple of tight circles across the green surface. He had options besides hopping from hot spot to hot spot around the globe. Less dangerous options requiring less high-octane adrenaline. He could secure diplomats or cargo ships or rhinos in the Congo. He could always contract with the CIA or FBI. He was patriotic. Loved his country. Red, white, and blue to his marrow, but he'd had enough of working for Uncle Sam. Of training for a mission for months, inserting and living in harsh environments, only to be told to step down once he had a high-value target in his crosshairs. And of course, the government paid a lot less than private military companies.

A doorbell rang and he turned his back to the lake. He assumed it was his doorbell. He'd never heard it before. He moved through the great room, past the wood and iron staircase, to the entrance. The blurred shapes of his neighbor and her daughter stood on the other side of the beveled glass. He could hear Charlotte wailing, and through the watery image, he could guess that her mother wasn't much happier.

He opened the door and didn't bother to hide his grin. Most definitely, Sweet Cheeks was not a happy camper.

Chapter Four

He wasn't wearing a shirt. Natalie opened her mouth to yell at the neighbor and call him a few choice names, but her mouth got dry and snapped shut. Without the safety barrier of a shirt, his testosterone hit her like an atomic blast. She was surprised it didn't blow her hair back and melt her face. Looking at all that skin, she couldn't quite recall why she'd marched up his steps.

"Mama won't let me keep Spa-ky." Charlotte hiccuped, and suddenly Natalie remembered exactly why she wanted to punch him. Not only had Charlotte always wanted a dog, she'd always wanted to name him Sparky after the dog in her favorite movie, *Frankenweenie*.

"You lost your dog," Natalie said.

Blake tilted his head to one side, and those cold gray eyes of his took a slow journey down the front of her trench coat, pausing briefly at her belted waist before continuing down her bare legs to her black pumps. "I don't have a dog."

Don't look, she told herself. *Don't look to see if he has a six-pack. Keep your eyes above the chin.* "You're not going to foist your dog off on a little girl." A little girl who'd been told she couldn't have a dog. A dog was a big responsibility. A puppy needed training and attention. Natalie liked dogs. She'd been raised with dogs, but she and Charlotte were not home during the day. It wasn't fair to leave a puppy crated all day while they were gone.

He lifted his gaze to her face and leaned one big shoulder into the door frame. "Someone left him in my truck, but he isn't mine." He looked pleased and relaxed, like he'd gotten away with something.

Natalie was neither pleased nor relaxed. "Your puppy bomb is not my problem."

"I'm not familiar with the particulars of property law in Idaho, but in most states, I believe possession is nine-tenths of the law."

What I Love About You

"Uh-huh." She folded her arms across the front of her coat. "Hand him over, Charlotte."

"But Mommy, I love Spa-ky." Charlotte buried her face on top of the puppy's head and cried. "Spa-ky loves me."

Without taking her gaze from the naked man in front of her, she said, "The dog belongs to Mr. Junger."

He shook his head and straightened. "Sparky does not belong to Mr. Junger."

"Give Mr. Junger the dog."

"Mr. Junger doesn't want Sparky."

"Too bad."

"But Mommy . . ." Charlotte cried as tears ran down her red cheeks. The puppy squirmed and yelped and fell from Charlotte's grasp. "Spa-ky!" She reached for the dog but it darted past Blake's boots and disappeared into his house.

"Shit." Blake looked behind him, then back at Natalie. His mouth slightly opened, bewilderment pinching his brow as if he couldn't believe what had just happened.

Natalie smiled. "We'll just say good-bye now."

"Wait." He glanced back inside the house.

She grabbed Charlotte's hand and took a step back. "Possession is nine-tenths the law. Remember?"

"Spa-ky!" Charlotte wailed and dramatically raised her free hand toward the door. "Come back. I love you." She twisted and pulled, and Natalie held on, shocked by her child's behavior. "You're mean to me," Charlotte managed between sobs, and Natalie felt like she'd been stabbed in the heart. Then Charlotte broke free and darted past Blake, her blond ponytail flying behind her as she disappeared into the house.

"What the hell?" He looked at Natalie, his brows rising up his forehead like he was baffled by a little girl's emotional outbreak.

"You," she said, and took a step forward. All the anger she'd felt for him when she'd marched over here rose up in her again. She loved Charlotte more than anything on the planet. She'd tried so hard to have her and was grateful every day, but raising her alone was hard sometimes. Being a single mom, she took the brunt of Charlotte's heartache and disappointments. The last thing she needed was for some asshole neighbor to make her life even harder.

"Me?"

"You did this to her." She pointed past him. "Now you're taking that dog back."

He looked behind him, then back at her. "How

can I take Sparky back now? You heard her. She loves Sparky."

"Don't call it Sparky." She moved to brush past but he didn't budge so she shoved her shoulder into his chest like a linebacker. "You took advantage of a child. Jerk," she added as she bounced off his hard muscles.

He stepped aside and smiled. He had some sort of military tattoo on the big ball of his shoulder. "Please come in, Natalie."

"It's Ms. Cooper." The last thing she wanted was to be on a friendly first-name basis with the man who'd told her child that he "shit bigger than you," then given Charlotte—no, Natalie—the responsibility of his dog. "Charlotte," she called out as she walked inside. Natalie had been in the house once before when it had been owned by Nick and Delaney Allegrezza and their six loud children. Now the big house felt empty as she moved through the entry and past the stairs. The sound of her heels echoed off the hardwood and she stopped in the great room. The house felt empty because it was empty. Or practically empty, anyway.

At one end of the large room sat a grouping of furniture and some boxes, dwarfed by the massive windows and space. Exercise equipment took up a portion of the middle of the room, as if he'd moved everything he owned in one spot and left it there. "Charlotte," she called out again as she moved to the kitchen. One single Crock-Pot sat on the granite counter, looking kind of sad. "I'm not playing games, Charlotte. You're going to be in big trouble if you don't come out." She glanced in the dining room, empty except for a nail on the wall. Either he'd lived alone in a little apartment, or he was divorced and his wife had taken him to the cleaners. If she liked the guy, she might think it was sad. Like his lonely Crock-Pot. But she didn't like him.

"Check the wine cellar."

Natalie turned as he moved toward her, his long stride and wide shoulders those of a supremely confident man. His pants were low on his hips; she could see the Under Armour elastic band of his underwear hid most of a heavy black tattoo. He pulled a gray T-shirt over his head and down his chest. No six-pack, but she could probably bounce a quarter off his abdomen. She didn't know where he got the shirt, she was just glad he got one.

"Down that hall." He pointed.

What I Love About You

He walked close behind her, and sure enough, through an open door on the left, she found her daughter kneeling on the narrow stone floor. The little black dog that had caused such chaos lay on his back in front of her, paws in the air, fast asleep. The wine racks lining the room from floor to ceiling were empty except for one bottle of Johnnie Walker. The room was just wide enough for Natalie to kneel next to Charlotte, and the hard floor chilled her bare knees. She brushed a strand of hair from her daughter's wet cheek. "Come on, baby."

Charlotte shook her head. "I love Spa-ky."

"I know, but I'm sure Mr. Junger loves him, too," she lied. "And he loves Mr. Junger."

"We could share Sparky."

Natalie looked over her shoulder and up. Way up into his Hollywood-handsome face and eyes, cool and watchful. "Share a dog?" She didn't even try and keep the aggravation she felt from punctuating her words. "Like parents share kids?"

"Why not?"

Because she didn't want to share a dog. Because he was devious, and she was sure she'd end up with it full-time. "Do you have kids?"

"No."

She supposed that answer was obvious given his interaction with her child.

"Yeah." Charlotte nodded as she looked up at the neighbor. "Like Mama shares me with Nana and Papa."

Every other weekend, Charlotte stayed with Michael's parents across the lake. Regardless of Natalie's relationship with their son, Charlotte was their only grandchild and they loved her.

"Pleeeeasse, Mama. I'll be weally good and eat all my celery and carrots."

"*Re*ally good." Natalie returned her attention to her daughter and corrected Charlotte's habit of dropping random R's.

"*Re*ally good," Charlotte repeated, all pitiful and heartbroken. "Rrrr-weally good."

"Okay." She sighed, giving in to her child's heartbreak. "We'll take the dog every other weekend."

"I was thinking half the time. Fifty-fifty."

Of course he was. "We're not home during the day." She grabbed a part of the empty wine rack and stood. "So, every other weekend and Wednesday night on our free week."

"Tuesday and Thursday nights on your free week."

She frowned because she was going to make

What I Love About You

a deal with the devil. A devil that smelled like soap and a cool breeze against warm skin.

"I'll throw in the food."

"Every other weekend. Tuesday and Thursday nights, and you pay for the first vet visit."

"I'll buy him toys," Charlotte threw in as if she had her own bank account.

He grinned and stuck out his hand. "Deal."

This wasn't exactly what she'd planned when she'd walked over earlier, and she wasn't quite sure how she'd ended up with part-time custody of the neighbor's dog. She slid her hand in his. His hot palm heated up her cooler skin and the pulse at the base of her wrist. If Charlotte hadn't been kneeling at her feet, Natalie might have forgotten that she didn't like Blake Junger. That he was arrogant and pushy. Not to mention rude and foulmouthed and judgmental. And those were just the qualities she knew from her few brief encounters. She might forget all that and wonder what it would be like to slide up his chest and smell his skin on the side of his neck. "I expect that dog to be house-trained by Wednesday."

His throat moved as he swallowed. "Tuesday." The word whispered between them like a heated ribbon. It brushed her cheek and slid beneath the collar of her coat.

"Yeah!" Charlotte stood and wrapped her arms around Natalie's waist. "I got half a dog."

Natalie laughed without humor because there was nothing funny about having half a dog. Nothing funny about lust tickling her skin and making her tingle. Nothing funny about wondering what it would be like if Blake Junger did something to satisfy all those tingles.

He'd been stuck with the dumbest dog on the planet. Blake folded his arms across his chest and stared at the puppy tangled up in the purple leash Charlotte Cooper had provided to match his collar. The leash was wrapped around the puppy's legs and body and wound around the lone branch of the tree stump where Blake had tied him.

Recruit Sparky just wasn't getting the hang of his training. Blake knelt down on one knee and felt the cool earth through the worn denim of his Levi's. He unwound the leash from the single branch. This was the third time the dog had gotten all caught up. The last time he'd nearly choked himself to death. The puppy barked and sank his teeth into the sleeve of Blake's old gray sweatshirt as Blake untangled the leash from his legs. Then Blake rose and crossed his arms over his chest.

"Sit!" Special Warfare Operator First Class Blake Junger ordered as if he was talking to a newbie. "Stay!" He leaned down and put a hand in front of the puppy's face. "Stay or I'll put a foot up your ass and wear you for a mukluk."

"Yip." Recruit Sparky bit Blake's finger and wagged his tail. Blake had clearly lost his touch. He'd worked with Sparky for five days now and the dog didn't sit or stay and it still shit in the house at will. This hadn't been the plan when he'd reassigned the dog to Charlotte Cooper.

"At ease," he said as he moved past his truck already loaded with wood. He continued to a stump where he'd left his gear and his embedded ax. Behind him the dog barked and pulled at his leash, and Blake had no doubt the puppy would eventually succeed at choking himself out.

His property was packed with lodgepole, white, and ponderosa pine. Aspen and huckleberries grew from the earth littered with decades of nettles and pinecones and blowdowns. He shoved his hands into his work gloves and pushed his safety glasses on his face. Then he picked up the chain saw he'd left on a log. He pulled the cord with one clean jerk, and the engine split the mountain air with the sound of raw power. He set his feet against the saw's biting teeth and cut a blowdown into rounds he would later chop for firewood.

Within the natural light filtering through the variegated shade of pine and aspen, a stream of sawdust shot through the crisp autumn air. Between cuts, he glanced at the dog chewing on a stick. He'd felt somewhat bad that his plan to re-assign or "foist" the little dog had caused a problem between Charlotte and her mom. He hadn't meant for that to happen, but he hadn't meant to keep a dog he didn't want, either. Not even part-time. He was still baffled by how that had all gone down. Usually he was a better negotiator. He blamed Natalie Cooper and her shiny hair and pink lips and deep blue eyes. Eyes that could flash with anger or simmer with sexual interest.

The dog's first visit to the vet had cost him several hundred dollars in shots and a checkup. He'd learned that Sparky was approximately three months old and was a mix of black Lab, some sort of spaniel, and perhaps a bit of Dalmatian. In other words, an all-American mutt. A mutt he'd agreed to share with a little kid and her hot-as-hell mother.

Blake paused to kick a few rounds out of his way before setting the teeth into the next section of log. When he'd first opened the front door and laid his eyes on Sweet Cheeks standing on his porch in her trench coat like she might be naked underneath, he'd lost the dog debate. His brain sank to the front of his pants and he'd worked at a disadvantage from that point. Then she'd shoved him and walked into his house, and his primitive instinct to shove her kicked in. To shove her down and climb on top. To shove up her coat and kiss her mouth. To shove inside her body and die.

He cut the saw engine and set it on the log. He had a hard-on just thinking about her, and he tossed his gloves on the ground. Time to think of something besides jumping on Sweet Cheeks. He moved to the CamelBak he'd left leaning against the stump and picked it up. For a lot of his life, the water reservoir had been a constant on his back. Like the sniper weapon at his side, SIG at his hip, and brain bucket on his head, he'd never left the wire without his hydration system.

The chilly October breeze rustled the leaves and branches of pine and brought with it the taste and feel of autumn. Blake hadn't felt a real autumn season in a long time. He'd always been stationed where it was warm and sunny or deployed to the desert or Afghan mountains. He liked the change of season. He liked the sharp contrasting color and the smell of leaves and earth on the crisp autumn air.

For the first time in his life, he didn't have to report to anyone or pack up his gear and hop a cargo plane destined for the latest hot spot. He was on self-imposed leave. He'd invested his bonuses over the years and could chop wood for the rest of his life if he chose. He could walk through the forest with nothing more than a camera. He didn't have to kit up or pack up an MK12. He didn't have to eat dust or crouch in a swamp. He didn't have to do anything.

But for the last twenty-one years, he'd lived on high octane. He was hardwired to go and do and conquer. To have a goal and achieve it. He wasn't sure how much longer he could run on a slower fuel before he got restless.

Probably two more weeks. Two more weeks to conquer this alcoholism. A month at the most, and then he'd review his options. Several private military contractors had contacted him recently. He was Blake Junger. His name alone cut through red tape and bullshit. His name gave him options. He could work six months on a cargo ship in the Gulf of Aden or on the Somali coast, then return to his Batcave here in Truly. Or he could hire on with crisis contractors to manage kidnaps around the world. Kidnap resolution was a specialized job for which he was uniquely qualified.

He glanced at the dog and set the CamelBak on the stump. Recruit Sparky was all tangled up again, and Blake scowled as he walked toward the furry black puppy. Three of his legs were trussed together and he shook with happiness when Blake knelt and untangled the stupid mutt.

He had eighty-three days of sobriety under his belt. He still wrestled with Johnnie, but today wasn't a white-knuckle day. Today his head was clear and filled with clean mountain air.

To his left, the distant crack of rifle power stopped his hands. His head jerked up. His senses instantly alert and heightened, he calculated the shot had been fired from 3.2 kilometers behind him. He heard a second shot, and even as he reminded himself that it was hunting season in Idaho, the green and yellow leaves in front of his eyes wavered like a heat mirage. Instead of rich earth and pine, the smell of rotting garbage, molding concrete, and baharat rose up to fill his lungs. His ears rang and the shifting ripples between what was real and what was not spun his head. He knew he was in the Idaho wilderness, yet his visceral memory had him crouched on a rooftop in Ramadi, sucking the smell of the Middle East into his lungs.

It wasn't real. One second. Two seconds trapped in visceral hell. He closed his eyes against the shimmering mirage. It would stop soon. It always did. Three seconds . . . Something wet slid across his cheek. Warm and sloppy. Something real, and he opened his eyes to a beady black gaze staring back at him. His tilted world righted, he took a deep breath of rich earth and dry leaves. Recruit Sparky barked and licked his mouth, and he was so relieved he almost kissed the dog back.

Almost. The stupid puppy tried to climb up his chest and nearly knocked him on his ass. Blake's ears still rang, and as always, he felt disoriented, confused, and foolish, but unlike the other times, he was distracted by a dog. A dog so happy he practically shook apart while his tongue assaulted Blake's face in a dervish of enthusiasm.

"Stand down," he ordered, but of course the dog ignored him. He untied the mutt and shut him in the cab of his truck, the bed loaded with firewood and few interesting logs he'd found. He loaded his chain saw and ax and shut the tailgate. He tried to ignore the pressure squeezing the back of his neck as he stowed the rest of his gear in his tactical rucksack.

His flashbacks had started several months ago. Before today, the last one had happened while he was staring out at Lake Mary when he'd first moved to Truly. The one before that in rehab. The first in his brother's Escalade in Nevada. Beau had taken him to his home in Henderson to sober him up before the trip to California. They'd been driving through the desert town, arguing over who was the biggest badass superhero, Batman or Superman, when he glanced in his side mirror. Within the reflective glass, a confusing image of a white Toyota filled with Iraqis sped toward them. They wore ski masks and keffiyeh, and dust rose from the truck's bald tires. The image wavered like smoke, and adrenaline shot through Blake's veins as he reached for a grenade in his chest gear and his

SIG Sauer on his hip. Innocent men did not wear ski masks in a hundred and thirty degrees.

"What are you doing?" Beau asked.

He looked at his brother looking back at him from the driver's side of the SUV. It was like staring at his own reflection. "Bad guys on your five."

Beau glanced into his rearview. "What's going on Blake?"

He looked back into the mirror and the image of the truck shimmered and disappeared. It had seemed so real. So real it spun his head and he grabbed the door handle. "Not sure."

"Do you have PTSD?"

"No." Jungers did not have PTSD.

"No shame in it."

"I don't have PTSD. Let it go."

A few silent moments passed as they sped across the Nevada desert. "One punch from Superman's powerful fists, Batman's head rolls like a gutter ball."

Blake had tried to laugh. Thinking back on it now brought a smile to his lips. "One punch from Batman's kryptonite boxing gloves," he'd said, "and Superman crumples like a pussy."

Blake missed his brother, but he wasn't going to call. Beau would want to talk about Blake's sobriety, and Blake didn't want to talk about it right now. Not when it tugged at his gut and whispered in his ear.

The drive home took ten minutes because of the rough terrain. Ten minutes of puppy barking, tail wagging, and window licking. To anyone else, this might seem normal, a man and his dog, but this wasn't normal. Not for him.

His head ached from the flashback. His hands griped the steering wheel a little too tight. He needed a drink. A couple of shots of Johnnie to blunt the sharp edges. The bottle was in the wine cellar. It would be so easy to pour it back.

No one will know, his addiction whispered.

Giving in would be so much easier than white-knuckling his way through it.

One drink. You can stop after one drink.

He'd never stopped after one drink. One drink led to two. Two to three. Three to a bottle and a shitload of beer. A bottle and a shitload of beer led to waking up with raw knuckles, a split lip, and a killer hangover. At the moment, a good old-fashioned bar brawl sounded like a good time.

Charlotte ran across her front yard as he pulled into his garage.

"Blake!"

He left the garage door up and climbed out of the truck.

"Blake!" She stopped at the rear of the truck, breathing hard. "It's my night for Spa-ky."

"I know." The dog jumped across the console and Blake lifted him from the driver's seat. He set Sparky on the ground and the dog barked wildly, then shot across the floor toward the little girl. He tripped on the leash and slid on his belly.

Charlotte laughed and picked up her part-time mutt. "We got Spa-ky a name tag," she said as the dog licked her face. He wiggled and squirmed and slipped out of her grasp. "It's purple. My favorite color." She tried to pick up the mutt up again, but he jumped and barked and bit the hem of her coat. "Stop, Spa-ky." She reached for him but he jumped back and barked.

Blake watched the dog's shenanigans for several more moments before he shut the truck door and picked up the mutt. At this rate, she was never going to get the dog home. "I'll carry him to your house." He subdued the recruit in a compression hold. "Settle your ass down before you piss yourself."

"You said a bad word."

"Are you going to tell your mom on me?"

She thought a moment as they moved down

the driveway. "No." She shook her head. "I won't tell. We're friends."

Friends? He wouldn't go that far. His friends were considerably older, male, and said as many bad words as they could fit into one sentence.

Sparky wiggled as Blake looked up the neighboring driveway and at Sweet Cheeks leaning into the open hatchback of her Subaru. His male friends would pause to appreciate her ass in those jeans.

"Mama, I got Spa-ky."

Natalie pulled out several bags of groceries and her blond hair swung across one shoulder. "Oh joy."

Blake set the dog on the ground and moved toward her. She straightened and he reached for the groceries in her hands. "I'll get those."

Her sunglasses slid down her nose and her blue eyes stared at him above the brown frames. "I've got these, but you can get the last few."

There was something about the eyes the color of the deep ocean, the aviator glasses, and her pink mouth that licked at the sharp edges of craving. Something white hot, and turned it into a different kind of craving altogether.

Blake grabbed the four remaining bags of groceries and shut the hatchback. He followed her and

Charlotte in through the garage door and set the bags on the kitchen counter. The house smelled like a woman lived in it. Like fresh baked cake and flowers and clean laundry soap. The house looked like a woman lived in it, too. A white tablecloth. A pink smiley cup sitting in the sink, and lacy curtains. Photographs of Charlotte all over the place.

"Do you need any more help?" he asked as he took in the sights and smells of the girly home. It was about half the square footage of his house and was semi-custom. Built from a builder's blueprint with some nice woodwork, stone, and tile. The back faced the lake, like his.

"No thank you." She shucked off her jacket and tossed it on a kitchen chair. "Can you hang around for a minute?" His gaze slid to the front of her thin white T-shirt.

The warm parts in his belly got hotter with the promise of a full-blown erection, and one thing was for certain, white-hot lust sure beat the hell out of white-knuckling it. "Sure."

"I want to show you something."

He wanted to see it. And when she was done showing what she had, he had something to show her, too. The way she'd looked at him the other day in the wine cellar was the way a woman looked at a man when she needed to get laid. He'd been with enough women to recognize that look. It wasn't teasing. It wasn't coy. It wasn't manufactured. It was a dark yearning in the depths of a woman's eyes. It was the drop of a full-bottom lip and a sweet inhalation.

She walked across the wood floor to the refrigerator, and the puppy barked as Charlotte giggled in the living room.

Standing there was a distraction. He didn't plan to have sex with Natalie. She was the kind of woman who wanted sex to *mean* something. She wasn't the kind to just get naked and have fun. She'd want some sort of commitment, but thinking about her thighs around his waist and bouncy breasts in his hands got him hard as a steel hooley.

Blake pushed his sweatshirt sleeves up his forearms. He could control his hard-ons. There were those who thought he was like his dad, a guy who jumped from woman to woman, and that was partly true, he guessed. But unlike his dad, he'd always been in control of his dick. Unlike his brother, he'd never believed he had to be celibate to do it.

Chapter Five

Natalie grabbed a drawing stuck to the refrigerator with a cupcake magnet and set it on the counter. "Charlotte made this last night." She pointed to a round figure with long dangly arms and legs. Charlotte had carefully drawn ten fingers and toes, and a big head topped with three strands of blond hair.

"What's that?"

Natalie pointed to the gray eyes and the straight red line for a mouth. "This is you." She slid her finger to the black furry circle with paws and tail. The puppy had a head with a red tongue and floppy ears. "This is Sparky. I've noticed that Charlotte's artwork has improved in the last few months. Everything used to be stick figures."

What I Love About You

His brow furrowed and he leaned in for a closer look. "Is that supposed to be my hair?"

Natalie smiled. "Charlotte doesn't have very much experience drawing hair on men. Her grandfather is bald." And her father has a prison cut.

"Is that a pot gut?"

He sounded so insulted her smile turned to soft laughter. Blake Junger had a full head of hair and his gut was definitely flat. "Your eyes are the right color." She moved to a lower cupboard and pulled out a pan. "And your smile."

"This thing isn't smiling."

"Exactly." She filled the pan with hot water and set it on the stove to boil. It was mac and cheese night at the Coopers. Living with a five-year-old, she'd learned it was easier just to keep the menu simple and hide veggies in things her daughter liked to eat. She'd learned to pick her battles. Over the sound of cartoons in the living room, Sparky barked, proving that she'd lost that one.

Blake straightened and she expected him to leave. To leave the part-time dog he'd conned on a little girl and run like hell. Instead he said, "I met a friend of yours a few weeks ago at the grocery store."

Her list of friends was short. She grabbed a box

of mac and cheese and looked over her shoulder at him. "Lilah?"

"Mabel."

She set the box on the counter next to the stove. Maybe he was sticking around because he was lonely in that big empty house next door. That made her almost feel bad for him, but not quite. "Mabel Vaughn?"

"Yeah."

"She was my grandmother's good friend." She added salt to the water. He didn't seem to have a job or family. He didn't seem to do anything but chop wood and shoot pictures. "I've known her all of my life."

He leaned a hip into the counter and folded his arms over his chest like he was settling in for a chat. Like he wasn't the rude neighbor who'd sworn at her child and questioned her motherhood. "She mentioned that." He wore a gray Navy football sweatshirt and a pair of Levi's worn in curious places. Curious places like the back pocket were he kept his wallet and his button fly where he kept something else. Not that she'd looked. Okay, she'd looked, but it wasn't her fault she'd noticed his bulge, like he was packing serious heat behind that button fly. Having him here in her kitchen was really strange. His testosterone was throwing off the feminine balance in her house. Like a storm cloud in the middle of her calm blue feng shui.

"She also mentioned your husband."

Natalie glanced toward the empty doorway of the living room and pushed her hair behind her ear. "Ex-husband." She wasn't surprised Mabel had gossiped about her. Annoyed, but not surprised. "No doubt she 'mentioned' he's in prison." She looked back at Blake watching her through those intense smoky eyes of his.

"When does he get out?"

Natalie rarely liked to talk about Michael, and this wasn't one of those rare occasions. "Around Thanksgiving." In the other room, Natalie listened to the sound of Charlotte's laugher over the puppy's barking and a *My Little Pony* cartoon. *My Little Pony* was okay, but ever since Lilah had rented *I, Robot* for them all to watch, anything with robots gave Charlotte nightmares.

"Is Charlotte excited?"

Natalie didn't like to talk about Michael, but he wasn't a secret. She learned years ago that secrets made a person sick. Sick like her former husband. She'd been in a really dark place during her divorce. She'd been pregnant and depressed and humiliated. Instead of medication, she'd been helped with cognitive therapy. She'd learned to disassemble overwhelming problems and break them into manageable parts.

"Charlotte doesn't know yet." Blake lifted a brow, and she explained as she put away groceries. "Michael's parents thought he was getting out last year. They told Charlotte he was coming home and got her all excited." Although why she felt compelled to explain anything to the neighbor was a mystery. "The state of Idaho had different plans, and I was the one who had to tell her that he wasn't coming home. She cried for three days. After that, we all agreed not to say a word until it actually happens." Which was coming up so soon it made Natalie's stomach tight. "What else did Mabel mention?"

He didn't answer and she turned from putting away a jar of peanut butter. His gaze was lowered like he'd been watching her butt. She supposed it was only fair that he look at her butt since she'd looked at his button fly.

"That you were a prom queen." He lifted his gaze up her stomach and breasts to her face. The difference between the two of them was that he got caught and was unrepentant.

"That was a looooong time ago." She picked up the box of mac and cheese and tore off the top. "I think the crown is still in a box somewhere." She pulled out the powdered cheese packet, then dumped the pasta into the water.

"And you were a cheerleader."

"Yeah." She tossed the empty blue and yellow box in the recycling bin under the sink. It fell onto the floor and she pulled out the heaping bin. "That was a lifetime ago, too." She obviously needed a container bigger than seven gallons. She pushed it down as much as possible, but it popped back up. Before she could try again, Blake was beside her. Towering over her as he put his big boot on top of the heap. He smashed it down like a trash compactor to half the size. Natalie was impressed. It had been a long time since she'd lived with a man and she had forgotten that they came in handy sometimes. Like for carrying in groceries and compacting trash. And for other things. Like for washing her back in the shower.

He removed his big foot and said, "She mentioned you still wear your little outfit sometimes."

She looked up so fast a few strands of hair swung from behind her ear and got stuck to her lip gloss. He stood close; a hand's breadth separated the front of his sweatshirt from her breasts. She looked into his eyes and the air between them changed. It got hot, charged with sexual awareness. "Mabel said *that*?"

He shook his head without taking his gaze from hers. "No. That's just my dirty mind."

Was he coming on to her? If he was, what should she do? God, it had been so long that she didn't know anymore.

He lifted a hand and brushed her hair from her lip. The tips of his fingers touched the corner of her mouth and cheek, and she couldn't breathe. Literally, her breath was caught in her chest. She tried to think of something to say. Something flippant, like his touch didn't affect her. Like hot little tingles weren't spreading across her skin.

His hand slid to the side of her throat, and he lightly pressed his thumb into her chin, tipping her face up. "Do you have a man in your life, Sweet Cheeks?"

A man? She shook her head and swallowed hard, past the clog in her chest. She fought an urge to turn her face into his hand and kiss his warm palm. "I don't date," she managed.

"That's what I thought."

He smelled good. Like the last time she'd been this close. Like mountain air and man. Whoa. Wait. What? How did he know she didn't date? Did she look like a loner?

He dropped his hand and moved closer. Closer until the tips of her breasts touched the front of his shirt. "You look like a woman who needs to date." What did that look like? She stood completely still as he told her, "You look like a woman who needs to date and with a man who knows how." He lowered his gaze to her mouth. He wasn't touching her, but it felt like it. "You look like you need a man to date you all night long."

She sucked the warm, tingly scent of pheromones into her lungs. She couldn't help it. They surrounded her like a sexually charged fog. "Are we talking about dating?" It felt like he was talking about something else. Something that made the clog in her chest get all hot and heavy and fall to the pit of her stomach.

He nodded. "No."

Was it yes or no? With him staring at her

mouth, she couldn't think. At least not beyond the urge to slide her hand up his chest and curl into him. "How can you tell I don't date?" she asked as if she wasn't getting bombarded with impulses and urges and dark cravings. "Do I have a sign above my head or something?"

He slowly raised his gaze to hers. "Your eyes."

"My eyes?" Her brows lowered. "You can see I want a *date* from my eyes?" Again, she didn't think they were really talking about dating.

"There's a difference between want and need." *His* eyes were sending her a message, too. Beneath lowered lids, he sent a message so hot it made the knot in her stomach tighten and threaten to burn up her thighs. "You need a man to get you in his bed and keep you there all night. You need it bad. Real bad."

She did. She hadn't realized how much she needed it until that day in his wine cellar. But it wasn't going to happen here. In her kitchen. Not now, with her daughter in the next room and her dinner boiling on the stove. And not with this man. This hot, sexy man who was rude and overbearing, and she was sure wasn't interested in any sort of relationship beyond sex.

On a purely physical level, she might like to

have sex and forget about it the next morning. She wouldn't mind just using a man for his body. For just one night she'd like to use men like Lilah did, but she was a single mother and a small-business owner. She had more respect for herself than to be any man's one-night stand. "I don't need anything that bad," she said, and stepped around him. "I'm a busy woman." She moved to the stove and took the boiling pot off the heat. "Believe me, I am not the kind of woman to answer a booty call. I have more respect for myself." She poured the hot water and pasta into a strainer in the sink.

"Uh-huh." She heard him move to the back door and open it as a cloud of steam rose to her face. "More respect for yourself than to stare at pictures of Frankie Cornell's monster junk?"

She turned, and her flushing face had nothing to do with the steam. He *had* heard her and Lilah that day in the store.

He smiled. "If you want to see a monster dick, you know where I live."

Then he was gone and she was left standing in her kitchen with an empty pot in her hand and a steam cloud around her head. Good Lord, she couldn't recall exactly what she'd said about Frankie. Other than his mutant penis, of course.

She set the pot on one side of the sink. Blake had a monster penis, too? She looked across her shoulder and out the kitchen window. Trees blocked the view of his house. She wondered if he was telling the truth about that. Her brain conjured the image of his button fly. No, he probably wasn't lying.

She moved to the refrigerator and pulled out a gallon of whole milk and some butter. Michael had always said he had a big penis. She'd been a virgin and a faithful wife, and hadn't had any personal experience when it came to size. She didn't have a lot now, but she was older and wiser and had enough to know that Michael was average. Nothing to lie about, but that was Michael. No way would he ever let himself be average at anything.

She looked at the clock on the stove. She had an hour before homework and bath time. Half an hour before she and Charlotte sat down to eat. She pulled out a casserole dish and reached for the phone. Everyone knew that Natalie couldn't keep anything to herself, and Lilah was going to love this.

How was she possibly going to look at her neighbor now? she asked herself as she dialed.

How was she ever going to look at him as just the jerk who'd stuck her with a part-time dog?

Of course Blake had sleazed out on the dog agreement. The day after he'd stood in her kitchen and told her he had a monster penis, he'd stopped by Glamour Snaps and Prints to tell her that he was going out of town for a while. He didn't know how long he'd be. That had been two weeks ago. Two weeks of full-time care of the part-time dog.

Natalie lifted her camera and took several shots of the newborn asleep in her daddy's hunting beanie. The camouflage hat was tucked around the tiny girl's shoulders and she wore a stretchy camo band around her small head. Behind Natalie the young mother wept with pride.

Natalie paused to move a few of the autumn leaves scattered on the table the baby lay on. Then she took several steps back and adjusted the focus of her Canon EOS. Personally, she was not a fan of the camo. She got down on one knee and took a few more shots before the mother carefully put the sleeping baby in a blue egg and laid her in a bird nest. Natalie changed the backdrop and moved the white reflective bounce card. The egg and nest were lined with lambskin and Natalie tucked the infant's hands beneath her chin. Much better than camo.

It was November first. Except for archers and muzzleloaders, hunting season was over. Natalie was happy the men in town had packed away their hunters' camo for another year. And it just went without saying that she could stand looking out the window of Glamour Snaps and Prints and not see an elk head riding down Main Street strapped to a car. Or pulling into the grocery store and not seeing deer legs sticking up from the bed of a truck. Or not hearing her child cry about poor dead animals.

As she snapped pictures of the baby girl, she remembered when Charlotte had been a baby. She felt a little nostalgic, and she might have been struck with a raging case of baby fever if she thought there was a possibility that she could have another child without going through infertility treatments again.

She paused to look at the pictures through the display screen before she showed them to the mother. Of course, before she even thought of IVF, she'd have to find a husband. A good man who'd be around to help raise his child. A good *law-abiding* man who'd love her and Charlotte. A man who wasn't a colossal liar.

"Turn the egg a little to the right," she told the young mother, and snapped several more photos.

Since Michael's release day was looming, she'd actually taken his call the other day. She wished she hadn't. He'd told her that he planned to spend a lot of time with Charlotte and acted like she should just want that to happen. He'd been real pushy. Pushy like he'd always been when she'd been young and naive and allowed it. She was no longer that person. She was a grown-up. A big girl. A woman and mother. She wasn't intimidated by Michael, but the closer it came to his release, the more she felt anxiety.

While the young mother changed the baby into a christening gown, Natalie staged the next composition. She changed the backdrop to a gray damask and pushed her great-grandmother's red velvet settee in front. The Victorian couch was bare in a few places but gave a photograph character and balance.

One of the last people she'd photographed had been Mabel and her smoky eyes. Thinking of Mabel made her think of Blake. Thinking of Blake made her think of his hand brushing her cheek that night in her kitchen. Maybe he was right. If the touch of a man's hand on her face made her go all tingly, maybe she did need to date. But not the kind of date he'd been talking about.

Tonight Charlotte was staying with the Coopers and Natalie was going on a date with Lilah. It was the Saturday after Halloween, and Natalie was hitting the town in her Robin costume. Mort's Bar was having its annual costume contest, and the winner would receive a jackalope trophy made by a local taxidermist. Natalie didn't plan to enter as she'd rather not win a stuffed jackrabbit with deer antlers.

The mother sat with the sleeping baby in her lap, and Natalie clicked photos from different angles and light settings. The problem with dating anyone but Lilah was that she lived in Truly, Idaho, population ten thousand—in the summer. Once the snowbirds left in September, the population dropped to about twenty-five hundred. She knew most of the men in town, knew them and knew their wives.

After several more shots, Natalie and the young mother moved behind the customer counter and plugged the photo card into the commercial printer. The woman looked at all the pictures, chose the ones she wanted, and ordered different sizes. The shop wasn't busy and Natalie printed the pictures before the woman left.

At five o'clock, she drove home to feed Sparky and let him out to do his business. He was housetrained now, and she'd even managed to get him to do his business in one area. The puppy took off for Blake's yard and took a dump on his lawn. Natalie smiled. He'd left town and left training the dog to her. It just seemed right that Blake had to pick up poop. She glanced up at all the dark windows in the big house.

He already had a two-week crap collection, if he didn't get home soon, he'd have to use a backhoe. There was neon pink in some of it, but Natalie wasn't about to investigate.

The puppy sniffed around and searched for another spot. Last night, she and Charlotte had taken Sparky with them while they'd trick-or-treated in their small subdivision. Charlotte had dressed up all nice and warm in a horse costume of brown corduroy. Her cute little face stuck out of a horse's head, and the costume had a long yellow mane and tail. Natalie had sewed a bow tie on the neck and Charlotte had pranced the neighborhood, neighing and stomping her foot. She'd been in full Bow Tie mode. Natalie loved when Charlotte was Bow Tie. She loved to make jumps and announce races, and last night Charlotte had added a new animal to her barnyard. Sparky the sheep. While Natalie had dressed as a cowgirl, they'd put a sheep costume on the puppy. Too bad the dog had spent most of the night trying to bite it off.

Sparky finished his business in Blake's yard like a good dog, and after Natalie put the dog back in her house, she grabbed her purse and garment bag and drove all the way back into town. Lilah lived in the apartment above the salon where she worked, and Natalie parked in the little lot behind the Cutting Edge and Allegrezza Construction. A freezing breeze practically blew her up the wooden stairs to the green door at the top.

"Get in here," Lilah yelled, and shut out the cold wind behind them.

The one-bedroom apartment was about as old as the town itself. The appliances had been replaced recently, but a few throw rugs covered the thin linoleum in the kitchen. Still, the big window seat that overlooked Main Street, and the old claw-foot tub in the bathroom, almost made up for the size of the apartment.

"Let me see your costume." Lilah grabbed the garment bag and moved into her bedroom. "Not slutty enough," she determined as she held up the shiny green and red costume.

"I wasn't going for slutty." The two of them got ready to go out for Halloween together as they had all through school. The difference was that now they drank wine and ate real fruit instead of Kool-Aid and fruit snacks. They laughed and joked about things that only the two of them would laugh and joke about. Like the time they'd taken Mildred Van Damme's obese goat for a power walk or lost their gloves hooky bobbing on Sid Grime's bumper.

At nine, they walked down the wood steps, Natalie in her shiny green shorts and a shiny red bustier. A yellow R on her right breast matched her yellow utility belt. The yellow satin cape tied at her throat and fell to her knees. Shiny green gauntlets covered her forearms, and she wore her black boots. Her costume was so tight she wasn't wearing underwear, but she wouldn't call it risqué. Her boobs weren't popping out—well maybe they were a little, but her butt wasn't hanging out. Not like Lilah, who'd tarted herself up like a dominatrix. She wore black leather and carried a whip, and Natalie was fairly certain it wasn't a Halloween costume.

She ducked her head against the wind whipping her curled hair about her face, and she would not have been surprised if it blew off the fake eyelashes Lilah had glued to her lids. Natalie had half a buzz, and she'd let Lilah do her makeup. Lilah made her look more like a vixen than a superheroine.

With the velvet cape tucked around her for warmth, they ducked between the salon and the construction company. A block down the street, Mort's Bar pulsed and vibrated with electric light and country music. There were four bars in Truly, but Mort's was more than a bar. More than just a place to drink cold beers and get into a fight on Friday nights. Mort's was an institution. Old like Princeton or Harvard, only for dumb people who wanted to get an education in getting tanked.

Natalie and Lilah passed devils and slutty

nurses as they walked down the sidewalk and ducked beneath the "No One Under 21" sign above the bar's door.

The heavy thump of the jukebox and the smells of hops and old wood filled Natalie's nose as she stepped inside. Her eyes adjusted to the dim light. She hadn't been in Mort's in years, but it hadn't changed. An array of antlers still hung above the long mahogany bar. The jackalope the original Mort had "bagged" back in '52 still hung front and center. Behind the cash register and bottles of alcohol, a mirror ran the length of the bar, while three bartenders pulled beers and blended drinks.

"What can I get you girls?" the owner of Mort's, Mick Hennessey, asked as they wedged themselves in at the bar. Out of the four bars, Mick owned two—Mort's and the saloon that had been handed down through generations and bore his last name.

"White wine," Natalie answered.

"Dirty Redheaded Slut."

A smile curved Mick's handsome face. "You got it."

Natalie looked at her friend within the shadows and neon glow. "Seriously?"

Lilah shrugged her bare shoulders. "I like them."

"You like the name."

Lilah flipped the ponytail of the sleek black wig she wore. "You should try one. Lighten you right up."

"No thanks. Charlotte goes to school with Mick's son. His wife is a Thursday helper. I'm not going to get drunk on Dirty Sluts."

"Dirty *Redheaded* Sluts," Lilah corrected her as she took off her jacket. "Are you going to wear that cape all night?"

"I'm cold." Which was true, but she discovered that she wasn't all that comfortable wearing a bustier in public. Not now. After a few glasses of wine, she might lighten up.

Natalie felt an arm slide around her shoulders before a voice said, "Hey sis. What's up?"

Lilah sighed and asked her brother, Tommy, "Is your wife here?" It was no secret that Lilah couldn't stand her sister-in-law, Helen. Helen owned a hair salon in town, but Lilah refused to work there. Helen had a reputation for giving shitty cuts and bad color.

Tommy hung one arm around Natalie and the other around his sister. "She's at home with the kids."

What I Love About You

Natalie had known Tommy Markham for as long as she'd known Lilah. At one time, he'd been a good-looking guy, but his lifestyle was quickly catching up with him.

"How are you, Nat?" he asked.

"I'm okay. Business is good. Charlotte's good."

Their drinks arrived and Tommy put them on his tab. They toasted with their glasses, then Lilah left her at the bar to chat with Tommy. They talked about his parents and his sons, who played junior high football. He bought her another glass of wine and a vodka shot.

"Are you trying to get me drunk, Tommy?"

He grinned, and a bit of his youthful charm shone through. "Maybe."

It was no secret that Tommy was a dog and a serial cheater. It was also no secret that the Markhams in general were horny people. Natalie shot the lemon-flavored vodka down her throat and let out a breath. "You're like a brother."

"But I'm not. No one would have to know."

"Gross, Tommy." She grabbed her wine and turned away.

"Ah, don't run away," he called after her as she moved through the bar toward Lilah, standing beneath a big moose head. She got halfway across the bar before she was stopped by Suzanne Porter. Suzanne was dressed as a sexy mouse, which fit. She'd gone to school with Suzanne, and the girl had always been quiet but wild.

They talked about kids and business, and Natalie's cheeks glowed with a happy buzz until Suzanne asked, "When's Michael getting out?"

"I'm not absolutely sure," Natalie answered. "Ask his mother and father."

"He won't be staying with you?"

Natalie looked at Suzanne's whiskers and red nose. "Of course not." She excused herself and found Lilah cozying up with none other than Frankie Cornell. "Hi, Frankie," she said, and kept her gaze glued to his vampire fangs drawn on his lips and chin.

"Hey, Natalie. I sent my Halloween pictures to your business."

She hadn't seen them yet, but she hoped they weren't photos of his magnum wang. "Thanks for the business."

"You're welcome. Just doing my part to keep my business local."

Natalie took a drink and looked at Lilah over the rim of her glass.

Lilah had a big grin that reached her eyes and made them shine with humor. "That's what we love about you, Frankie."

Frankie beamed beneath the attention. "I hear Michael's getting out soon."

Natalie lowered her glass. "That's what I hear."

"That's great!" Frankie, never good with social cues, rattled on about high school and football and how nice it was going to be to see Michael again. "Remember that game against the bull-dogs when Michael threw that touchdown pass in the last three seconds?"

Lilah, who *was* good at social cues, tried to change the subject several times, but Frankie was stuck on the same track. Finally Lilah just gave up and threaded her arm through his. "Come buy me a drink, Frankie," she said, and led him through the crowd toward the bar.

Natalie found a group of friends at a high table in one corner of the bar. Some of them had children around Charlotte's age, and they chatted about kids and jobs. They talked about the upcoming Truly Winter Festival, speculated who might win the ice sculpting trophy, and laughed about last year's spectacular snowmobile wipeouts.

Then the subject turned to Michael, and Natalie wasn't laughing anymore. She'd buried her past with Michael long ago, but with his impending release, it was brought up fresh, and suddenly her life was the subject of speculation. Everyone wanted to know when Michael was getting out. Where was he going to live? Did he have to pay restitution? What did Charlotte think of her daddy coming home?

Natalie finished her wine and excused herself. She wrapped her cape around herself and found Lilah by the bar hanging out with her brother and some guy named Steve.

"If one more person asks me about Michael, I'm going to crack a chair over somebody's head."

Lilah took a bite of a green olive on a toothpick. "You're not a brawler."

She looked into her friend's smoky eyes. Either Lilah had smeared her makeup or Natalie was getting drunk. "I can throw down." She held up the forearms covered in shiny green gauntlets. "I have superpowers." She knew it was the alcohol, but she kind of felt like she could kick some butt tonight.

Lilah laughed. "You ran home crying when Linda Finley threw bird poop on you."

"That was the sixth grade and it landed in my hair." She dropped her arms. She'd never been in a fight in her life, but if one more person asked about her ex-husband, she could probably go all flying snooker crazy on someone.

Lilah shook her head. "Steve, dance with my friend Natalie." She patted the guy on the shoulder and warned, "Behave."

"And don't mention Michael."

"Who's Michael?"

"Exactly."

She and Steve moved to the small crowded dance floor and he wrapped his arm around her waist. All respectable like a real gentleman. "I like this Catwoman costume."

Catwoman? "I'm Robin. Batman's sidekick."

"Robin's a guy."

"Not tonight." Over Tyler Farr's "Redneck Crazy," she told Steve how long it had taken her to find the costume on the Internet. "Most were inappropriate."

"I like inappropriate." To prove it, Steve slid his hand down her green shorts and cupped her butt. She pushed at his shoulders and left him standing on the dance floor. What had she expected from a friend of Tommy's?

She found Lilah chatting with a cute young bartender. "I'm going home."

"Are you going to crash at my place?"

She'd love to. "I can't leave the dog alone." She was too tipsy to drive and Truly didn't have taxis. "Are you sober?"

Lilah shook her head. "I know who is, though."

Ten minutes later, Natalie sat in the back of Frankie's piece-of-crap Ford Taurus. The heat didn't seem to work and Natalie wrapped her cape tight around herself. Lilah sat in front, chatting nonstop like Frankie's car was all nice and toasty and Natalie wasn't in the back turning into an icicle.

When they pulled up in front of her house, Lilah looked over her shoulder at Natalie, "Are you going to be okay?"

Natalie nodded and looked past her friend's head to the lights from the big house next door spilling into the darkness and onto the long drive. Light that hadn't been burning hours ago. "Oh yeah. I'll be just fine."

Chapter Six

Blake laughed and raised a bottle of water to his lips. "Cliff was uglier than a bag of smashed assholes," he said into his cell phone, then took a drink. "But there was no one better in the comm center during a firefight."

Retired Navy SEAL buddy Vince Haven added, "And drank anyone under the table. Even you and your brother."

"True. Remember that bar in Memphis when we took out a couple of firefighters and some of those mixed martial arts pussies." Fighting was just a fact of life in the teams. Blake never went looking for a fight. A fight just always seemed to find him. Usually it started with a little dog itching to take on a big dog. Or it happened when a man insulted a woman, and Blake felt it his duty to tap him on the shoulder and tell him to shut his pie hole. And it just went without saying that all bets were off when someone disrespected a fellow serviceman or woman while sitting on their ass in a micro brewery, sipping pumpkin beer.

"You got arrested that time."

Arrested because he'd been so shit-faced he'd kept fighting once the cops arrived. Blake took another drink, then set the bottle on the counter. "The charges were dropped," he said as the doorbell rang. He raised his wrist and looked at his watch. It was midnight. "What the fuck? Someone's at my door."

"Booty call?"

He thought of Natalie. "Nah. That's the big drawback of small-town living. Not a lot of booty to call."

"Damn. I remember those days."

Now Vince had a good-looking woman in his bed every night. He'd even put a ring on her finger. "My nut sack is about to explode from lack of action," Blake said as he walked to the door. On the other side all he could make out was a yellow blur through the glass.

Vince laughed. "Go take some Motrin."

The military handed out Motrin for everything from tooth pain to sucking chest wounds. "I don't think Motrin can cure my blue balls," he said as he opened the door and came face-to-face with someone who could. By the look on her face, she didn't seem to be in a real accommodating mood.

"You're finally back."

Her hair was big. Her shiny yellow cape was not. "I'll get in touch later, brother." He hung up and slid the phone into his back pocket. He guessed it was too much to hope that she was naked beneath that thing. "What can I do for you, Ms. Cooper?"

She pointed down and listed to the left as if she were taking on water. "Your dog."

He lowered his gaze from the little red smear of lipstick on the bottom of her lip, down her chin to the yellow cape tied around her throat. The shiny cape fell to mid-thigh, and his gaze continued down her long legs and black boots to the puppy lying at her feet like she'd dragged him out of his dog bed. For once, Recruit Sparky wasn't bouncing around being a maniac.

"You can't just take off any time you feel like it and neglect your responsibilities." She righted herself and stood up straight. "Your actions affect other people, you know. You're a bad dog owner and neighbor."

Yet another affirmation why he was not the marrying kind of guy. "I was at a friend's funeral in Oklahoma."

"Oh." She frowned. "I'm sorry for your loss."

"Thank you."

He waved her inside and got a whiff of booze as she passed. "Are you drunk, Sweet Cheeks?" He shut the door behind her.

"I had some wine." The dog finally recognized him and barked like the maniac Blake remembered. "Some vodka and maybe a shot of tequila." Natalie leaned down to unsnap the leash and almost took a header into his crotch. She knelt on one knee, and the yellow cape parted around one of her smooth thighs. "How did your friend die?"

He looked down at the top of her blond hair so close to his button fly, and his blue balls turned a few shades bluer. "His convoy was hit with an IED in Ramadi." Blake squatted down on the heels of his running shoes and petted the wiggling dog. She smelled like booze and perfume and temptation. A temptation that tugged at his belly and told him to slide his hand from the inside of her knee and up her thigh.

"He was a soldier?"

"No." He looked into her eyes a few inches from his. "Navy SEAL Team One, Alpha Platoon. We graduated BUD/S together." She looked like she sincerely felt bad and, if she offered to give him a hug, he didn't trust himself not to throw her down and pin her to the floor.

"He was a SEAL?"

"Yeah." He didn't talk about his dead buddies with people who'd never lived in a war zone. "How many shots of vodka did you have?" he asked, purposely changing the subject.

"Two. Maybe." Natalie put her hand on his shoulder and straightened. Put it on him like her touch meant nothing. As if her warm palm didn't send fire down his chest and straight to his crotch. She dropped her hand like she didn't notice. "I feel bad," she added.

Sparky licked his face and he stood. He hung the dog upside down against his chest and scratched its belly. He'd never admit it out loud, but he'd kind of missed the little guy. "Wine, tequila, and vodka is a bad combo."

"No." She pushed one side of her bouncy curls behind her ear. "I feel bad because I've been all annoyed that you stuck me with the dog for two weeks. I thought you'd gone on vacation, but you were at a funeral."

He supposed now was not the time to mention he'd spent the week and a half after the funeral in Texas with Vince, refurbishing his ranch house and shooting skeet.

"Don't feel bad." The dog stretched and yawned and Blake patted Sparky's round gut.

"So I trained Sparky to poop only in your yard."

He looked up.

"There's a lot of it." She moved toward his kitchen. "You might want to pick it up soon."

Blake set the dog down and brushed black fur from his white Henley. He wanted to get pissed off, but he'd dumped a puppy on her so he didn't suppose he could get indignant about it now. "I don't imagine you're going to pick up your half."

She shook her head. The heels of her boots tapping across his wood floor drew his gaze to her long bare legs in black fuck-me boots. "Possession is nine-tenths the law. Remember?"

Yeah. He remembered.

What I Love About You

She reached for his bottle of water on the counter and made herself at home. "Do you cook?" She unscrewed the cap and lifted it to her lips.

"I Crock-Pot," he answered as he watched her drain the bottle. "Do you want some water?"

"No. I'm not thirsty." She wiped the back of her hand across her red mouth and set the empty bottle back down. "Are you recently divorced?"

"No." He took his phone from the pocket of his jeans and set it on the island. "Never married."

Again her heels tapped across the floor as she wandered into the living room. Tap-taps like a sexual code. A relay of information. It was late. She was in his house. He needed to get laid.

Copy that.

"You don't have much furniture." She turned in a slow circle while she looked up at the vaulted ceilings. "I thought maybe you got wiped out in a divorce."

"Before moving here, I lived in a condo in Virginia Beach. I wasn't there a lot."

She looked over her shoulder at him as she walked to the big front windows. "Are you anti-marriage?"

What was this? Twenty-question night? "I think marriage is great. For other people." His ran his gaze up the backs of her legs. "But it's not for me."

"Get your heart broke a time or two?" She stopped in front of her reflection.

"No." He moved behind her, and his gaze met hers in the window. "Are you anti-marriage?"

"No. I've been married." She looked out at the darkness, and the smattering of town lights across the lake. "I'd get married again if I met the right man." She turned to face him and her cape brushed the front of his jeans. "A man around the house would come in handy for those things I can't do myself."

Sex. She couldn't have skin-on-skin sex by herself.

"Like lifting heavy objects and opening pickle jars."

Pickle jars? That's why she wanted a man around?

"The problem with living in Truly," she continued, "is that I went to school with most of the men in town, and none of them are the right one, either." The corners of her lips turned down as her brows pulled together. "If one more person asks if Michael's living with me when he's getting out, I'm going to go all flying snooker crazy."

He'd been trained and tested in hand-to-hand combat. He knew where to hit a man to take him out for a while or for good. "What the hell is 'flying snooker crazy'?"

"I don't know. It sounded lethal when I thought it up in my head, but I'm kind of drunk." Her hand slipped from behind her cape and she twisted the cord around her finger. "I think it's a combination between a flying kick and a snooker punch."

"I guess I won't ask about your ex and risk a flying-snooker butt kicking." He watched her long fingers and short pink nails work the cord and felt it twist his nuts. He wanted her. He wanted to feel her fingers sliding down his chest and diving beneath his pants. She'd told him she wasn't a booty call kind of woman. He bet he could get her to change her mind.

After a few seconds of twisting she asked, "If you aren't anti-marriage, and you've never been married, why do you think it's not for you?"

He raised his gaze from her hand to her red mouth. The lipstick smear tempted him to smear her up a bit more. "I don't have to get hog-tied and barbecued to know getting a spit shoved up my ass isn't for me."

"Ouch." The corners of her mouth turned up. "Have you ever lived with a woman?"

"Yeah." He took the cord from her finger. "My mother." She looked down at his hand as he slowly pulled. "She used to pack my lunches for school. Peanut butter and grape jelly sandwiches. I liked the crusts cut off." The bow slipped free. "But I don't need a mother now."

She lifted her gaze and looked at him like she had in his wine cellar. Like she had a few weeks ago in her kitchen when he'd been so tempted to smash her against him and stick his tongue down her throat. "What do you need?" she asked just above a whisper.

To get laid, temptation answered. Her question hung in the air as he pulled the cord until her cape opened like a shiny present all wrapped up just for him. "What are you wearing, Ms. Cooper?"

"I'm Robin."

Seemed only fitting. "Batman's sidekick." The cape slid from her shoulders and pooled at her feet. Blake's tongue stuck to the roof of his mouth as his gaze landed on a red bustier pushing her plump breasts together. Red-hot lust landed a flying snooker punch to his groin.

She raised a hand over her cleavage. "My costume is kind of tight and slutty."

He reached for her wrist and pinned her hand to the window next to her head. "Tight and slutty is my favorite." He slid his free palm along the side of her warm throat to the back of her neck. "I love tight and slutty." He *needed* tight and slutty.

"You're one of those guys."

He tangled his finger in her hair and pulled her head back. "What guys?"

"The kind who pick up women in bars but never call again."

"I don't go to bars." Not anymore.

"Why?"

"I'm into clean living," he answered. Rehab had pounded the importance of honesty into his head. They'd also pounded the importance of AA, but Natalie didn't need to know about his addiction anymore than he had to attend a meeting to control it. "I'd call a woman again if the sex was good and she wasn't crazy." He lifted his gaze to the lust shining back at him through her blue eyes. "I might even call a crazy girl again if the sex is crazy good." He pushed her back against the window. She gasped, and he took advantage of her parted lips. He kissed her soft mouth, and she tasted like sweet wine and intoxicating pleasure. He had tasted neither in a long time.

It didn't matter that she wasn't a booty call woman. It didn't matter that he *was* a booty call man. It didn't matter that she was drunk. All that mattered was the hot, moist pull of her feeding mouth. Her slick tongue and the rise and fall of her breasts against his chest. Her hands slid up his ribs, and her touch made him want more. A lot more. A lot more of her hands and mouth. A lot more of her hungry mouth sliding south, down his hot flesh. It had been a long time since he'd kissed and touched a woman. A long time since a woman had taken him into her hot, wet mouth.

Instead of sliding south, Natalie curled into his chest and pressed her soft parts into his hard places. He groaned deep in his throat, and slid his hands to the sides of her bustier. He hooked his thumbs beneath the satin top, and all he had to do was yank it down.

What I Love About You

Her head tilted to one side and the kiss got deeper. Deeper and hotter and tempting him to pull the bustier down until her breasts popped out and her hard nipples poked his chest through the thin cotton of his shirt.

As if she read his thoughts, she moaned into his mouth and he had to lock his knees to keep from falling. Through his denim button fly, he rocked his hard penis into her. Into her little shorts and crotch. All he had to do was push aside her shorts and drop his pants. Then he'd be in. Inside where she was hot and wet and her orgasm would grab his erection and pull him deeper.

The tips of his fingers dug into the satin covering her ribs, and he hung on as if she was a mirage. A shiny illusion that would shift and disappear.

He was a man. He needed to get laid. She was in his house and hands and it would be easy to get her into his bed and make everything real.

He was a man living in temptation hell. From Johnnie and Natalie, and it would feel so good to give in to one of them. To drown in it for just one night.

He was a man, but he wasn't that man. He pulled back and looked into her blue eyes sleepy with lust and her mouth wet and swollen from his kiss. "You need to go."

"What?" Her voice was a husky whisper.

"You need to go or you're going to end up my booty call."

She blinked as if his words made no sense.

"Do you want to be my booty call?"

She sucked her bottom lip into her mouth and broke his heart. "No," she said.

He let out a breath he didn't even know he'd been holding. He was a man with more honor than to take advantage of Natalie. "I don't take advantage of drunk women. I want you fully aware when I take advantage of you. So you need to go."

And she did. She stepped around him and disappeared. Like a mirage, but unlike a mirage that wavered, then disappeared completely, she'd left behind the lingering scent of her perfume and the cape at his feet. The imprint of her shoulders on his window and the painful erection in his pants let him know that she wasn't a flashback from the past.

Blake tilted his head back and looked up at the ceiling. He was sick of temptation. He'd had a belly full of living with it. Of it riding him hard and him not giving in. Ever. Not to his desire for booze or the neighbor. He was tired of white-knuckling his way through life.

Natalie was gone. The temptation of her body, naked and pressed against him, was out of his reach, but Johnnie wasn't. The number one temptation in his life sat in a dark wine cellar, chilled to a perfect fifty-five degrees. All he had to do was take a few straight shots, and his biggest temptation would take care of the second. It would dull the edge of addiction and the ache in his groin.

A win-fucking-win situation.

Instead he turned off the lights and headed upstairs. He took a shower and himself in hand. Beneath the warm flow of water, he gave himself relief. Relief from the desire pounding his groin, but it did not last long.

Twice he woke from dreams of Natalie. Dreams of her mouth and hands all over him and his mouth and hands all over her. *What do you need?* she asked. In his dreams he was free to show her. Free to touch her anywhere. To kiss her where he liked to kiss a woman. To part her thighs and shove himself into her soft body.

Each time he woke, frustration turned to anger, and by the time he got out of bed, he was in a foul mood. The kind that squeezed the back of his neck and burned a hole in his gut. The kind that loaded his addiction on a one-way train to relapse if he didn't find a way to stop before he ran his life off the rails.

He pulled on his running shoes and jogged a five-mile trail into the mountains, but his mood didn't improve. It didn't improve much more when he busted out his camera and snapped shots of the lake. It certainly didn't improve when he discovered Sparky had chewed a hole in his leather sofa or when he had to shovel the dog poop in his backyard.

Blake wheeled the big gray garbage can down his drive toward the curb. How had his life become this? How had he ended up an alcoholic, sexually frustrated, dog-poop scooper?

"What are you doing, Blake?"

Blake parked the gray garbage can at the curb, then turned his attention to Charlotte, standing by her mailbox in a puffy purple coat and a knit unicorn hat. "I just cleaned up about ten pounds of dog shit."

Charlotte gasped. "That's a bad word."

"Did Sparky eat some of your hair ribbons?"

She nodded. "He ate my Hello Kitty bow."

"Yeah. I found it." He moved the few feet toward her. "It was in his crap."

Her little nose wrinkled and she shook her head. "I don't want it back."

He tried not to smile. "Are you sure? You could probably dig it out of his poop and put it in your hair."

"Gwoss!" She shook her head harder. "You can keep it for *your* hair." Then she laughed like their conversation was hysterically funny. "You're a poopy head!"

Christ. Poop talk with a five-year-old. "I like your hat." He pointed to the gold horn and white ears on top of her head. "Nice horn."

Her laughter died suddenly and she frowned. "It's a corn."

"Really?" He looked a little closer. "It looks like a horn to me."

"It's a corn." She rolled her eyes. "Uni-*corn*."

"Jesus."

"That's a bad word."

"Yeah. I know." Was this really his life? Picking up dog shit and arguing with a five-year-old? Lusting after her mother and masturbating like a teenager?

"Guess what?"

He looked at his watch. The Niners were playing the Packers at six-thirty. If he hurried, he could catch the last hour of the pregame show. "What?"

"I got a secret." She looked behind her toward her house. "I can't tell my mom."

His hand dropped to his side. That wasn't good. He'd never really been around kids but he knew keeping secrets from a mom didn't sound good.

"My daddy is coming home from jail."

"Yeah?" He looked down into Charlotte's little face. Her cheeks were pink from the cold.

"I heard my nana talk to my papa."

"I think your mom knows."

"No. She didn't tell me. She always tells me stuff." She shook her head and her horn wobbled. "I have another secret."

He glanced at the front door and back. "Yeah?"

"I have to tell it in your ear." She motioned with her hand for him to bend down.

142

So he did. Way down.

"Don't laugh," she whispered, and her small breath tickled his ear. "I'm scared."

"Why?"

"I don't know him." She placed her hand on his shoulder and leaned in a little closer. "Nana told Papa I can stay with Daddy sometimes. She said I can live with him, but I want to live with my mama. I'm never leaving my mama's house."

He shouldn't say anything. It wasn't his business, but Charlotte's small hand on his shoulder and her little voice in his ear made him feel strangely protective. Like he should do something even when he knew it wasn't his place.

"What if I don't like him?"

He doubted Charlotte would be living with her dad anytime soon. No, it wasn't his place to say anything, but he pulled back and made the mistake of looking into her blue eyes, like she expected him to tell her something to make it better. Like she expected him to *do* something. Blake was a man of action. He made things better for a living, but this was above his pay grade. She kept looking at him like he had the answer so he said, "You'll like him."

"How do you know?"

Yeah. How did he know? He shouldn't have said anything, but since he had, he was involved. "You didn't like me when you first met me."

She nodded. "You were mean."

"And now we're friends." He straightened and shook his head. Friends with a five-year-old. A five-year-old who rolled her eyes at him and called him poopy head. His friends didn't call him poopy head.

"Yeah." She looked at him, and her hat shifted toward the back of her head. "And now we have Spa-ky."

Recruit Sparky was currently in his crate, rethinking his behavior.

The front door swung open and Natalie stuck her head out. "Charlotte, come in and wash your hands for dinner."

At the sight of her blond hair across the yard, Blake's anger and frustration pinched his skull. He should tell her about his conversation with Charlotte, but with the previous night still very fresh in his head, it would be best to avoid Natalie for the next few days. Or months, when the taste and touch of her mouth beneath his was just a distant memory.

Chapter Seven

The whir and hum of the commercial printer filled Natalie's ears with the sound of money. The photo printing side of her business had picked up so much lately, she'd hired a part-time employee just the day before. Brandy Finley was a senior at the local high school and the hours were perfect for her. Natalie needed help at the front counter when everyone in the county decided to pick up their prints at five o'clock. She especially needed someone to help package photos to mail.

"Sometimes people send inappropriate photos and we don't know it until they are already printed," she told Brandy as she showed her how to load the machine with new ink. She thought of

Frankie and this young girl getting an eyeful of his junk. "If you come across naked pictures, or anything you find personally disturbing, set the order aside and I'll take care of it."

"People send in naked pictures?" Brandy looked at her through the lenses of her glasses. Even if Brandy hadn't written on her application that she was a member of the science club and played clarinet in the marching band, the nerdy cat T-shirt she'd worn her first day would have given her away. Today she wore a Team Voldemort T-shirt with a wand on it, reminding Natalie that she needed to order Brandy several work shirts like Natalie wore. Crisp white blouse with the logo over the breast pocket. Khaki or black pants, but no jeans.

"Unfortunately, yes." Natalie understood why a person would want to order twenty or more photos from her, but she didn't understand why they wouldn't keep their personal pictures personal and print them off at home.

She showed Brandy how to package the photos to be matted and mailed out. While the girl arranged mailers, Natalie took the opportunity to grab a stack of prints Blake had sent a few hours ago. It had been two days since she'd seen him standing by her mailbox when she'd sent Charlotte out to put away her bike. Three since she'd made out with him. She recalled little about that night. Just bits and pieces of his kiss and his hands on her waist. His hard chest against hers and his muscles beneath her palms. If her memory was right, and not just part of a drunken fantasy, Blake Junger knew how to kiss a woman. He didn't ask and didn't hesitate. He just lowered his handsome face and burned up any resistance with his hot, powerful mouth. Not that she remembered giving any resistance. Not even a token effort.

She also remembered something about him comparing marriage to a barbecue spit up his butt and asking her if she wanted to be his booty call. She remembered that she'd been tempted. So tempted to peel off her Robin costume and curl up on his naked chest.

She'd like to blame her lack of any sort of resistance on alcohol. She *had* been drunk that night. Irresponsible and drunk. She was the mother of a five-year-old and never drank like that. She certainly never mixed alcohol that was sure to give her a hangover, and she blamed her two-day headache on Michael. Obviously his impending return was getting to her more than she'd imagined. She'd expected to feel apprehension, but not the heaviness that grew with each day. She worried about Charlotte and how she would take the news that her father was really coming home this time. She worried that Michael would expect to breeze into their lives and play the long-lost daddy. Mostly, she worried that he would break Charlotte's heart like he'd broken hers.

Natalie looked at the first photo Blake had shot of Lake Mary, through branches of ponderosa and yellow aspen. He'd obviously set the aperture at a higher value and increased his depth of field to kept the edges nice and sharp.

It didn't do any good to make herself crazy and drink like a sailor on leave. Michael had either changed or he hadn't. There was nothing she could do about it today. She slid the photo to the bottom of the stack and looked at the second. Blake had taken advantage of natural light filtering through variegated shade to snap a picture of a squirrel perched on a stump. He had snapped a series of Sparky playing in leaves, chewing a stick, and partially lifting his leg on a pinecone. It was such a guy photo that she chuckled.

There was nothing she could do about the

other night in Blake's living room, either, but the more she thought about it, the more bits and pieces she recalled. She remembered him pushing her against the window and pulling the back of her hair, and she remembered that she'd liked it. She liked the hot little shivers of pleasure up and down her spine as he took charge and the choice from her. She remembered that he'd pulled away and sent her home because she was drunk. Maybe beneath all that testosterone and badass aura, he was actually a good man.

The bell over the door rang, and she looked up as the source of all those hot shivers strolled in wearing a gray and white flannel shirt tucked into those jeans with the interesting button fly. The door swung shut behind him, and he pulled a pair of dark sunglasses from his face. His gray gaze met hers, and all the bits and pieces of her memory flooded in on her at once. The memory of his lips on hers and his long, deep kiss made her cheeks flush like a girl's. Embarrassed, she broke eye contact. She lowered her gaze to his squirrel picture, and . . . Crap! She'd been caught snooping through Blake's pictures, and he was too close not to notice. "Are you here for your prints?" she asked the obvious, trying to act all natural like snooping was a service she provided for her customers.

"Yeah." He stopped on the other side of the counter as she scooped up his prints. "You about done being nosy?"

"I was just checking to make sure the printer stayed on line. It's called quality assurance."

"Uh-huh." He pointed at the photos with his glasses, then shoved them on top of his head. "More like you're checking for dick pictures."

Her mouth fell open. That had not occurred to her. Now it did though. Had he sent in a penis pic? Was it beneath his Sparky and squirrel photos?

"No," he answered as if he'd read her mind, and planted his hands on the counter. The sleeves of his shirt were rolled up his thick forearms. "I don't need to take a shot of my package to get a woman's attention."

A piece of her memory fell into place like a missing shard and was embedded with the recollection of his "package" pressed against her. She shoved the prints into a photo envelope and wished she could shove aside the memory of his big erection shoved up against her crotch. "Charlotte told me Sparky chewed up your leather sofa," she said, changing the subject.

What I Love About You

Blake frowned. "Down to the wood." He reached in his back pocket and pulled out his wallet. "His chew toy was on top of the stuffing like a cherry on a cake."

"He got one of my blue suede pumps." She rang up his photos and he swiped his American Express black card. She thought only rappers and rock stars had black cards, which made her again wonder what the man did for a living.

"I finished the mailers, Natalie," Brandy said behind her. Natalie turned and introduced her new employee to Blake. Brandy blushed and stared at a spot on the counter. Natalie knew how she felt. Blake Junger was the biggest and best-looking thing to hit this town in years.

"How many Horcruxes have you created?" Blake asked as he put his card back in his wallet.

Horcruxes? Natalie looked from one to the other. What was a Horcrux?

"One," Brandy answered.

"Let me guess. Your cat."

"No!" She glanced up. "I would never hurt Pixel." A shy smile tilted her lips. "My car."

"You have an evil car?" Blake chuckled.

Brandy nodded, and Natalie had to ask, "What is a Horcrux?"

Her employee looked at her through her glasses like she was surprised Natalie didn't know. "An object where a witch or wizard hides a part of their soul so they can live forever. It's evil."

What?

"It's from Harry Potter," she explained further, and Natalie felt like she had a big arrow above her head, pointing to the only person on the planet who hadn't read the books. But evidently Blake had read Harry Potter and knew about Horcruxes. He was just full of surprises.

He shoved his wallet into his back pocket, then turned his gaze to Natalie. "Do you have a few minutes? We need to talk."

No doubt he wanted to talk about Saturday night, and that was the last thing she wanted to discuss with him. She just didn't want any more of the blanks filled in. "I'm kind of busy."

"It's about Charlotte."

"Oh." That threw her a bit, and she turned to Brandy. "Do you think you'll be okay if a customer comes in?"

Brandy nodded and looked so earnest, Natalie felt comfortable leaving her for a few moments. She led Blake to her office and left the door open just a crack. "Did Charlotte do something?"

"No."

Charlotte was usually such a good girl, it was hard for Natalie to imagine that she'd done something so horrible it warranted a conversation behind closed doors. She sat on the edge of her desk stacked with stray photo paper and invoices, and she folded her arms under her breasts.

"She knows her dad is getting out of prison."

Her arms fell to her sides and her heart skipped a painful beat. "How?"

"She told me she overheard her grandparents talking about it."

She'd told *him*? "When did she tell you all this?"

"Sunday. By your mailbox."

Natalie lowered her gaze to the buttons closing the flannel shirt over his big chest. A myriad of emotions tumbled and twisted in her stomach. Among them anger that the Coopers hadn't been more careful, and Natalie wasn't so sure Charlotte hadn't been meant to overhear them. The Coopers were good to her and Charlotte, but sometimes they did an end-run around her. "What else did she say?"

"That you don't know he's getting out because you would have told her."

"Crap." She raised her gaze to his eyes. "I didn't tell because the last time he said he was getting out, he didn't." How was she going to tell her child that she'd known about her father but hadn't told her? What could she say? God, she hated Michael. "I try really hard to never lie to that child. I sometimes might leave things out that might scare her, but I don't lie. Never. And now she'll think she can't trust me to tell her the truth."

"Everyone lies just a little."

She shook her head and looked into his face. "I don't lie, Blake. I hate lies and liars. Lies ruin lives." She rubbed her forehead and closed her eyes. "Did she say anything else?"

"She's scared that she won't like him."

"She doesn't know enough about him not to like him." She stood and turned to her desk. "She talks to him sometimes on the phone when she visits the Coopers, but she's never met him in person." Her hands shook as she reached for the invoices on her desk. "Maybe she's overheard me and Lilah talk about him." She spoke her thoughts out loud. "Or maybe me and my mom. God knows what I might have said throughout the years."

"I think she's afraid she might have to live with him."

Natalie spun around and dropped the papers at her feet. "That will *never* happen." It was just like Michael to think the world still revolved around him. "He didn't want Charlotte." She felt her temper rise, and she didn't bother to contain it. "I tried for five years to conceive that child. Five *years*, and the day after I told him I was finally pregnant, he skipped town with his twenty-year-old girlfriend and several million dollars of investors' money. He was planning to start a new life in Sweden or Switzerland . . . or wherever!" She raised a hand and dropped it to her side. "If he hadn't gotten caught, I never would have known if he was dead or alive. His own parents wouldn't have known!" She let out a breath and shook her head. "I wish he hadn't gotten caught. I wish he'd gotten away. I wish he'd frozen to death in the Alps. I wish his prison bus had caught on fire on the way to the big house. I wish he'd gotten shanked!" She covered her mouth with her hands. Okay, she shouldn't have let that last wish out for anyone but Lilah to hear. Lilah understood. She dropped her hands to her side and glanced up at him. He looked more amused than horrified by her bloodthirsty outburst. "Sorry to vent. I'm done. It's just that I hate him for what he did." She swallowed past the dry rage clogging her throat. "The last time I talked to him on the phone, he said he wants to see a lot of Charlotte and me." She guessed she wasn't quite done venting yet and felt it pressing in on her like a black fog. "He asked me to think about working on our relationship." She held up quote fingers. " 'For Charlotte's sake.' "

She didn't love Michael anymore, and she certainly didn't trust anything that came out of his lying mouth. "That will *never* happen, either. He doesn't really want to be a family. It's just a con. Plain and simple. That's all there is to it."

"Probably not all."

God, was Blake like everyone else and thought Michael deserved a second chance?

"I imagine he wants to get laid."

She stared at him without saying anything, but her eyes spoke for her.

What I Love About You

"Hey." He held up both hands. "The guy's just getting out of prison. It's a given he wants to get laid."

She frowned. "Then he should probably hire a hooker. I'm not the young girl he dated in high school or the naive wife he married and dumped." She took a few short breaths and stared at the bump of his Adam's apple above his plaid collar. "It's not like he went to war for the past five years or got stranded on a desert island. He's been in prison for stealing retirement money from old people, but everyone around this town is acting like they can't wait to welcome him back. Michael Cooper, star quarterback and all-around good guy. I can understand why his parents forgive him. But everyone else?"

His touch under her chin brought her attention back to his cool gaze. "Breathe or you're going to pass out."

She shook her head, and the tips of his fingers brushed her skin. "I never passed out."

He tapped a finger on the tip of her chin, then dropped his hand. "Humor me and take a few deep breaths."

She did and felt the fog clear a bit.

"Are you afraid of your ex?"

157

She was afraid he'd charm her daughter's susceptible heart. "I'm afraid he'll try and take Charlotte from me."

The cool in Blake's gray eyes turned frosty. "When the lead starts to fly, I'm a good man to have around."

Lead? Did he mean bullets? "I don't think Michael will shoot me. I hate him but I would never kill him." She'd just admitted that she wanted Michael dead, and she paused for half a second to collect her scattered thoughts. "No. Really. I mean . . . I'd get caught. The ex-wife is always the first suspect. Just last week, a lady in California was arrested for hiring a hit man she met in a bar. The hit man got caught and turned on the woman." She shook her head with disgust. "There's no honor among assassins."

"Never look for a hit man in a bar, Sweet Cheeks." He took her hand and dipped his face to look into hers. "Professional contractors don't get work out of a bar."

Natalie's eyes widened. *Professional contractors?* "Are you a hit man?" She probably shouldn't have just come out and asked that out loud, but it made sense. He didn't work nine to five but had money.

"If I told you, I'd have to kill you."

What I Love About You

She opened her mouth but nothing came out. Was he a hit man? A soldier of fortune?

He chuckled, and humor lines appeared at the corners of his eyes. "No. I'm not a hit man. I am a professional security contractor."

"What does that mean?"

"It means I'm a retired Navy SEAL, special operator first class, with a toolkit full of skills. Private military companies pay me a lot of money to use those skills."

"Is it legal?"

"Yes." He grinned and pulled her against his chest. "Mostly." He slid one arm across the small of her back.

Her hand found his shoulder as she fell against his flannel shirt and wall of muscles. She had more questions about his skills and exactly what that meant, but she suddenly couldn't think beyond the heat rolling off him like a radiator and warming up her breasts and belly.

"I'm on my way out of town." He pulled her onto the balls of her feet so her nose was level with his. His eyes a soft, sexy gray. "I stopped by to let you know so you don't bitch me out like last time."

Inside her crammed office, everything pressed in

on her until there was only he. His eyes shone a seductive gray and his big hand slid to her butt. "What are you doing?" came out on a shocked breath.

"I got skills. Skills the military didn't teach me. Skills I've learned all on my own." He lowered his face to hers and his lips brushed hers when he said, "You're going to love the skills in my own personal toolbox."

She should push him away. They were in her office. Really she should, but his lips brushed hers, teasing her with warm touches, and the memory of deeper kisses. Bits and pieces of hot kisses, and she decided to wait a minute. One minute to determine if the memory of his kiss was as good as she remembered or just her drunken imagination. She tilted her face to the right and tested her recall. He smelled good, like soap and skin and cool breezes, and he tasted better. Like warm mouth and hot sex. Yes, she remembered that part.

One minute of light, chasing kisses turned into two. She told herself it was just kisses. Nothing more, and she wrapped her arms around his neck. The moment she ran her finger through his short hair, the air inside the office turned carnal and possessive. Her tongue touched his, and he tasted so good she didn't give another thought to stopping.

Against his solid chest and soft flannel, her breasts felt heavy and her nipples tightened to hard, aching points. He fed her hungry mouth with deep, soul-sweeping kisses, and she ate them up. Hot threads of fire ran through her veins and pooled low in her abdomen. Low where her thighs met, and she squeezed her legs together against the onslaught of sensation. Sensation that wanted him to slide his warm hand from the curve of her backside and slip it between her thighs. Hot, liquid sensation that made her forget she stood in the office of Glamour Snaps and Prints, and a mere cracked-open door separated her from the rest of her business.

Then he tilted his head to the side and deepened the kiss, and she wanted even more. He forced her to take a few steps back, and he lifted her. Her backside hit the top of the desk and he moved between her parted thighs. The pockets of his gray cargo pants brushing the inside of her legs.

The tips of his fingers brushed her collarbone and slid to the top button of her shirt. She held on to his shoulders, and her lips clung to his as every breath filled with sensuous longing. The kind she'd let herself forget as she'd fought to survive.

His shoulders were so solid beneath her touch. Solid and warm and so powerful, she arched her back toward the heat of his chest. His fingers teased her skin and brushed her cleavage as he worked each button from its hole. Then his big hand slid inside and she moaned deep in her throat. Deep down in the primal part that wanted and lusted. The part that needed pleasure. He cupped her breast, weighing her in his hot palm, and his mouth kissed the side of her throat, leaving a moist little path just below her ear. Shivers ran down her spine to her bottom, and his thumb brushed her nipple, back and forth through the thin nylon of her bra.

"Your skin tastes sweet," he whispered against the patch of her neck he'd wet with his mouth. "You smell good. God, I want you so much I'm about to explode."

"Yes." A warning bell rang in her head and she shut it out.

"Take me out." He lightly bit her just below her ear. "Take me in your hand."

"Mmm." She slid her palm from his shoulder

and down his chest. His muscles bunched beneath her touch. His breath brushed the side of her neck, rapid and heavy, then caught and held in anticipation of her touch.

The warning bell rang again and Natalie's fingers curled around his belt buckle. Something wasn't right. The bell sounded a lot like the service bell at the front counter. It rang again, and everything in her stilled. The noise beyond her office reached her foggy head and she heard Brandy's voice and a deep male response.

"Stop," Natalie whispered, and pushed at Blake's shoulders. "Someone is out front."

"So." His hand on her breast tightened. Not painful but not like he wanted to let go, either.

"We can't do this here."

"Yes we can."

"No." She pushed him and he dropped his hand.

"Great." He moved back far enough for her to stand. "We'll go to my house. I have an hour if we hurry."

"I have a business. I'm a mother." Her fingers shook as she buttoned her blouse. "I don't do this sort of thing."

"You didn't do anything. Yet."

"I'm not going to, either." She glanced up into his eyes, all stormy now beneath his lusty lids. He was so handsome and she was so tempted to go to his house and fall in bed for an hour. "Ever," she added for emphasis, more to herself than Blake.

He took a deep breath, and he looked like he wanted to hit something. Instead he pointed at her. "Then don't come near me, Natalie Cooper. 'Cause I can guaran-goddamn-tee the next time I'm not stopping. I don't care if you're drunk or standing in the middle of Main Street." He yanked the door open. "You're getting naked and I'm climbing all over you."

She dropped her hands and watched his retreating back as he walked out of her office. He moved past the printers, and she wondered how many customers were out front.

Act natural. Anxiety tumbled with the lust still warming her stomach as she followed close on Blake's heels. She put a smile on her face and pretended like nothing happened. Like Blake Junger hadn't just stormed out of her office looking all hot and sexy. *Act natural.* Like he wasn't a dark, angry cloud rolling past Frankie Cornell.

"Hi, Natalie." Frankie stood at the counter with a pack of photos in his hand, all cheery and pleased like he didn't know he'd just dodged Hurricane Blake.

"Hello, Frankie," she said, a little too friendly to be natural.

Blake yanked opened the door but stopped in his tracks. His shoulders looked so wide framed by the entrance. Then he slowly turned and pinned poor Frankie with his gaze. "Let me give you some advice, my friend." He took the sunglasses from the top of his head and shoved them on his face. "Keep your camera out of your pants. No one wants to see your cock."

Chapter Eight

A crescent moon hung like a pale sliver above the mud wall and the compound beyond. It was the perfect moon. A sniper's moon in the dead of night.

"You all asleep?" team leader and retired Delta Force operator, Fast Eddy, asked the four-man team through the headset.

"Junger's getting twitchy."

From his position on top of a small hill, Blake chuckled. "I'm staying frosty." All his senses were definitely on high alert, but he was relaxed. He lay on his belly, behind an MK11 mounted on a swivel base bipod. The weapon was a semi-automatic, with a twenty-round box filled with 7.62 NATO rounds, accurate up to fifteen hundred feet. Three additional magazines sat next to the rifle in case things went sideways and he had to light up the night. He and three other contractors had been airdropped from twenty-five thousand feet, then walked under the cover of darkness two miles to the compound in South Yemen.

Through his thermal optics scope, he watched the three other contractors make their way toward the mud wall surrounding the compound.

Blake hadn't been behind a rifle since before rehab. It felt like coming home. Like picking up his life where he'd left it before drinking had completely taken over. Looking down the sights of a sniper scope was familiar. He knew what to do. There was no confusion. Not like looking into a pair of blue eyes and lusting so hard he didn't recognize himself.

This direct action mission was what he needed to clear his head. To remind himself that he was a security contractor. A man who spit and swore and scratched his balls. A man whose buddies spit and swore and scratched their balls. Not a man who had a five-year-old for a best friend and whose mother gave him blue balls.

He'd trained for two days with this team of contractors, each retired from different Special Forces units. He knew the layout of the compound like the back of his hand. Beyond the mud wall, oil executive John Morton was being held hostage in the smaller of the two buildings. Mr. Morton had been taken from his hotel in Turkey and transported to South Yemen, the heart of al-Qaeda. His captors were demanding the release of four terrorists currently held in Guantanamo.

The U.S. government did not negotiate with terrorists, but that didn't mean the CIA wasn't tangentially involved with several private military firms around the world. The State Department provided them with the latest intel as well as billions of taxpayer dollars; in turn, they provided the government with plausible deniability.

According to the latest intelligence, there were half a dozen armed guards loaded with AKs at the compound. Two stood guard at a locked gate and four more occupied the larger of the structures. At 1800 Zulu every night, one of the terrorists took bread and water across the compound to the smaller building that held Mr. Morton. The fact that they bothered to feed him was a good sign that he was still alive and still chained to a bed. But even though it was a good sign, it wasn't a certainty. If they knew for certain he was in the smaller building, they'd send some RPGs through the windows of the larger of the two and go home.

"See anything, Junger?"

Through the green glow of night optics, Blake looked for hot spots in the small windows in the buildings below. There was no movement, just a little light. He dialed in the scope to a position beyond the back wall and the desert terrain beyond. "Just some sheep twenty meters southeast." One of the first rules of intel gathering was to relate all activity for analysis. Even if it didn't seem significant. "They appear ass-raped as hell."

All four men chuckled softly into the mics built into their helmets.

"Benson was ass-raped in a hut just like that," a tall, redheaded SEAL named Farkus informed the group.

Benson looked like Ving Rhames in *Pulp Fiction*. Big, glossy black, and ready to go medieval. He was also the father of six and claimed to work for the "firm" because he needed a vacation. "By your mama."

A weak flash of light caught the corner of Blake's eye and he swiveled the rifle around and doped the scope. Adrenaline ran up his spine and raised the hair on the back of his neck. He said in a calm, clear voice, "Target six o'clock." It got real quiet. "It appears to be a white truck." This wasn't in the intel they'd been given or part of the battle plan.

"Roger. Target six o'clock," Fast Eddy responded. From his position, he wouldn't be able to see the truck. "Just one?"

"Correct." But no matter the planning, Blake had been on many missions that didn't go down as planned. There were too many variables. The known unknowns and the unknown unknowns. This truck was somewhere in the middle. "Two headlights about one kilometer."

"Roger. How many individuals?"

"Looks like two in the cab. One standing in the back. They're just entering range." If the truck rounded the small hill, the terrorists inside the compound would see the headlights. "I can take care of them or we can wait and see what they're up to."

"They're up to no good. Take them out."

"Roger." To compensate for distance and air temperature, Blake put the crosshairs below and to the left of the glowing red and yellow turban peeking over the roof of the truck. Intrinsic as his own heartbeat, Blake squeezed the trigger. The silencer on the end of the barrel suppressed the gunfire to a high-pressured pop of air. He lowered the sights and sent two more rounds into the headlights and four into the cab, delivering each terrorist a double tap. The truck veered off the road and slowed. Through the night scope, Blake watched for movement. The passenger door opened and one individual sprang out. His hijab was a bright yellow glow as Blake squeezed the trigger and sent a round center mass. The man crumpled. "Target down."

"Roger. Anything moving?"

"Not anymore." He twisted the rifle around toward the compound and looked through the scope. He watched the three Americans move in the shadows. Near the gate, Fast Eddy gave the signal to eliminate, and Blake fired four rounds. The terrorists were dead before they hit the ground. Farkus loaded the gate with a dose of

C4 and stepped back into the shadows. The lock blew and the three Americans were through the gate and inside the compound before the smoke cleared. Benson kicked in the door of the bigger building and he and Fast Eddy entered while Farkus ran to the smaller of the two where the hostage was thought to be held. The boom of flashbang and the *pop-pop* of gunshot split the air. Within moments, the fight was over and Fast Eddy's voice spoke in Blake's helmet. "Structure clear. Targets eliminated."

Blake kept the crosshairs on the door where Farkus had disappeared. "Hostage located and alive," the former SEAL reported, and everyone could hear the relief in his voice.

Blake adjusted the four magazines strapped in his chest gear. Eight dead terrorists, and one hostage alive and soon to be reunited with his family. Blake felt good. The juice running through his veins felt good. This was his life. His element. He knew what he was doing here. It was black and white. No gray areas.

Through his headset, he listened to the chatter below and kept watch over the compound. The hostage was alive, but by the sounds of it, roughed up pretty good. Eddy made the call to the Black Hawk half an hour out. Half an hour to watch the area from his position, then load up and head back to Oman. In the past, he and his buddies had found the nearest bar. In the past, he'd unwound with beers and straight shots and a warm woman.

Now that the mission was over, now that the rush of it flowed from his body, the thought of booze rushed in, bigger than it had in several months.

He removed his finger from the trigger and looked down at the slight tremor in his hand. He made a fist and shook it out. For the first time that night, for the first time since he'd stepped out of the DHC–3 and felt nothing beneath his feet, a little bump of fear broke through his calm. Whether in a rehab in California, a small town in Idaho, or a patch of dirt in South Yemen, his addiction followed and bit him on the ass.

His addiction was weakness.

Weakness was not an option. Not in Yemen or Qatar or the other NATO bases he landed in as he crossed the globe. Not on his flight back to the States, not two days later as he drove to Truly.

No, weakness was not an option, but by the time Blake pulled into Truly, he was dead tired. Tired of flying and fighting the one demon he couldn't take out with a well-placed bullet. He'd beaten his demon. Hadn't given in to the whisper in his head, the need in his gut, or the tremor in his hand. But it hadn't been easy. His back ached. His eyes were gritty, and his feet hurt.

Willie Nelson's "Nothing I Can Do About It Now" filled the cab of his truck as he drove through town and took a left around the lake. His dad was a huge Willie fan and Blake had grown up on his music. As Willie sang about regret written on his brow, Blake thought about the big spa tub waiting for him at home. As he'd sat in first class from Chicago to Boise, and on the two-hour drive from Boise to Truly, he'd thought about hot jets of water massaging the knots out of his muscles.

Blake turned his truck onto Red Fox Road and his attention immediately caught on two familiar figures walking up the street and the dog pulling at the leash. Rays of orange sunlight shone on them as they walked between the deeper shadows of pine.

Blake slowed the truck and pulled to the other side of the road. Charlotte wore her unicorn hat and raised a white-gloved hand to wave. "Blake!" He saw more than heard his name on her lips. Through the gray tint of his windows, he raised his gaze to Natalie and her deep blue eyes. She wore a navy peacoat on her slim shoulders and a blue beret on the top of her long blond hair. The last time he'd seen Natalie, he had her breast in his hand and his tongue in her mouth. Her cheeks turned pink, as if she was thinking about the last time, too. Or perhaps it was the cool air brushing her face and tossing the ends of her hair about her shoulders.

He turned off Willie and rolled down the window. "Hey there, Charlotte." He kept his gaze locked with Natalie's when what he really wanted was to lower his attention to the open buttons of her coat and think inappropriate thoughts. "Ms. Cooper."

"Mr. Junger."

Charlotte jumped up and looked into the window. "We're walking Spa-ky."

"Yeah. I can see that."

She jumped up again and the horn on her hat

bobbed. "Come with us." She went down and jumped again. "We like to walk him to the paw-k."

A walk to the park was about the last thing he wanted.

"I'm sure Blake has better things to do," Natalie said, giving him an out.

A November breeze blew several strands of blond hair across Natalie's lips and tickled her cheek before she pushed them behind her ear. It was cold out but Blake looked hotter than usual. He looked like he hadn't shaved since he'd left town. The bottom half of his handsome face was covered in a blond scruff. He gazed at her from across the cab of his truck, his eyes a dark gray, tired and alert at the same time.

"I'll catch up with you."

The tinted window slid up and Natalie turned and watched Blake's big red Ford roll down the road, then pull into his driveway. She reached for Charlotte's hand and almost tripped over Sparky. She'd enrolled the dog in an obedience school that started in a week. "We'll have to get Sparky's school to teach him how to walk on a leash." She took a few steps but Charlotte didn't budge from her spot on the side of the road.

"We have to wait for Blake."

"He said he'd catch up with us." Although she doubted he meant it. The last time he'd seen her, he'd been so mad he'd threatened to climb on top of her in the middle of Main Street. Then he'd yelled at Frankie.

Together, she and Charlotte and Sparky continued down the street. She hadn't wanted a dog. Not yet. Not until Charlotte could take more responsibility in the day-to-day care of a puppy, but Natalie had to admit, he was kind of growing on her. Especially when he slept after a long walk.

Sparky barked and pounced on a leaf, more like a cat than a dog. Charlotte laughed, and Natalie's heart pinched just a little. From the day of Charlotte's birth, Natalie worried that her daughter would suffer for the choices that her parents made. Natalie's own parents had divorced when she'd been nine, but at least she'd had those first impressionable years when a father was important in a child's life. Charlotte had her grandfather Cooper, but Natalie worried he wasn't a significant enough role model to keep her child from becoming a sad statistic. And she especially worried how Michael's sudden appearance would affect Charlotte.

The day she'd learned that Charlotte knew when Michael would be released from prison, she'd talked to her daughter about it. She'd waited until Charlotte's bath time to bring it up. Bath time was girl time. Time when they talked while Natalie shampooed her child's hair. Charlotte had told her she was happy and excited to finally meet her dad, but she didn't want to live with him. Natalie assured her daughter that she wasn't going to live anywhere but her own home with her mom.

"What if I don't like him?" Charlotte had asked as she scrubbed her feet. Charlotte had been so serious that Natalie had had to bite her lip to keep from smiling. It didn't occur to Charlotte that Michael might not like *her*. Charlotte always assumed that everyone just naturally loved her and thought she was wonderful. Perhaps Natalie and her mother and Lilah had overcompensated a bit.

"What if Spa-ky doesn't like school?" Charlotte asked as she pulled the dog away from a neighbor's hissing cat. The neighbor came out and Natalie waved as they passed by.

What I Love About You

"He'll get to meet other dogs and learn some tricks." She adjusted the beret on her head. "Think of it like you going to school. You like school."

"No, Mama. I don't like school anymore."

Natalie looked down at the top of Charlotte's unicorn hat. "I thought you liked playing with your friends and learning to read."

Charlotte shook her head. "Nope. Amy said I couldn't be a hoss today and made me be a chicken. I didn't want to be a chicken."

Across the street, they passed the house where Gordon Loosey had jumped off the second story roof after pounding back a twenty-four pack of Bud Light.

"I wanted to be a hoss."

"Did you tell her you wanted to be a horse?" Needless to say, the house had remained vacant now for the last three years.

"Yes. She said if I wanted to play farm with her and Madison, I had to be a chicken."

Natalie stuck her cold hands in her pockets. Playground politics could be brutal. "Well, that's not very nice."

"So I told her she was a big poopy head."

"Charlotte!"

She turned her face and looked up. "What?"

"You can't call people that."

She shrugged her shoulders inside her puffy coat. "Blake doesn't care if I call him a poopy head."

"You called Blake a poopy head?" They stepped up on the curb and started down the paved trail to the park.

"Yep."

"When?"

"Umm . . . that one day." They cut across the cold grass to a colder bench.

"What one day?"

"That one day when he picked up the poop." She thought a moment longer and added, "The day I told him about my dad."

"Oh." The day of her Halloween hangover. The day after he'd kissed her for the first time.

"Can Spa-ky get off his leash now?"

"Yep." Natalie bent down to unhook the dog as Charlotte took off her mittens and worked a ball from her pocket. "You have to stay where I can see you. Remember?"

"I wememeber."

Natalie stood. "*Re*member with the R sound."

"Re re," Charlotte practiced and handed Natalie the ball to put on her mitten. "*Re*member."

"Good job." Natalie handed the ball back. "We're not going to stay too long because it's cold."

Sparky saw the ball and barked like a lunatic as Charlotte cocked back her arm and threw. It sailed through the air for about fifteen feet, and the puppy pounced on it the second it touched the ground. He looked at Charlotte, then took off with the neon green ball in his mouth.

"Come back, Spa-ky!" She patted her knees and the dog stopped and looked at her. He turned his head to the side and dropped the ball. "Good dog," Charlotte said as she walked toward him. Of course the "good dog" grabbed the ball in his mouth and took off again. Charlotte ran after, calling the puppy's name.

"I see that dog isn't any better behaved since before I left," Blake said from behind Natalie.

She turned and watched him move toward her and was surprised to see him. Surprised that he'd actually shown up.

He walked toward her wearing his tactical

boots and Levi's. The worn denim cupped his package, and she raised her gaze to his brown jacket with pockets on the chest and arms. It had darker brown shapes on the shoulders as if it had once had several patches and he'd ripped them off. His scruffy beard made him look a little ruthless and wildly hot.

She felt heat rise up her neck to her cheeks, and her stomach got a fuzzy feeling inside. "No." She didn't want a fuzzy feeling. Fuzzy feelings led to other feelings. Purely physical feelings and thoughts and urges. "He's still naughty."

"Blake!" Charlotte called out, and waved. "I knew you'd come."

"I told you I would." He stopped next to Natalie and stuck his hands in the pockets of his jeans. "How's business at the photo shop?"

She frowned at him. His attempt at small talk was actually a sore subject with her. "I'm lucky I have any business after what you did in my store."

"No one saw what we were doing. The door was shut."

She felt her cheeks burn hotter as she looked up at him through rounded eyes.

What I Love About You

His gaze followed Charlotte and Sparky's antics. "When you want to take up where we left off," he said as if he was talking about the weather, "let me know."

"I wasn't talking about *that*." Good Lord. "You yelled at Frankie about his monster junk pictures in front of Brandy. Brandy told all her friends at Truly High and before—"

"Wait!" he interrupted, and looked down at her. "The school here is called Truly High?"

"Yes." Several times throughout the history of the town, someone had petitioned the city to change the name. To no avail.

Blake chuckled. "No shit?"

She glanced at Charlotte, who had managed to wrestle the ball from Sparky. "Anyway, now the whole town knows about Frankie's monster junk pictures."

"Isn't that what he wanted?"

"It's not what I wanted." She placed a hand on the front of her wool coat. "Now everyone thinks that I look at their pictures."

"You do."

"For quality assurance purposes!"

"That's what you say." He chuckled. "Is your business down?"

"Not yet." He seemed as worried about her ethical business practices as Lilah had been. And speaking of business . . . She couldn't remember what he said he did for a living exactly. He'd said he was a retired Navy SEAL, and some sort of contractor. "How was your job?" she asked as she brushed her hair behind her ear. She was definitely prying.

"Good. Went down as well as could be expected."

That was it? She watched Charlotte run and Sparky chase her. "Where did you go?"

"Yemen."

She looked up at him out of the corners of her eyes. His beard made his lips more noticeable. "Yemen?" She wasn't exactly sure where that country was located. "What were you doing in Yemen?"

"Have you heard about John Morton?" He glanced at her, then turned his attention back to Charlotte and Sparky. "The oil executive kidnapped in Turkey a few weeks ago?"

"Vaguely." She didn't watch the news. Sometimes she turned it on while she made dinner and did laundry. She was usually too distracted to pay attention, but she'd have to be dead not to have heard about the American businessman held hostage. "I think he was rescued a few days ago."

"Saturday. In a compound in South Yemen."

"Wait." She put her hand on the sleeve of his jacket and he turned toward her. "Are you saying you rescued that guy?"

He looked down at her hand. "I was part of the extraction team."

He was certainly big enough, and the timing of his return matched, but she was a woman who didn't believe everything a man told her. Just a few days ago, Chris Wilfong had tried to sell her a fake lottery ticket outside the Maverick. He'd wanted only five thousand dollars for a ten-thousand-dollar scratch-off, like she was that dumb. Then there was Michael. He'd lied to her for years.

"You don't believe me?" He rocked back on his heels and frowned. "Oh for fuck's sake."

"You swear too much." She dropped her hand to her side. "I actually don't know what you do for a living."

"I told you I'm a private military contractor."

"What does a military contractor do?"

"We're highly trained specialists."

That still didn't really answer her question. "What is *your* specialty?"

He thought a moment. "I'm tasked with a lot of things, but my specialty is hostage extraction."

He could be somewhat charming, but she couldn't see him sweet-talking kidnappers. "Like a negotiator?"

"If I'm called in, Natalie, negotiations are over."

Oh. "Like a sniper?"

"No. Not *like* a sniper." He scratched his scruffy cheek, then shoved his hand in his coat pocket. "I am a sniper. I told you that."

"No you didn't." She glanced at Charlotte, then back at him. "You said you're a retired Navy SEAL. I think I would have remembered the word 'sniper.'"

He gazed down at her through those watchful gray eyes of his. "Now you know," he said, his voice lowered on the breeze.

Yeah, now she knew, but she really didn't know anything else. She knew he'd lived in Virginia, cooked out of a Crock-Pot, and had a brother. He'd never been married and didn't ever see himself married. That was pretty much it, except now she knew he was a retired Navy SEAL and a sniper. Somehow it fit him. Sometimes coolly detached. Sometimes intense. Always alert.

Silence filled the cold air between them and she struggled with something to say. She couldn't exactly ask him how many people he'd . . . sniped. Kind of. "I'm a fairly good shot with my .22 revolver." He watched her through those cool gray eyes of his, making her even more rattled. "Well, I mean, good enough to shoot the tail on a beaver target."

A wrinkle furrowed his brow as if he was in pain. "That's not very good, Sweet Cheeks. That's hardly a flesh wound." He dropped his hands from his hips and walked toward Charlotte before she could argue.

Her gaze moved down his wide shoulders to the bottom of his coat and Levi's-covered butt. Not just every man could make Levi's look good. Warm lust brushed across her belly and breasts. Some men had flat butts. Like her dad. And Michael, for all his good looks, had always had a disappointing backside. Kind of long instead of perfectly rounded like Blake's. She lifted her shoulders and buried her nose in the collar of her peacoat. She wondered how many squats he did daily.

Her attraction was purely physical, and she tilted her head to the side. It wasn't her fault, really. There were just so many stare-worthy places on Blake, so many yummy, lick-worthy parts, she was afraid she might actually drool.

Charlotte screamed and Natalie looked up to see Sparky jump on Charlotte's back and flatten her on the ground. Natalie rushed forward as Sparky bit the horn on Charlotte's unicorn hat and shook it like a chew toy.

Blake got to the dog first. "Off," he commanded, and lowered to one knee. Charlotte's scream got higher-pitched and she flailed about. He pried the horn out of the puppy's mouth and asked, "Are you hurt, Charlotte?"

"Yes!" she wailed.

Natalie knelt down and rolled her daughter onto her back. "Where are you hurt?"

"My knee. Spa-ky knocked—me—me down and bit my hat."

Natalie turned her attention to Charlotte's legs and the little hole in her purple leggings. The hole hadn't been there before, but there wasn't any blood. "It looks like you fell hard on your knee."

Charlotte sat up and tears poured down her cold cheeks. "I think it's bw-woken."

"I don't think it's broken."

"Uh-huh." She rubbed the back of her gloved hand under her nose. "It hurts."

"Let me see," Blake said, and put the dog aside. For once, the puppy sat and didn't move. "I've had some experience with broken knees."

Charlotte swallowed and managed between sobs, "You have?"

"Yep. I had to have surgery on mine. I have a big scar." He lifted Charlotte's leg and bent her knee a little bit. "Does that hurt?"

"Yes." Charlotte nodded. "I don't w-ant surgery and a scar!"

Blake's gray gaze met hers and his mouth twitched a little like he was trying not to laugh. "I don't think you're going to need surgery."

As Natalie looked into his eyes, at the humor creasing the corners and his scruffy beard on his cheeks, the air between them seemed to change. At least for Natalie. It got thicker and her lungs burned. Her pulse pounded *boom-boom-boom* in her chest and ears. Blake turned his attention to Charlotte's leg, and his big hands carefully touched her knee and shin. "That was a pretty nasty fall," he said, and shifted her booted foot from side to side. "Does that hurt?"

She shook her head and sniffed. "I need a Band-Aid."

"Definitely a big Ace bandage. I have four. We can wrap both legs." He looked so serious, Natalie wasn't quite sure if he was joking. "Maybe we can find more to wrap your arms like a mummy."

"Mom has Tinker Bell Band-Aids. I don't want to be a mummy."

Blake's deep laugh started low in his chest and worked its way up. It warmed the air around them. At least it felt that way to Natalie as she breathed his laughter into her lungs. It warmed up her chest and burned her heart like a brand. She sat back on her behind as if the wind had been knocked from her and gasped.

"Are you feeling better?" Blake asked, and she almost answered before she realized he was talking to Charlotte. Before she realized he didn't notice that the world had shifted beneath them. "Are you going to be okay?"

No! No, she wasn't going to be okay. How could he not feel the shift and change? It overwhelmed and pressed in on her from all sides. She was falling in love with a man who didn't believe in marriage or relationships and had never felt emotion stronger than lust.

She turned her face away before he did notice. "Can you stand, sugar?" she asked Charlotte.

"Maybe." Charlotte wiped the tears from one cheek and Natalie rose and helped her to her feet. "It still hurts."

"I know." She wiped Charlotte's other cheek with the arm of her coat. She couldn't fall in love with Blake. It was unacceptable. "But we have to walk home."

"I can't, Mama." Often it was hard to tell if Charlotte was really hurt or if she was just turning on the tears. Natalie shoved aside the scary feelings entwining her heart and concentrated on her child. Maybe Charlotte was hurt worse than

Natalie suspected. She'd been obsessing over the neighbor and was a horrible mother.

She looked at Charlotte's knee again, but still didn't see blood. "I didn't drive."

"You have to carry me."

"I can't carry you all the way home."

"I'll pack her out," Blake volunteered as he scratched the puppy's head between the ears. "You can't weigh any more than a rucksack."

There it was again. The unacceptable little shift she was going to completely ignore. "You don't have to carry her all the way home." She picked a few pieces of grass from the yarn in Charlotte's hat, quite sure that if she gave her daughter several more moments, she'd be okay to walk.

"It's only about a quarter of a mile and I've carried a lot heavier." He handed over the leash. "I had to sprint a hundred yards with Mouse Mousley on my back during SQT. Believe me, for a SEAL, he was a lard ass."

Charlotte gasped. "That's a bad word."

"'Lard ass' isn't a bad word." He turned and motioned for Charlotte to climb on his back. "It's a sad condition."

"Can I say it?"

"No!" Natalie helped Charlotte wrap her arms around his neck and lifted her as he locked his elbows around her knees. She smelled the cool breeze in his hair and on his skin, and it was all so unreal and confusing. "It's not a condition. It's not like cellulite. It's a bad word."

He easily stood with Charlotte like he had indeed carried a lot heavier. Natalie couldn't recall a man ever carrying her child. Maybe Charlotte's grandfather Cooper, but not since she'd been a baby.

Natalie walked beside the two of them, holding Sparky's leash. Thoughts raced around in her head and she couldn't control any of them. Any more than she could control her out-of-control heart.

At the edge of the park, Charlotte's grasp around Blake's neck nearly cut off his oxygen. He "tapped out" and they stopped for Blake to lift Charlotte onto his shoulders.

"Look, Mom. I'm weally weally high!"

Natalie gazed up at Charlotte, and her laugh mixed with Blake's. "That's music to my ears."

He wrapped his big hands around the ankles

of Charlotte's Ugg boots. "Your mom's right. You're heavy. What does she feed you? Lead?"

"No!" Charlotte laughed. "Mama feeds me spaghetti."

Natalie paused to untangle Sparky's feet from the leash and Blake waited for her to catch back up. Anyone who didn't know better might mistake them for a family, but they weren't. Their closest connection was an unruly puppy. Other than Sparky, there was nothing between them.

As if he read her mind, he turned his head and proved her wrong. He looked down at her lips and cheeks and finally her eyes. Her skin got hot and tingly, reminding her that there was a whole lot of lust between them. But sometimes lust had nothing to do with love. Sometimes lust was just lust.

Blake chuckled at something Charlotte said, then turned his smile on Natalie. A charming flash of white teeth and curve of his sexy lips. A warm spark in his eyes that could be misinterpreted for stronger feelings.

Natalie looked down at the toes of her sneakers. Falling for Blake would be a mistake. A huge one. Perhaps even bigger than believing

Michael's bullshit for so many years. At least with her former husband, she could tell herself that he'd changed from the man she'd married and it wasn't her fault. With Blake, he'd been unapologetically upfront from the beginning. He was emotionally unavailable, had commitment issues, and didn't believe either was a problem. She'd known it all along but was falling in love with him anyway.

No, Blake didn't have a problem. She had the problem. She was falling for an emotionally stunted, hot, hunky man, and her problem was that she had to figure out how to fall right back out of love.

Chapter Nine

His brown eyes melted her heart in middle school. The first time Michael Cooper kissed her, she'd fallen in ooey-gooey love. From her head to her toes, Natalie had loved Michael. She'd loved his hair and the color of his skin and how tan he got in the summer. She'd loved his chest and long legs and that his middle toe was shorter than the others. She'd even loved to watch him breathe in his sleep. Then he'd broken her heart and ruined her life. It had taken years to heal, and now he was back, standing in front of her. His brown eyes watching her and their child, and she felt nothing. No heart-cramping love. No gush of joy, and most surprising, no urge to punch him in the forehead. Not yet.

"She looks like you."

She stood in his parents' living room with Charlotte by her side. "Yes." Natalie helped Charlotte off with her purple coat. "She has your weird toe."

"Oh yeah?"

Carla took Natalie and Charlotte's coats and laid them across the arm of the couch. "And she's smart as a whip. Just like you when you were at that age."

Natalie felt a subtle shift in the Coopers' support of her. It wasn't anything she could pinpoint. Nothing specific, it was just a feeling.

"And she loves macaroni and cheese just like you did." The joy of having her son home lit up Carla's whole face, and Natalie could appreciate that joy, even if she didn't share in it.

Most kids loved macaroni and cheese, Natalie thought as she and Charlotte sat on the old floral sofa that had been in the Coopers' living room since 1999.

"Only in the blue box," Charlotte said, and she practically sat on top of Natalie. "I don't like the yellow box."

Michael took a seat in his father's leather La-Z-Boy a few feet away. As teenagers, they'd made out in that chair. "Do you like hot dogs cut up in it?"

"We never had that." Charlotte looked up at her mom, color high on her pale cheeks. "I don't like wrinkly hot dogs."

Natalie smiled and took her daughter's hand in hers. She rubbed Charlotte's back and felt her relax a fraction. "Overcooked hot dogs get wrinkled," she explained.

"And ice cream." Carla sat on the end of the couch beside Charlotte. She had short brown curls and a round face, and Natalie could almost see her bubble over with happiness. Michael was her boy. Her only child. "She loves to have ice cream with her papa."

Natalie thought Carla might be selling things a little hard. Charlotte was a good girl. She was kindhearted and loved animals and people. She could be overly dramatic, get struck deaf with convenient hearing, and had a freaky little fear of robots, but she was wonderful and irresistible all on her own. Natalie knew all mothers thought their children were beautiful, funny, and gifted. That couldn't be true of every child, but it was, of course, true of hers.

"What did you do in school today?" Michael asked, his attention on his child, and Natalie had to wonder what he thought. Could he love Charlotte or would he leave her again?

"Computer lab and I sang a song about tu-keys."

Michael raised his gaze to Nicole's. "Turkeys?"

"Yes. Charlotte sometimes forgets to pronounce her R's, but she's working on it."

"Tu*rrrrr*key."

"Michael couldn't pronounce his L's." Carla chuckled. "He told everyone his name was Mich-o."

"You told me that already, Nana." Charlotte sighed and rolled her eyes. "About five hundred times."

Michael laughed. "That's a lot of times."

"Well, maybe not that many." Charlotte crossed her ankles and swung her feet. "Maybe only seven hundred."

"Seven hundred is more than five hundred," Natalie told her. "Like seven is more than five."

"Oh." Charlotte nodded and her little ponytail bobbed. "That's right."

"Perhaps you and I should go in the kitchen." Carla looked at Natalie while she rose. "Michael and Charlotte need a few minutes to get to know each other."

Beneath her hand, she felt Charlotte's back stiffen. "That's okay. They can get to know each other with me here."

Carla's lips tightened. Natalie rarely countered Carla's wishes because there was really no need. She felt her former mother-in-law's disproval as she retook her seat. The last time Carla had looked at her like that was the day Charlotte was born and Natalie had named her after her great-grandmother and not Michael's grandmother Patricia. She and Carla rarely butted heads these days, but she suspected that might change.

For the next half hour, the four of them talked about little things like Charlotte's dog and her swimming lessons last summer. She was signed up for ski lessons after Christmas and her favorite color was purple. It was all extremely surreal. The Coopers' house hadn't changed since the nineties. It was a time warp of Carla's Precious Moments collection, the huge entertainment center filled with the big-screen TV, and photos, mostly of Charlotte and Michael in his glory days.

Strange. Definitely strange sitting in this room with Michael. Everything looked the same, yet everything was different. Physically, five years hadn't changed Michael much. He looked the same and his voice sounded the same. She'd spoken with him on the telephone from time to time, but it was odd to see and hear him at the same time.

When it was time to go, Natalie helped Charlotte on with her coat and waited while she gave Carla a hug good-bye.

"I'll walk you girls out," Michael said, and grabbed a blue coat from a closet by the front room. He held the door open, then closed it behind them. They moved across the wide porch and down the steps of the home where Michael and Natalie had married fourteen years ago.

"I'd forgotten how good the air in Truly smells," he said.

Natalie buttoned her coat and wrapped her red scarf around her neck. She imagined any air outside of the prison smelled good.

"I'd like to take you two girls to dinner one night this week."

"I don't know about that." She opened the door to her Subaru and Charlotte climbed inside. "Do you want to say good-bye to your dad?"

Charlotte raised one hand. "Bye."

Natalie leaned into the car and buckled the seat belt. "Are you okay?"

"Yes, Mama." She looked beyond the window

to Michael. Charlotte was usually an open book, but Natalie couldn't read her expression. That concerned her. She straightened and closed the car door. She turned, and Michael stood right in front of her. Close. Too close. His cocoa brown eyes had a little crease at the corners that hadn't been there before. He didn't seem as big as she remembered and he was shorter. She was fairly sure he was shorter. She had on flats, so it wasn't her shoes.

"You are as beautiful as always, Natalie."

"Don't, Michael." Warning bells went off in her head. What did he want? "I'm the mother of your child. Nothing more."

A cool breeze brushed across his short, spiky hair. "You are the first girl I ever loved."

"You left me when I was pregnant. You ran off . . ." She shook her head and moved to the other side of her Subaru. "I'm not going to do this, not with my child in the car. I'm not going to rehash the past with you. Ever."

"You can let me apologize."

She glanced at him across the roof. "It doesn't matter now. I've moved on. I don't need you to apologize to me."

"Maybe," he said on the breeze, "I need to apologize for me."

She got in the car and turned the key. He needed to apologize for him. She backed out of the driveway and headed home. She knew what Michael meant. In order for him to forgive himself, she had to forgive him. That surprised her. Never in a million years did she suspect that he needed to forgive himself.

But there was just one problem. She didn't know if she could. Yes, she'd moved on, but she'd never forgotten the past. She'd never forgotten sitting in their home alone, thinking the man she loved was missing. Hurt or dead or any number of things. But none of those things had involved fleeing with a new girlfriend to start a new life without her and the baby they'd worked so hard to conceive. At least she'd worked hard to conceive. He'd just shown up.

"Mom?"

Natalie glanced in the rearview mirror. She held her breath waiting for Charlotte to say something about her father. Her daughter had sat so quiet on the couch. Well, quiet for a little girl who usually talked nonstop. There had to be something important brewing in that little brain.

"Can we have corndogs for dinner tonight?"

That was it? "I don't have corndogs."

"What do we got?"

"I'll look when we get home." She glanced back at the road lined with pine and ponderosa. "What did you think of your dad?"

"I don't know. Okay, I guess."

"Do you want to see him again?"

Natalie would be okay with the answer no.

"Yeah. When I go to Nana's house." Charlotte paused, then said, "I got a book about a lost dog from the library at school. It's called *A Lost Dog* book."

Conversation about Michael was obviously over and she didn't push. "We'll read it in bed tonight." She turned onto Red Fox Road.

When she got home, she called Lilah, and her friend showed up half an hour later with a pizza—half pepperoni, half cheese—and a bottle of wine. She'd dyed the tips of her spiked hair white and was dressed almost conservatively in a color-block blouse and pencil skirt. Almost conservative except for her furry knee-high boots.

"Your hair's going to fall out one of these days," Natalie told her as she set the table.

"I never overprocess anyone's hair. Including my own."

"I like it." Charlotte took a bite of pizza. "It looks like Buddy, our school iguana."

Natalie laughed and Lilah chuckled. They ate dinner, and afterward, Charlotte had a small bowl of ice cream for dessert while they waited for Charlotte to bring up the subject of Michael. They waited while they helped her with homework and while they all played "Bow Tie on Parade." Bow Tie, of course, was always the fanciest and fastest horse in the show. They waited for her to mention her first meeting with Michael while she took a bath and while Lilah read her a bedtime story, but she never mentioned her father.

"That was weird," Lilah said as she walked down the hall and joined Natalie in the laundry room. "I thought she'd be excited to meet her father for the first time."

"I know." Natalie reached beneath the pink "Makin' Bacon" T-shirt Lilah had bought her last year. The shirt had two pigs kissing on the front and was only suitable for wearing to bed. She unhooked her bra, pulled the straps down her arms, and tossed it on the pile of white underwear in a laundry basket. "I tried to talk to her about him, but she just kind of clammed up."

"How did Michael look?"

Natalie changed into a pair of red polka-dot pajama pants and didn't bother to tuck in the bottom of her T-shirt hugging her waist and hips. "Good." She tossed her black pants in the washing machine, and measured out soap and fabric softener. "Kind of pale now that I think about it." Changing in the laundry room was a convenient habit that she'd developed when Charlotte had been a baby and thrown up on everything Natalie owned.

She turned on the washer and flipped off the laundry room light. She grabbed her glass of wine off the kitchen counter and moved to the living room. "Michael's shorter, maybe." She sat on the blue sectional made of microfiber for easy cleaning. "Either he's shorter or I'm taller."

"Shorter?" Lilah sat down the couch from her. "Do men get shorter in the joint?"

Natalie pulled one bare foot beneath her and took a sip of her chardonnay. "I wouldn't think so. Maybe I just forgot how tall he was." Maybe she'd subconsciously compared him to Blake.

Which wasn't fair to any man. Blake was taller and hotter. Bigger than life.

"Hmm. Does Michael have a prison tat?" Lilah pointed to the corner of his eye. "Maybe a teardrop?"

"A teardrop for his dead homies?" Natalie made a pistol out of her fingers. "Or do you get a tear when you bust a cap in a homie?"

"Listen to you talkin' all gangsta." Lilah chuckled and shook her head. "Have you seen Elliot Perry's tattoo?"

"No." They'd gone to school with Elliot and about five other Perrys.

"It's a big skull that takes up the back of his head. It's kind of disturbing when you see it from behind."

"Does it have bloody eyes?"

Lilah nodded and took a drink.

"Last week, Kim came in and picked up some prints," Natalie said, mentioning Elliot's third wife. "A picture of that skull on someone's bony head was in the order. I should have known it was Elliot." She swirled her wine in her glass. "Kim took a picture of *her* new tattoo."

"What is it? Some cheesy saying like: 'Believe

in Love' or 'Never Stop Dreamin''? 'Keep It Reel' misspelled with two E's."

Natalie smiled and raised the glass to her lips. "A kitty right next to her kitty."

Lilah's nose wrinkled. "Yuck."

"Guess what she named her kitty?"

"Stinky?"

Natalie laughed. "No, but that fits Kim. She named it Pussy Galore."

"That's so stupid. No one can ever accuse those two of having any class." She turned to the side and stretched her furry black boots out on Natalie's sofa.

Speaking of class, Lilah looked like she had goat legs. Not that Natalie would tell her. Or if she did, not that Lilah would care.

"Is Michael still as good-looking as ever?"

Natalie thought for a moment and nodded. "He's still a very handsome guy. I'm sure he won't have any problem finding some desperate female to bone."

"Are you sure there isn't any part of you that wants to get back together with him and bone?"

Now it was Natalie's turn to wrinkle her nose in disgust. "No."

"Good. I read that some people keep boning

after a breakup because it's easier than finding someone new to bone."

"Relax, Dr. Cosmo. Seeing him today didn't make me want to do anything with him. Let alone have sex." Actually, when she thought about sex these days, the neighbor popped into her head. His bare chest and arms and mouth that sucked out her pitiful resistance. She adjusted the striped pillow behind her. She liked blond guys with gray eyes and square jaws. Guys who kicked down doors to rescue hostages, and who carried little girls on their shoulders, both with equal ease. "He wants to take me and Charlotte to dinner, though."

"Are you going to go?"

The problem with a guy like Blake was that he wasn't dependable to stick around after the door was kicked down. "I don't know if I want to be seen with Michael." She shrugged one shoulder. "Not because he's been in prison, but because everyone in town will talk and wonder if we're back together. Then I'll have to explain we're not, and I don't want to explain my life because it's no one's business." Natalie turned behind her and set her empty glass on the iron and wood end table.

"Do you remember how his mom used to iron his T-shirt and jeans for him?"

"Yeah. When Michael and I first got married, Carla had a problem with me because I wouldn't iron his clothes." Or make sure he was hydrated.

"Carla was always a pip." Lilah crossed her furry legs and yawned. "It's too cold to drive home, do you care if I crash in the spare bedroom?"

Natalie stretched her arms above her head. "Of course not. Your toothbrush is in the bathroom." The doorbell chimed, and she dropped her hands to her lap. She glanced at the ornate iron clock on her stone mantel. It was eight-forty. The only person rude enough to show up this late without calling sat on the couch across from her.

"Are you expecting company?" Lilah bit her lips and her eyes lit up.

"No." Natalie got up and walked across the short beige carpet. Perhaps because they'd been talking about him, she kind of expected it to be Michael. If it was, she was sure she'd get a delayed urge to punch his forehead, and she couldn't promise not to act on it. Besides the fact that she didn't like Michael, a man just couldn't show up on a woman's porch this late at night. It was bad-mannered and rude.

What I Love About You

The stone floor entry chilled her bare feet as she looked through the peephole. It wasn't Michael, but someone definitely bad-mannered and rude. Blake stood on her porch, the shadow from the beige Navy ball cap on his head hiding the top half of his face.

He held up Charlotte's unicorn hat and she opened the door.

"Where did you find that?" Cold November night air rushed into the house and chilled her face and arms as she took the hat from him.

He didn't answer right away and stood perfectly still like he was suddenly frozen in place.

"Blake?"

"I found it in Sparky's crate," he finally answered. "Are you alone?"

Natalie took it from him and looked for tooth marks and holes in Charlotte's favorite hat. "Lilah is over and we're talking."

"Just Lilah?" He'd shaved since she'd last seen him and he almost looked respectable. Respectable in a big, bad, kick-your-door-down sort of way.

"Yeah." There was one little snag in the hat, but it was in good shape otherwise. "Thanks, but you could have brought it tomorrow."

"I'm leaving in the morning." He walked inside, forcing her to take a few steps back. "I'll try and bring Sparky over before you leave for work."

He shut the door behind him, and Natalie guessed that meant he was staying. "Does it do any good to ask where you're going this time?"

"South America."

"Big country." His hip and bare arm bumped hers as they walked into the living room. Natalie was fairly sure there was room for both of them without bumping into each other. She was also fairly sure she liked the touch of his cool forearm sliding against her warmer skin. "You can't be any more specific?"

"Yeah. Not Brazil."

Lilah stood by the couch, shoving her arms into her black wool coat. "I gotta go."

"What? I thought you were staying the night?"

"I got stuff to do tomorrow. I can't spend all night drinking with you." Lilah glanced at Blake as if she didn't know which piece of him to stare at first. Natalie knew the feeling. Having him in her house was like having G.I. Joe jump off the silver screen and land in her living room, minus nothing but his submachine gun and gritty sweat. He wore a body-hugging T-shirt and cargo pants and his hat shading his eyes and nose. "Hello, Blake."

"How are you, Lilah?"

"Good." She moved toward Natalie. "Call me if Michael tries anything. I know people."

She didn't know who Lilah was talking about. They knew the same people. "Okay." She walked her friend to the door and hugged her good-bye.

"Please," Lilah whispered in her ear, "get laid by that man."

"He just came here to return Charlotte's hat."

"Bullshit. He looks at you like you're sex on a stick. His eyes got so hot, I'm surprised your clothes aren't singed."

How had Lilah seen his eyes beneath his hat?

"Now pull your stick out and get in there," Lilah said, suddenly sounding like a football coach. "Take notes. Take pictures. Take one for the team and tell me everything."

Natalie wasn't going to pull or take anything. She watched Lilah until her Honda drove away before returning to the living room. "We looked all over for that hat this morning." Blake stood in front of the mantel, with Charlotte's school picture in one hand.

"Without a doubt, those were the scariest boots I've ever seen," he said as he looked at the picture. "And I don't scare easy."

"I think they might be made of goat."

The corner of his mouth tilted up. "I thought she maybe skinned a black Lab." He set the frame on top of the heavy wood mantel. "Where's Charlotte?"

"In bed asleep."

He looked across his shoulder at her, the shadow from his hat slipping across his top lip. "What happened with your ex today?" he asked. "Did he get out of line with you?"

"No." She tossed Charlotte's hat on the coffee table.

"Then why does Lilah think he'll try something?"

"Because I'm the first girl he loved and he thinks that means something?"

"Does it?"

"Maybe to him."

He took off his hat and tossed it next to Charlotte's. His pupils were very black and his eyes a hot, steamy gray she recognized. She didn't know if those eyes singed clothes, but they singed her thighs.

"Does it mean anything to you?"

"No. I don't love Michael anymore, but even if I

did, I could never forgive him. He's a cheater and a liar. The cheating hurt, but I hate when people lie to me." She squeezed her legs together against the hot ache pooling there. "Any more questions?"

"Just one."

His gaze slipped from hers to pause on her lips before sliding to her chin and throat. "Are you cold?" he asked, his voice dropping to a velvet hush as his eyes dropped to the front of her shirt. "Or just happy to see me?"

Natalie looked down and her mouth fell open. Her hands came up to cover her hard nipples poking the eyes out of the two kissing pigs on her shirt. "I'm not wearing a bra." She stated the obvious as heat rose to her cheeks, so hot and fast she feared she might pass out.

"I noticed." Blake took a step forward and wrapped his hands around her wrists. "Your shirt is the sexiest thing I've seen in a very long time." He pulled her palms away and held her wrists wide.

She should pull her wrists free. He couldn't just grab her and force her arms to her sides. She should tell him to stop and make him leave. Except that was one of the things that turned her on about him. He didn't ask. He pushed her up against windows or tugged her hair or grabbed her wrists. He was a little rough and she liked it. Maybe she shouldn't, but she did.

"You make me want to bury my face in your shirt and suck you through the cotton."

God help her, she wanted that, too. He'd been in her house less than five minutes and she wanted him to touch her. She stood perfectly still to keep from arching her back toward him. It was shocking really. How much she wanted him and how much she wanted him to take what he wanted from her. "Charlotte is just across the house." Yet at the same time, she wanted a man who cared about her. Enough to make some sort of commitment beyond one night. As much as she tried to ignore her problem or get over it, she was falling for Blake and it didn't feel wrong.

"We'll be quiet."

"We can't have sex with my child in the same house," she said, even as her nipples got tighter beneath his gaze.

"Who said anything about sex?" He frowned like she'd misunderstood. "I just want to play a little."

She didn't believe him for one second. "Play what?"

"Grown-up games." He let go of her wrists and placed his hands on her waist. "How long has it been since a man kissed you all over? Starting at your top and stopping at your bottom?"

Oh God. Oh no. She wanted that. She wanted her top and bottom kissed. He pulled her hips toward him and pressed her thin cotton PJ pants against the front zipper of his cargo pants. He let her feel the power of his erection, and her stomach clenched. Instead of pushing him away like she should do, she put her hands on his warm forearms and watched him rub against her. "A really long time. I've been super busy."

"A beautiful young woman like you is never too busy to play around." He put a hand beneath her chin and brought her gaze to his. "Where do you want me to kiss you first?"

Lord, but she was a weak woman suffering a moral dilemma between what she *should do*, and what she *wanted to do*.

"I'll give you options, and we don't have to do anything you don't like." He rocked his erection into her again and she got all light and fuzzy and tingly at the same time. "I can start at the little warm spot just below your ear where you taste like flowers and skin."

That was innocent-enough sounding.

"Then I take off your shirt and pop your nipples in my mouth."

She licked her lips as the skin all over her body got tight and she couldn't think anymore. Not beyond the hard, thick pressure shoved against the apex of the thighs and the promise of passion in his eyes. She was an adult. She knew where this was all leading.

"Or I can start at the inside of your knees and eat my way up your thighs to your honey pot."

Oh. That didn't sound innocent at all, but if they had rules and options, she could respect herself later. Maybe. Probably. Probably not. She was rationalizing. She didn't care.

"I have choices? Like on a menu?"

"Yes. Just tell me what you want and how you want it. If you can't make up your mind, I have several suggestions." He brushed her hard nipples. "If you can't pronounce something, just point."

She knew exactly what she wanted, and she

knew how to pronounce it, too. She liked the idea of choices and ordering off his menu. It gave her some control. Over her body, if not her heart. "When you say 'bottom,' you don't mean my back bottom?" She'd never let any man touch her butt. Not that any had tried. "Just my . . . front. Right?"

"Front door or back, I'll play wherever you want. It's up to you."

She felt a little hot and dizzy now. Hot, dizzy, and beyond ready for the touch of a man. His hands and mouth and hard penis. "How fast are you?"

"As fast as you want me to be."

"Okay." She could almost hear the gavel come down on her side. "I want a front quickie from behind."

He looked down at her from beneath heavy lids and smiled. "You got it."

Chapter Ten

He lied. There wasn't going to be anything quick about tonight, and he wasn't playing around. The second she'd opened the front door, his gaze had immediately landed on her nipples straining against those kissing pigs. His dick had gotten so hard so fast, he feared he'd fall over from lack of blood to his head. He almost got brain damage and he figured she owed him. For that and the blue balls he'd been packing around for a couple of months now. He'd wanted Natalie the first time he'd seen her ass-deep in flowers, and he'd certainly waited for her a long time. Certainly longer than he'd waited for any woman.

"You've got a beautiful bottom." He slid his

hands to her backside and cupped her cheeks through her thin pants. He tilted her pelvis and pushed his erection against the inside seam. She sucked in a breath and his testicles drew up tighter than a coin purse. He looked down into her gorgeous face and sunny blue eyes, shining with lust just like that day in her office. But unlike that day, he knew her better now. Had her figured out. When it came to women, it usually didn't take this long. Natalie was an open book, an open book of contradiction and complications.

"My hands are full," he said. "Take your shirt off for me." Natalie owned a business. She was her own boss and was in charge 24/7. Her head told her to hold out for a relationship, but her body told her something else. He was happy to tip the scale in his favor.

She curled her fingers around the bottom of the pink cotton and pulled it up. Up past the waistband of her pants and navel, up her flat stomach and abdomen and the plump undersides of her breasts. She was killing him and he had to wonder who was really in control. He held his breath waiting. She smiled a little, either from shyness or a practiced tease, he couldn't tell.

Then the she pulled the shirt up past her tight pink nipples and over her head. Her hair swung back down and brushed her shoulders and the top of her right breast. His stomach fell, a painful whap that felt like a roundhouse kick.

"Beautiful." He lifted a hand and brushed her with the tips of his fingers. Beneath his touch, she shuddered and pressed her breast into his hand. She lifted her face to him and he kissed her mouth. She tasted good, like Natalie and sex. She rose on the balls of her feet, and her nipples grazed his chest through his T-shirt on the way up.

He took his hands from her long enough to pull off his shirt and toss it aside. Then he was on her. Kissing. Touching. Feeling as much skin as possible. The hard tips of her breasts poked into his bare flesh. Two points of sheer pleasure as she ran her fingers through his hair. Her short nails scraped his skull and sent a shockwave of fiery lust down his spine to his feet. He had to slow things down. Slow it down before it ended. Before he tossed her on that big couch and jumped on her. He pulled his face back and looked into her eyes, sleepy with desire. She licked her wet lips and he felt it in his groin. He pushed her pants down her legs until she stood in nothing but little white panties. Too late he realized he didn't have a condom, but that did not stop him from picking her up and setting her on the padded arm of the couch. Her hands grabbed the couch behind her and her back arched as he lowered his mouth to her breast. Her nipple was tight and he rolled it like a berry with his tongue.

"Yes," she whispered between little pants of breath. "Do that, Blake."

"You like it?"

"Mmm. Yes."

He stabbed and nibbled and cupped a handful of her crotch. Her panties were wet and he slid his fingers beneath the leg band and touched her slick flesh. She moaned so deep and long he feared she'd orgasm. He wasn't quite ready for that to happen. He wanted to be deep inside when the walls of her body clenched and pulsed around him.

"Don't come yet," he warned, and slid her panties from her legs and dropped them to the floor.

"Then hurry," she ordered, and reached for the front of his pants. "I don't want to wait." He helped her with the button and zipper and her hand dived inside. "You said you'd be quick."

"Yeah." But he hadn't meant it. He wanted to see her naked. All of her. He wanted to touch and taste her everywhere. Then she wrapped her hand around his dick and he had to take several long, deep breaths before he embarrassed himself and unloaded in her palm. He spun her around and pushed her feet apart. "Grab the arm of the couch," he ordered, and positioned himself between her legs. She was wet and ready and moaned deep in her throat as he pushed into her incredibly soft flesh. She was tight around him, and he had to pull out and slide into her a couple more times before he was buried so deep his lower belly was pressed against her pretty behind.

"Are you good?" he asked as he caught his breath.

"Yes." She pushed back and looked over her shoulder at him. "Don't stop."

His hands palmed her smooth butt as he gave her what she wanted in long, even thrusts. Again and again he drove into the hot, gripping pleasure of her body. He leaned forward and pushed her blond hair to one side. "More?" he asked next to her ear as he planted a hand on the arm of the couch.

"Yes, Blake. You feel good. Don't stop."

His heart pounded in his chest and head. He was going to come before her. God, he didn't want to do that. He tried to hold it back. Tried to hold it back even as he moved faster in her tight walls. "Come for me, Natalie," he whispered into her throat. Then he heard her long, drawn-out moan and felt the first pulse of her orgasm. It milked him hard and seemed to go on forever. Squeezing him tighter and tighter, torturing him as he held back. Back against the hot, intense pleasure that didn't stop. She orgasmed longer than any woman he'd been with, and he couldn't hold back against the tsunami of fierce pleasure from deep in his belly. It gripped his balls and curled his toes. Then he set his jaw and prepared to pull out of her hot body. He was a pro at pull-outs. Had control where he spilled without a condom. He tried once and once more before he gushed deep inside her body. The most intense orgasm he'd ever felt in his life ripped through his body. It sizzled across his skin, grabbed his insides, and set his lungs on fire. He thought he just might die. Die bent over a beautiful woman on a blue couch, and he didn't care. He couldn't move. He couldn't breathe. He couldn't think. She'd killed him, and as soon as he caught his breath, he wanted her to kill him again.

Then he heard a little giggle.

"What?" he asked, and softly bit her shoulder. He'd get up in a minute. Once he could move.

"Nothing."

He slid his hand to her behind and gave her a soft little slap. "Tell me." He rubbed her skin.

"That really was quick."

"You came a long time."

"I know. That's the best quickie I've ever had. Thanks."

"You're welcome. I think I deserve a medal." He slid out of her body and wrapped his arms around her waist.

"What? Best quickie on a couch?"

"Best stamina." He stood and pulled her up with him. "Like a racehorse." He wrapped his arms around her shoulders. "That was just a warm-up. I'm even better in the long stretch."

She stepped away from him and reached for her panties. "We agreed on a quickie." She pulled them on, then stepped into her pajama pants. She looked up at him through her hair. "A front quickie from behind off your menu."

She reached for her shirt and pulled it over her head. "You bent me over and served your part of the deal."

Wait. Was she kicking him out? He was just getting started. "I've got all night to bend you lots of other ways." His pants and underwear were around his ankles and he pulled them up.

"It's late."

He adjusted himself and watched her pull on her shirt. It wasn't that late. "Are you kicking me out?" he asked, because women didn't kick him out. Not after he'd given them a quality quick one and they had an entire night to take it slow.

"Charlotte and I get up early." She reached for his T-shirt on the floor. "We'll probably be gone when you bring Sparky over. I'll leave the side door open for you." She threw the shirt, and he caught it just before it wrapped around his face. "Make sure he's pooped first."

She was kicking him out. Un-fucking-believable.

The next morning, Natalie lifted a cup of coffee to her lips and smiled. She stood in the stock room of her shop and pulled a stapler from a drawer beneath her worktable.

Last night, Blake's face had been priceless. He'd looked truly baffled when she'd told him he had to leave. He'd had the same look the night Charlotte and Sparky had darted past him and into his house after he'd been so sure he'd dumped the dog and somehow his carefully crafted plans had been countermanded.

She set the cup on the table, then wrapped a canvas photograph of one of the ugliest cats she'd ever seen over a wooden frame. She would guess that not many women had ever kicked him out after sex. They probably kept him locked up all night ordering off his menu. It might be true that Natalie hadn't had sex in a very long time, but she did remember that quickies weren't always satisfying. At least not for the woman. Women needed more buildup. More lead time. More foreplay.

Blake was right. He *did* deserve a medal.

She carefully stapled the edges of the canvas to the back of the frame. Blake was good at quickies. Like he'd practiced them a lot. She was sure he'd been bending women over for a really long time. Probably since puberty.

She hated to admit it, but the thought of him touching other faceless women the way he'd touched her bothered her more than it should. More than she had a right to be bothered. She'd ordered from his menu and he'd delivered the goods. In fact, he'd delivered amazingly good goods. She'd known what she was getting. She'd known that sex with Blake had nothing to do with a relationship and feelings. He didn't connect the two, like he thought they were mutually exclusive.

She carefully placed the canvas-framed photo of Ted Porter's hairless cat in a shadow box. She couldn't be mad at Blake. Or at least she shouldn't be mad at him. She was the one who wanted to have some sort of loving relationship with a man before she had sex with him. She was the one who'd made that personal choice years ago, and she was the one responsible for compromising her principles.

Until Blake, that choice hadn't been hard. Most of the men in Truly were married or living with their mom and a dozen cats and smelled like Friskies. She held up the canvas photo. Men like Ted. Until Blake, her stance on sex and relationships hadn't really been an issue. Her willpower had never been tested because there hadn't been any men that interested her. Certainly no man had tempted her like Blake.

She grabbed a pencil from the bib of her apron and marked the inside of the shadow box. Blake hadn't lied. She knew where he stood. If she had deeper feelings for him than he had for her, it wasn't his fault. She wasn't sure that she'd call her feelings for him love. Blake Junger wasn't the kind of man a smart woman fell in love with. He was the kind of guy a woman could depend on if she was kidnapped or chased by jewel smugglers in Cartagena. He'd said it himself, when the lead started flying, he was a good man to have around. A woman could depend on him to keep her safe. Physically safe, but she could never depend on him to keep her heart safe.

Natalie measured the inside of the shadow box, then placed dabs of glue on the canvas frame. Blake was also the kind of guy to carry a five-year-old home if she hurt her knee and was being dramatic. That was the guy who made her heart pinch and warmed her up inside. That was the guy who confused her and made her susceptible to his menu. That Blake was far more dangerous than the private military sniper.

They were both the same guy. Both the same Blake. He was a guy who was physically perfect but emotionally stunted. He was a break-your-heart kind of guy.

Natalie set the framed photo aside and stared on a second canvas cat picture for Ted. She and Blake shared a dog. They were neighbors, and Charlotte thought he was her best friend.

She knew Blake liked her, but liking her didn't mean he wanted to be with her, anymore than a quickie meant they were lovers. He liked her, but that didn't mean he wanted to share his life with her anymore than the bits he shared of his life meant he was an open book.

The bell in the front of the store rang as Natalie finished the second shadow box. She was expecting Lilah to come in for coffee and to talk about some photos Lilah wanted taken for her portfolio. That was the reason Lilah gave for coming in, but they both knew better. Lilah wanted to grill Natalie about last night. Natalie didn't want to spill the details, but Lilah would get them out of her. She always did.

She moved from the stock room and past her photo press. Instead of Lilah, Blake stood on the other side of the front counter. He wore his brown coat, a khaki and black shemagh around his neck.

It had started to snow, and melted drops caught the light and shone in his hair. His face was expressionless. Purposely blank, but his eyes watched her move toward him, so hot she feared her hair would start smoking. The singed look that Lilah had mentioned. The one that made Natalie susceptible to his menu. The one that made her world shift and spun her head around.

"I thought you left."

"I'm leaving now." He combed his fingers through the droplets in his hair. "I put Sparky inside your house and locked the door behind me. You shouldn't leave your doors unlocked."

He hadn't come by to tell her he'd locked her side door. "I leave it unlocked for Tilda and Charlotte." She'd made the babysitter keys before, but she'd lost two sets. "Will you be back by Thanksgiving?" she asked. She didn't want to talk about last night. She wanted him to stay on his side of the counter and keep his hands to himself and talk about the weather or something. Not about sex with Blake. He was good at talking about sex, and talking about it always led to doing or almost doing it.

"No." He shoved his hands into his pants pockets. "Once I'm back in the country, I'm meeting up with my brother in San Diego to spend Thanksgiving with my father." He pulled one hand from his pocket and checked his watch again. "When I get back we're going to talk about last—"

"I'm making an appointment for Sparky with the vet," she interrupted to avoid the conversation.

"—last night—"

"He needs to get neutered."

He frowned. "You're changing the subject."

She smiled. "No more balls."

Blake moved his hands like he was going to cover his crotch but thought better of it and crossed his arms over his chest instead. "He's getting his nuts whacked?"

She made a scissor motion with her fingers. "Snip. Snip."

"Jesus." Then he did move a hand to shield his manhood. "I can fence my yard. He can't walk around humiliated with an empty nut sack."

"He's a dog. He'll get out of your yard and make more puppy bombs just like him."

He looked like he might argue in favor of Sparky's nuts, then he dropped his hand to his side. "Keep the receipts. I'll pay for the poor guy's castration." He looked at his watch, then at her. "You're avoiding the reason I came to talk to you."

She was, and she wasn't all that surprised the he'd figured it out. Most of the time, Natalie just wasn't very tricky.

"If I'd known you were serious about a quickie and nothing else, I'd have done things a little different." He dropped his gaze to her mouth. "I would have taken the time to make it better."

"It was exactly what I wanted you to do. Don't worry about it."

"I'm not worried. When I get back, we're going to try that again and get it right."

It had felt right to her. "No." She shook her head. "We can't do that again. I was good with once."

He reached beneath his shemagh and unzipped his coat. "I knew you were going to say that and make me prove you wrong."

She held up one hand, palm out. "Wait."

"Scared?" He moved around the counter and smiled like a hunter stalking prey. "Scared I'll make you feel so good you'll demand more from my menu starting right now?"

"I'm not scared." She was terrified. "I've always

told you that I can't go around having sex just because it feels good."

He grabbed her hand in his strong grip. "I want to be with you more than just once. I want more from you."

For one awful beat of her heart, she looked up into his eyes that could go from cold to hot in an instant, and the warm bubble in her chest got painfully bigger. "What do you want?"

"I want kisses that lead to long, lazy days in bed."

"I have a child." Of course he hadn't meant more than sex.

He kissed the palm of her hand. "Nights that get so hot the sheets stick to your skin."

"I have a child," she repeated.

He slid his mouth to her pulse and sucked little tingles to the surface of her skin. "I know. A funny, sweet girl who loves dogs and thinks she's a horse. Having a child doesn't mean you can't have sex."

"It means I have to be responsible." She pulled her hand away from the temptation of letting him suck tingles in other places. "We didn't use a condom last night."

"Yeah. I remembered when it was too late."

"I remembered this morning. It's been a while

since I had sex, but that's no excuse not to be responsible about it."

"I'm clean," he assured her. "I'm so clean I squeak. I routinely get tested for everything from typhoid to HIV. If you need proof, I have a copy of every test result for the past year. I'll bring them by."

"Okay." Typhoid?

He took a step closer until she had to tip her head back to look up at him. "And you're not sexually active, and from what you've said, I don't have to worry about getting you pregnant."

It was the sad truth. She hadn't had sex in a while and she couldn't have a child. At least not without a lot of work. "You're going to just take my word for it?" Shouldn't he demand some sort of proof?

"Yes. You're one of the most honest people I've ever met." He put his hand on the side of her neck. "That's one of the things I like about you. That and your nice smile and great butt." His thumb brushed her throat. "And when I get back, we're going to hump and bump until neither of us can move."

"'Hump and bump'?" She pulled the corners of her mouth downward.

"You don't like that expression? How about: knock boots, bang bellies, fuck like wild monkeys. Or your personal favorite, makin' bacon. Pick one."

Makin' bacon wasn't her favorite. It was a T-shirt Lilah had given her. "Make love." He'd probably never really made love. Just banged boots or whatever.

"That's a good one, too. When I get back, we're going to knock bellies and make wild monkey love."

She opened her mouth to object to monkey love but was saved a response by Lilah breezing in the front door, bringing in snow and two Styrofoam cups of coffee. She turned around to look at her friend, who wore a fur hat and coat like she was living in Imperial Russia instead of Truly, Idaho. "Oh hi, Blake," Lilah said as she set the to-go cups on the counter. "If I'd known you were going to be here, I would have brought more coffee."

"Thanks, but I had about a pot already this morning." He was so close, the front of his coat brushed Natalie's back, and she had to fight the urge to lean back into the comfort of his hard chest.

"What happened after I left last night?"

"We chatted," Natalie answered, and squinted her gaze across the distance at Lilah.

"It was a quick chat," Blake added, and zipped his coat. The backs of his knuckles brushed up her spine. "Next time we'll chat longer."

"Long chats are always better." Lilah took off her hat and picked up her coffee. "Nice looooong chats." She took a sip and looked like she was going to behave. "On the bone phone," she added behind the cup.

"Lilah!" Natalie blinked several times, like Morse code for her friend to shut the hell up. "We're not in sixth grade."

"In the sixth grade, I used to call it the blow horn." Blake laughed and put his hand on Natalie's shoulder. "My brother called it the meat mike."

His heavy hand brought warmth and felt oddly comfortable on her shoulder. Lilah had obviously found a comrade in sexual euphemisms, and Natalie looked up at him over her shoulder. "I thought you liked knock boots."

He gazed down into her eyes as if he was considering his words. Odd since he'd just said "meat mike." "I believe we were talking specifically about oral sex. As opposed to sexual position."

"I've never heard 'meat mike.'" Lilah laughed. "That's a good one."

Natalie turned to scowl at her friend. Get Lilah in a room of adults and somehow the subject always turned to sex. Natalie wondered what she was going to come up with next or if she planned to behave now.

Blake said next to her ear, "If you don't understand the difference, we'll have an in-depth lesson when I get home."

She didn't need an in-depth lesson, and she didn't know why they were talking about it at all. She could feel her cheeks get a little hot. She'd had a one-time quickie with Blake. That was it, and she didn't feel comfortable enough with him to talk about sex, and that included an in-depth conversation about the bone phone, blow horn, or meat mike.

"Don't get mad," Lilah told her from across the store.

"I'm not mad. Just super uncomfortable and wondering what's coming up next to make everything a little more awkward."

As if in answer to the question, the front door swung open and her ex-husband breezed in on a gust of frozen air and a flurry of snowflakes settling in his dark hair. He stomped his boots on the mat and looked up. His attention lit on Natalie, then Blake behind the counter. "Hello."

Great. Just great.

"Hello, Michael Cooper," Lilah said, and set down her coffee.

A frown pulled his brows as he looked at her amid all that fur. Then he smiled. "Delilah Markham." He held his arms out. "Come give me a hug."

Lilah being Lilah said, "I don't know. Are you going to steal my wallet?"

Natalie's eyes widened and she gasped a little. Behind her, Blake chuckled.

Michael just shook his head and smiled. "My days of stealing are behind me."

"Your ex-husband?" Blake asked as Michael hugged as much of Lilah as he could get his arms around.

"Yes," she answered, then things got even weirder when the door opened again and Ted Porter blew in with his hairless cat. "Michael Cooper!" he said, all excited like it was high school

240

reunion time at Glamour Snaps and Prints. Like it hadn't been fifteen years and Michael hadn't spent some of those years in prison. Like Ted wasn't standing there holding a cat with enormous blue eyes staring out from beneath a pillbox hat and wearing a perfectly matched leopard-skin coat.

"Hello, Ted." Michael shook hands with the other man, then his gaze sought and found Natalie again. "How are you?" he asked Ted as he looked over the man's balding head at her. "How's your mother?"

"Good." While Ted and Lilah oohed and aahed over Diva the cat's nifty outfit, Michael continued to look across at Natalie as if he was trying to figure something out.

She turned and tipped her face up to Blake. "I have to get Ted's shadow boxes for him." Really, she just wanted to escape for a few moments and catch her breath. This morning reminded her of Charlotte's favorite book, *Wacky Wednesday*. With each turn of the page, something even more wacky happened until pigs were flying and alligators were driving cars. She wouldn't be surprised if Mabel rolled in on a pink scooter with purple grips and streamers.

Blake wrapped one arm around her waist and kept her from escaping anywhere. "Remember what I said." He pulled her against the front of his coat and up on the balls of her feet. "When I get back"—he lowered his face to whisper against her lips—"hot, sticky nights." Then he placed his palm on the side of her face and pressed a soft kiss on her lips. "Wild monkey love." He deepened the kiss a few seconds past appropriate for the workplace. A few seconds past hot enough to blot out all the wackiness before he raised his face. "It's going to be a long week." He lightly tapped her chin with his finger, then dropped his hand. "Behave while I'm gone."

Shock kept Natalie frozen in place as she watched him move from behind the counter. The sound of Blake's boots filled the sudden silence, but he didn't seem to notice as his long legs carried him out the door, leaving a whirl of snow and silence in his wake.

"Well." Lilah was the first to speak. "I think someone just marked his territory."

Chapter Eleven

"I don't like bacon," Charlotte said as she stabbed a bite of pancake. "I tried it once and it's salty."

"That's why I love it." Michael held up a piece of crispy bacon and took a bite. "Yum."

Natalie leaned back in the booth at the Shore View Diner as Meg Castle refilled her coffee cup. "Thank you."

"You're welcome. Can I bring anything else?"

"I think we're good." Among the smells of coffee and grease, the chatter of diners mixed with the sounds of plates and coffee mugs. Saturday mornings were always busy at the Shore View, and Natalie wished that Michael had chosen someplace less busy for his second meeting with Charlotte.

Someplace where they weren't the subject of open stares and covert whispers.

Natalie took a bite of her English muffin as Michael engaged Charlotte in conversation. She didn't have to hear the whispers to know the other customers were gossiping about her and Michael's past and speculating about their future. She didn't have to hear with her own ears how they were talking about Michael and her and the big fella living in the old Allegrezza house.

Apparently Ted had taken his cat and his shadow boxes home and told his mother what he'd seen at Glamour Snaps and Prints four days ago. His mother had blabbed to her friends, and by the next day, she, Michael, and the big fella were the topic of conversation around town, everywhere from Grace Episcopal on Pine to Hennessey's Saloon around the corner.

Natalie blew into her coffee cup, then took a sip. She'd managed to live gossip-free for several years now. She'd lived down Michael's scandal and their divorce. She'd lived down speculation over her involvement in his legal problems and proved she was an honest businesswoman, a good citizen, and a single mother trying hard to raise her child.

She hadn't given the gossips of Truly anything to talk about. Not until that day the big guy kissed her in front of her ex-husband, her best friend, Ted Porter, and his hairless cat. Now she was supposedly involved in a love triangle thanks to Blake, who was conveniently out of town.

"I can write my whole name." Charlotte pushed her plate to one side and made room for her kid's menu. She dug around for the eight-pack of crayons that Natalie carried around in her purse, and she wrote on her paper menu. It took her a few minutes but she did it, sort of. Some of the letters were higher than the rest and, when she ran out of room, she wrote the last half of her last name at the top of the paper. "There." With a smile she turned the menu and handed it across the table to Michael. "Charlotte Elizabeth Cooper."

"Wow." He studied it as he ate his hash browns. "That's really good." He looked up at Natalie. "Are other kids at her school writing their whole names?"

"Some." He didn't know anything about a five-year-old's development and milestones, and his question just illustrated his absence in his child's life. "Charlotte and I worked on it over the summer."

He lowered his gaze to his daughter. "What else can you write?"

She shrugged and took a bite of her pancake. "I can draw weally good pictures." She took a drink of milk, then sucked the mustache from her top lip. "Do you have paper, Mom?"

Natalie fished around in her purse and pulled out a power bill envelope. "Draw on the back."

"Okay." Charlotte chose a blue crayon and got busy.

"What are you two girls doing for Thanksgiving?" Michael asked.

"Probably just staying home. My mother is living with my aunt Gloria now."

"I heard that. How's your mother?"

Her mother hated Michael, and she was fairly certain the feeling was mutual and had been since long before Michael's arrest. Her mother blamed Michael for Natalie never going to college. For everything that she could blame on him, that one was not his fault. "Mom's good. She sold her house after she retired and bought a fifth wheel." Sitting here, in the diner where they'd eaten as teens, was just bizarre and uncomfortable. She knew the man across the table from her. Knew he had a birthmark on his shoulder and a triangle of freckles on his knee. Yet she didn't know him at all. "They hook it to Uncle Jed's truck and the three of them travel a lot." She hadn't known the Michael who'd run out on her, and she didn't know this Michael, either. "They'll probably still be in Arizona this Thanksgiving." Her mom loved that camper. Charlotte, too, but Natalie couldn't think of a worse way to spend the holiday.

"Then you two should come to my mom and dad's for Thanksgiving."

Except with the Coopers. "No." Natalie shook her head.

He flashed a cajoling smile that used to melt her heart. It didn't anymore. "It's my first real holiday in a long time and I'd love to spend it with you girls."

And she'd love to spend it in pajama pants and a T-shirt. All day. She always closed the photo store the few days after Thanksgiving and just wanted to veg. "Charlotte doesn't even like turkey." They were going to have junk day and eat Tater Tots and Pizza Rolls. "We just want to stay home."

"Are you spending the day with your boyfriend?" His smile disappeared.

She didn't bother to tell him that Blake wasn't her boyfriend. If it helped to keep Michael from trying to charm his way into her life, that was fine with her. "He's not your business."

"If he's around my child he is." He sat back and reached for his mug.

Suddenly he was a concerned father? "Don't." She pushed her plate aside and leaned forward. "You don't get to say who's in . . ." She paused, aware of little ears and bigger ears of diners around her. " . . . you know who's life. You haven't been around for five years."

"I'm here now, and I'm not going anywhere."

Right. "You don't have any credibility with me." She sat back. "I have raised . . . you know who . . . by myself, and you can't come back in our lives and start ordering me around." She cast a glance at Charlotte, who was busy drawing. "If you're here this time next year, then we'll talk."

"I said I'll be here."

"I heard you." Natalie tossed her napkin on the table and glanced about to make sure no one in the diner was eavesdropping before she continued. "You may have forgotten the past, but I haven't."

"I haven't forgotten. I live with it every day."

Sorrow creased his brow. "I live with regret and shame and things I can't change. I can only make amends and show people I've changed."

That might take a while, she thought. Then she felt bad because he seemed sincere. Then again, Michael was a good liar and had tricked her in the past.

"I'm done." Charlotte turned the envelope around. She'd drawn a sun, three spindly stick figures, and a ball of black fur with short legs. "That's Mama and me." She pointed to the two stick figures with yellow hair, one longer than the other. "That's Spa-ky my dog." Then she pointed to the other figure. "And that's Blake."

Michael lifted his gaze to Natalie as Charlotte chattered on.

"Blake's my best friend. He picks up Spa-ky's poop," she said, picking up speed before her mother could stop her. "One time Spa-ky ate my Hello Kitty bow and it was in his poop. Blake saw it and said a weally bad word!"

"Charlotte, that's gross." She'd gotten in two poops and one tattle. Banner day in her life. "Please don't talk about that at the table."

Charlotte giggled and covered her mouth with her hand like she just couldn't help herself.

Michael's lips turned up at the corners and he started to laugh. "I had a dog who used to eat rocks. Do you remember Henry, Natalie?"

"Of course." Henry had been an extremely obnoxious beagle.

"Henry used to *always* have rocks in his poop."

Charlotte fell sideways against Natalie like Michael had knocked her over with a funny bone.

"Your papa used to run over it with his lawn mower all the time."

"Michael," Natalie warned.

"One time the mower shot a rock into Nana's garden and broke the head off a stupid gnome."

Charlotte pushed herself up and her eyes got big. "Was Nana mad?"

"Yeah. She glued it back together. Never did find one of the eyes, though. I think she still has that busted-up gnome somewhere."

"I wanna see it."

"Maybe if you come over for Thanksgiving, I'll show it to you."

"Can we go, Mama?"

Natalie's brows lowered. "I'll think about it."

"That always means no." Charlotte sighed.

"I have a lot to make up for, Natalie." He looked

at the picture Charlotte had drawn, and Natalie knew what he was thinking. That should be him in the picture instead of Blake. If he'd made different choices, it would be him with Charlotte and Natalie. Then again, perhaps not. He'd been bored with her and had found someone else. He could say he was a changed man, maybe he even meant it, but he couldn't change history. His or hers. And Charlotte was right, "I'll think about it" always meant no.

The Cowboys and the Ravens cracked helmets on Ron Cooper's big-screen television. Or maybe it was the Steelers and the Lions, or the Packers and the Raiders. Natalie didn't know and couldn't keep the football schedule straight. Mostly because she just didn't care.

She placed knives and forks and linen napkins on the Coopers' Thanksgiving dinner table. Growing up, she'd been a cheerleader, but she'd never been a sports fan.

So how had she ended up here today? Setting the table while Carla basted the turkey and Michael and Ron watched the game, everyone looking and acting like they were a happy family? How had this happened when she'd specifically said no last week at breakfast with Michael? She'd told him that she and Charlotte were going to stay home. Home in cozy pajamas pants and lamb slippers, but somehow she was in the Coopers' dining room, wearing her brown sweater dress, T-strap pumps, and panty hose. She'd curled her hair and put on makeup, and all because for one weak moment, she'd felt selfish and hardhearted. For that one weak moment inside the Shore View Diner, she'd felt bad because Charlotte had drawn Blake instead of Michael and she'd told him that she'd think about Thanksgiving. Everyone knew that "I'll think about it," meant no. Just like "I'll see" meant no, and "Maybe" meant "I can be nagged into it."

Too bad no one had told Carla. She'd called the day after the Shore View to assign Natalie a Thanksgiving dish. Michael's favorite cranberry Jell-O, of course. She and Charlotte had tried to make it in their rooster-shaped mold. It hadn't set up quite right and ended up looking more like a bloody mess.

"I'm so glad you came today." Carla hugged Natalie about the shoulders. "It's so nice to have the family together."

"Carla—" Natalie shook her head as she placed

the last knife and fork on a cloth napkin. In the other room, Michael and Ron yelled at that game on TV, and for the first time since moving back to Truly, Natalie felt uncomfortable and out of place in the Coopers' home. "I'm the ex-wife. Not part of the family anymore."

"Sure you are."

Carla and Ron had helped Natalie in more ways than she could even recall at the moment, but things were bound to change now. Michael was home. He was their son. Their loyalty would always be with him, and the reality was that she was not a part of their family. She wasn't blood. She set down the last knife and turned to her former mother-in-law. "Carla, you and Ron have been such a huge help to me these past five years, and I want you to know that I appreciate everything you've done."

"We were happy to help."

Natalie swallowed. She didn't want to ruin Thanksgiving, but she felt everything needed to be clear and out in the open. "A few months ago, Michael talked to me about getting back together."

Carla smiled and placed candles in the center

of the table. "He told me. Ron and I would be tickled if that happened."

That was what Natalie was afraid of. "It's not going to happen, Carla."

"I know you don't think so now, but—"

"I'm not going to change my mind," she interrupted. "I don't love Michael."

Carla straightened and her smile fell. "Maybe not now, but you could fall in love again."

Natalie shook her head. "No. It's never going to happen."

Carla blinked several times and her brown eyes filled with tears. "He's changed. He's sorry for what he did and he's owning up to his mistakes."

"I truly hope so." Crap. She'd made Carla cry. On Thanksgiving. She tried to make it better. "Don't you want Michael to find a woman who can love him like he deserves to be loved?" How had this happened? How had she become the bad guy? "That woman isn't me."

"But you haven't even dated anyone for years."

Had her holding out for the right man given the Coopers false hope? "I never wanted to bring a man into Charlotte's life unless it was serious, but that doesn't mean Michael and I are ever going to get back together. We're not."

Carla seemed to deflate right there in the dining room as if Natalie had stuck her with a pin. Tears ran down her cheeks and she mumbled something about a broken heart before she ran from the room.

"What . . . ?" Natalie just wanted to do the right thing. She just wanted this new chapter in everyone's lives to start off on the right foot. In a good place, but she'd ruined Thanksgiving, instead. After that, everything that could go wrong, did. Carla burned the rolls, and the turkey was as dry as plywood. Charlotte rolled around in her chair and wouldn't eat. She spilled her milk, then pulled her poufy dress over her head. "Sawwee," she said from beneath the big, puffy skirt.

"Sorry," Natalie pronounced for her daughter, perhaps more sternly than usual. She cleaned up the mess, then pulled Charlotte into the kitchen to talk to her. Charlotte's lip trembled, then she burst into tears. Great, who was Natalie going to make cry next?

She and Charlotte returned to the table while Ron and Michael kept the conversation light, as if they were just one big happy family. Across the table from Natalie, Carla fingered her knife with one hand and wiped at her eyes with the other. Okay, the finger-her-knife thing might be Natalie's imagination.

"I bought that fairy movie for Charlotte. It's Disney," Carla said as she set her knife and fork on her plate and pushed it aside.

They weren't offering to send it home. "Charlotte's tired. We can watch it next time."

"I wanna stay and watch the fairy movie, Mama." Charlotte turned and looked at Natalie. "It's my favorite. I'll be weally good now. I promise."

"Honey, I'm tired." Natalie took a breath and let it out. A dull ache pressed in on her temples, and she'd rather be beaten over the head with Carla's garden gnomes than spend one more second than was necessary with the Coopers. "We can watch it another time."

"I'll bring her home later," Michael offered.

Natalie lifted her gaze to her former husband and looked into his brown eyes. He didn't have a cheesy grin or a charming smile. He simply looked at her, waiting for her response.

"Please, Mommy."

What I Love About You

"Okay," she gave in because she wanted to go home so bad she feared she might be the next to cry. Besides, she could soak in the tub all by herself for a few hours without interruption. Or she could nap or watch what she wanted on TV or vacuum.

"She can spend the night," Carla slipped in.

Before Natalie could say no, Charlotte jumped up from her chair. "Yea! I can watch the fairy movie two times. Or maybe five." She pawed the air and shook her head. Then she took off, galloping from the dining room to the kitchen, running off her excitement.

"It's too soon." Natalie felt pressured and pushed and she didn't like it.

"She spends the night here all the time," Carla reminded her.

True. Charlotte had her own room at the Coopers'. She wanted to stay, and was Natalie saying no just because she felt pushed and manipulated? That wasn't fair to Charlotte. "Okay," she relented, but she wasn't happy about it. She set her napkin on the table and stood. "I'll help you with the dishes before I leave."

"No need." Carla stood, too, suddenly cheerful, and practically ushered Natalie out the door.

Probably out of fear that Natalie would change her mind.

"Have her call me tonight before she goes to bed," Natalie said as she buttoned her peacoat and grabbed her black purse.

"Of course."

She kissed Charlotte good-bye, and Michael walked her out to her car. The heels of her pumps sank into the inch of snow on the Coopers' sidewalk. Michael took her arm. It was the gesture of a gentleman. Something he would do for any woman, but she wasn't just any woman. There had been a time when his touch would have made her feel secure. Another when it would have sent little tingles up her arm. Today she just felt uncomfortable.

"Sorry I ruined your mother's Thanksgiving and made her cry," she said as they walked to the driver's side door of her Subaru.

"What was that all about?" Michael wasn't wearing a coat, just his blue dress shirt and navy slacks. A chilly breeze ruffled his sleeves and short hair and gave color to his cheeks. He looked good. Handsome as the boy she'd dated and man she'd married.

"She was holding out hope that you and I would get back together. I told her it wasn't going to happen."

He dropped his hand and shoved it in the pocket of his pants. "That's probably my fault. She knows I want my family back."

"We're not family, Michael." She pointed to him and then herself. "I'm not married to you. You left me for a foreign bank account and a younger woman. Why am I the only one who seems to remember?"

He looked down at his shoes and his brows furrowed. "I remember, Natalie. I remember what I did. To you and my family and people who trusted me with their money." He shook his head. "I could tell you why I did it, but right now isn't a good time."

She didn't think there was ever going to be a good time. "You told me you left because I was boring."

He looked up. "I don't remember that."

"I do."

He took a deep breath and let it out. "You weren't boring. It really didn't have anything to do with you. It was me."

"Didn't have anything to do with me?" Was he

serious? "It sure felt like it had something to do with me."

"I meant it wasn't your fault. I lost the principles and values my parents instilled in me. I lost myself and I lost you." He hunched his shoulders against the cold. "I lost a lot."

She'd lost a lot, too.

"Are you ever going to be able to forgive me?"

She shrugged inside her wool coat. He hadn't said much beyond he was sorry, and she wasn't sure she wanted him to say more. She wasn't sure there was anything he *could* say for her to forgive him for the unforgivable. "If you'd left just me, I probably could forgive you. I'm not a perfect person. I've certainly made mistakes, but you left Charlotte. You left your baby and you were never coming back." She blinked back the sting in her eyes. "I love that child so much my heart can't hold it all. Every time I look at her, my love gets bigger. She is everything to me. Everything, and you left like she was *nothing*. I don't think I can ever forgive you for that."

"She wasn't real to me then." He took a step forward and put his hands on her arms. "That's not an excuse. We tried so hard for so long to have her. By the time you got pregnant, my life was headed down a whole different path." His hands squeezed her arms, and he shook his head. "I think we forgot how to be together. We forgot how easy it was between us. We forgot that we'd loved each other since the tenth grade."

She hadn't forgotten how to be with him. She hadn't been unhappy. She'd been too caught up with her infertility treatments and trying to have their baby to think about being unhappy. "I've wondered if it wasn't too much for you. I've often wondered if, while I was so wrapped up in trying to have a baby, you were unhappy and I didn't notice." Not that anything excused what he'd done, and she'd stopped second-guessing herself years ago.

"You were always so easy to be with." He slid his arms around her waist and pulled her against him. "I've missed you, Nat."

For a few seconds she let him hold her. While a cold breeze rattled the tops of the pines, she let herself feel the weight of his arms and his cheek against her temple. It felt strange. Like someone she should know but didn't. She didn't love him. She didn't hate him. She just wanted to go home.

She pushed out of his embrace. "Don't, Michael."

"I love you and want you back."

She looked into his eyes and told him the truth. For his sake and hers and Charlotte's. "I don't love you, Michael." She hurt him and took no pleasure in the pain crossing the brown eyes she'd once loved beyond anything. "I don't think you love me. I think I'm easy to be with, like you said."

"Don't tell me I don't love you, Natalie. I spent a lot of time in prison getting my head straight." He sniffed and dropped his hands. "Do you love him? That big guy who picks up dog poop?"

Blake? Did she love Blake? She looked down at her shoes and dug her car keys out of her coat pocket. Her feet were freezing.

"Do you?"

She was very afraid that she did, but the last person she wanted to talk about it with was her ex-husband. Especially since Blake did not feel the same for her. "Go in the house, Michael. It's freezing out here and my feet are numb."

"Do you love him, Nat?"

She also knew Michael. If she didn't answer the second time, he'd fill in the blanks. She looked up. "Yes."

What I Love About You

He closed his eyes and she was afraid he was going to cry. First Carla, then Charlotte, and now Michael. She was batting a thousand today.

"I'll bring Charlotte home tomorrow." He opened her car door for her, and his dark lashes looked suspiciously wet and the color in his cheeks a little too bright. "I'll call first."

"Happy Thanksgiving," she said as if it wasn't too late. She climbed in her car, and Michael shut the door. It wasn't her fault everyone was crying, she told herself as she turned the ignition. Charlotte was five and cried at the drop of a hat. It wasn't her fault Carla and Michael cried. She didn't love Michael, and that was Michael's fault and not hers. There had been a time when he had been her everything. A time when she would have done anything for him. He'd been her lover and best friend, and she would have happily spent the rest of her life loving him. It wasn't her fault she didn't love him now.

She put the car in reverse and looked behind her. If it wasn't her fault, then why did she feel so bad?

Chapter Twelve

I took the mutt.

Natalie reached for the paper towel stuck to her refrigerator with a cupcake magnet. The bold, blocky words had been written with the pink marker sitting on the counter. She guessed this meant Blake was back in town. She'd never seen his handwriting, but it had to be he. Either that, or someone else had walked into her house and kidnapped the dog. After the day she'd had, she wouldn't be surprised if she found a ransom note and a lock of Sparky's fur.

Natalie shrugged out of her coat and tossed it on the kitchen counter. She was tired. Emotionally drained and on the verge of a panic attack.

What I Love About You

The day had started with a disastrous Jell-O mold, had escalated to Natalie making everyone cry, and had peaked with being railroaded into letting Charlotte spend the night.

The smart thing to do would be to get in the bathtub and relax. Yeah, that would be the smart thing she should do, but that wasn't what she wanted to do. She stared at the note in her hand and felt a funny little glow in her chest. It grew bigger and bigger, and she took a deep breath around it. She'd only had this feeling one other time in her life. With the man she'd left crying in his mom's driveway, and if she wasn't careful, she'd find herself drawing hearts on the paper towel and circling Blake's house on her bike.

When I get back, Blake had told her, *we're going to knock bellies and make wild monkey love.*

Natalie bit her bottom lip and set the note on the counter. Then he'd kissed her in front of Michael and Lilah, Ted and his cat Diva. Lilah thought that meant something. Natalie didn't know what it meant. When it came to Blake, she didn't know what anything he did meant. Why had he taken Sparky when she wasn't here? Why hadn't he waited until she got home? Did he want to avoid her?

I want kisses that lead to long, lazy days in bed. The memory of his seducer's voice brought with it the memory of his touch, on her face and belly and between her legs. Warm, liquid memories that made her stomach turn warm and her thighs liquid.

Had he left the note on her refrigerator hoping she would see it and walk the short distance to his house? He wouldn't know that she didn't have Charlotte. She glanced at the clock on the stove. It was five-thirty. Would he return Sparky after Charlotte's bedtime, thinking he could spend the night getting her sheets hot and her skin sticky?

She thought of the other night. Of his hot mouth on her breast and how good it had felt to order off his menu. He'd promised she could have sex any way she wanted it. He'd promised that when he got back, he was going to take his time.

She wanted that. No, he hadn't come right out and said they were in an exclusive relationship or even dating, but by kissing her in her shop, he'd made everyone in town think it was true. He'd created the kind of gossip she'd tried to avoid for years. She might as well enjoy what people had her doing anyway.

What I Love About You

Natalie grabbed a bottle of merlot out of the refrigerator and walked next door before she could talk herself out of it. She put her head down against the wind that had kicked up. Cold air lifted her hair and seeped through her sweater dress. If the whole town thought they were a couple, that meant the whole town assumed they were having sex. If the whole town thought they were having sex, why not order off the big fella's menu?

And yes, she knew she was justifying what she planned to do. She didn't care. She'd had a horrible day, and spending the night with Blake sounded a whole lot better than spending it alone. She was falling in love with Blake. Head over feet, and she wanted to make love with him. She wanted him to make her forget her crappy day.

The choice was easy.

The heels of her pumps tapped up the stone steps and across Blake's porch to the door. She took a deep breath and held the bottle of wine against her chest. For a few brief seconds, she thought of opening the wine and taking a few slugs to calm her shaking hands and jumpy nerves. She didn't have a corkscrew so she knocked on the door instead. Sparky barked from within, and through the wavy glass, she watched Blake's big, watery outline move toward her. Her heart pounded and her mouth got dry as she frantically reconsidered her decision to walk over here. Maybe he was tired. What if he didn't want to see her? He hadn't mentioned wanting to see her on the paper towel note.

The door swung open and her tongue stuck to the roof of her dry mouth. He wore a black long-sleeved T-shirt, tight across the muscles of his developed chest. He'd cut his hair a bit shorter, more spiky on top. She liked his hair long enough for her fingers to comb through, but it didn't matter. The man had a large menu. He looked good enough to eat, and she'd skipped breakfast, eaten a burnt roll and some green beans for dinner, and she was starving.

His gray eyes looked at her. Watching her as if he wasn't quite sure what to make of her standing on his porch with a bottle of merlot clutched to her chest.

"Hello," he finally said.

Lord, she loved his voice. It just kind of slid to the pit of her stomach. "I've been thinking about what you said." She swallowed past the lump in her throat and the expanding glow in her chest. Then she said fast before she lost her nerve, "And you're right. We're both adults and Charlotte's at the Coopers' until tomorrow. We have all night. I want to do what you promised."

One brow rose up his forehead. "What exactly did I promise?"

"Really?" There was something a little different about him tonight. Something subtle that she couldn't quite grasp. Maybe his new haircut made his forehead look a bit broader. Or maybe it was his eyes. There wasn't the usual flash of interest in his storm-colored gaze when he looked at her. "Are you going to make me say it?"

He grinned and folded his arms across his big chest. "Oh yeah."

She swallowed past the lump in her throat and clutched her wine tighter. "Knock boots. Bump bellies. Hot monkey love." She could feel her cheeks burn and not from the cold. "But I still prefer make love."

"Hot *monkey* love." He tipped his head back and laughed. "No shit?"

He was acting weird. Like maybe he got hit real hard on the head during the super-secret military thing he did for a living.

"Maybe I should leave," she said, and took a step back. Just as Blake shook his head like he wanted her to stay, a woman with dark hair looked around his shoulder.

"What are you laughing at?" the woman asked. Big blue eyes stared back at Natalie, and a long curtain of her black hair fell across Blake's arm.

"Oh," Natalie managed, and took a step back. The glow in her chest popped and she felt like she'd been punched in the stomach. Like she was going to be sick. Blake had company. Female company with blue eyes.

"You must be a friend of Blake's." She was young and beautiful and smiled like she was happy to see a woman on Blake's doorstep.

"I'm a . . . his neighbor." Maybe the woman was a relative.

Blake looked across his shoulder. "Hey, baby, could you get him."

Baby? A man didn't call a relative "baby."

"Come in." The woman motioned with her hand. "It's cold outside."

"No. Thank you." Blake didn't call Natalie "baby." He called her Sweet Cheeks. Maybe he called all the women in his life by different names to keep them straight. "I'm obviously interrupting."

"We finished an hour ago. Now we're just watching the game." The woman looked behind her. "Here he comes."

Finished? Natalie about choked on the ball of pain and anger and embarrassment in her throat. She opened her mouth to tell him he was the raging asshole she'd thought the first time she'd met him, but just as the first word sputtered out, an identical copy of Blake muscled his way past Blake.

"I didn't expect to see you today," the second Blake said. This Blake's T-shirt was navy.

Natalie looked from one to the other. Her brain seemed to shut down and refuse to process what stood before her. "What?" was the only thought that leaked through her mental block and escaped her lips. Her ears rang and she blinked against the sudden blur at the edges of her vision. A dizzying wave tingled down her neck and chest, and the bottle fell from her hands. It smashed between her feet as the identical Blakes rushed forward.

"Natalie." Blake carried her limp body over his shoulder. Not exactly the most romantic way to carry a woman, but the quickest and most effective. With one arm around her long legs and his other hand on her behind, he moved through his house.

"Did she hit her head?" his brother, Beau, asked as he tossed several cushions off the brand-new couch.

"I reached her first." He sat down and carefully laid her out on the dark brown leather. Her blond hair covered part of her face and he pushed it from her cheek. "Natalie. Can you hear me?" She didn't respond and he lightly shook her shoulder. She'd looked so pale standing on his porch. He'd watched the blood drain from her face and he'd rushed forward as her eyes rolled back. "Natalie." He shook her lightly again. "Wake up." It didn't look like she was wearing anything constricting, but he ran his hands over her body and dress before he placed two fingers against the carotid pulse in her neck. "Can you hear me?"

"She's got glass in her shoes," Beau said as he shoved a cushion under her feet.

Blake glanced down her body and legs to her feet. Her dress looked like a long, skin-colored sweater. It hugged her body and had ridden up to mid-thigh. Red wine splattered her shins and up her legs through her thin hose. "She needs those shoes off, and those hose probably have glass in them, too."

Beau lifted a brow as he grabbed the remote and turned off the football game they'd been watching. "You want me to take off her panty hose?"

"No." He'd seen a hundred guys faint in his life, but watching it happen to Natalie had been scary as hell.

"I didn't think so." Beau's fiancée, Stella, stood slightly behind him. Looking worried and upset. He still couldn't believe his twin was getting married.

"Could you bring me a cold cloth?" he asked her, more to give her something to do than anything else. "Natalie, wake up."

"Has she ever done this before?" Beau took off Natalie's shoes and set them on the floor.

"Not in front of me." She looked gorgeous, in a fainted Cinderella sort of way. Or was it Sleeping Beauty? He wasn't sure. As a kid he'd never really been into those Disney chick cartoons. "Wake up, Natalie."

"She should be coming around any second."

"Has it been about a minute?" He shook her again and looked into her face. She hadn't been out long enough to worry about yet. So why did his heart pump a little harder in his chest?

"A minute, three seconds."

"Natalie!" It seemed longer. He shook her harder and raised his voice. The next step to revive a fainter was pain. He didn't want to do that and stared into her face, willing her eyes to pop open. "Wake up."

"Stop that," she whispered.

"Can you hear me?"

Her eyes sprang open.

"There you are." He let out a breath, more relieved than he let on. "It's good to see you."

Confusion pulled her brows together. "Where am I?"

"At my house," he said as Stella handed him a damp washcloth. But before he could put it on her forehead, Sparky barked and squeezed between them. The puppy licked her face and nuzzled her with his head. Blake knew how the dog felt. He was so relieved he wanted to nuzzle her, too.

"Sparky?" She lifted a hand to weakly push the dog away.

"How do you feel?" He pushed the dog behind him and lightly put the cloth on her head.

"I don't know. What happened?"

"You fainted." He looked in her eyes, a little

glassy but clear. "Is Charlotte at home?" he asked. He didn't believe she was the kind of mother who'd leave her child at home while she drank wine with the neighbor, but he needed to know she wasn't sitting over there waiting for her mom and Sparky.

"She's at the Coopers'." She raised a hand and placed it on the washcloth on her forehead. "I fainted?"

"Yeah. Have you ever fainted before?"

"No. Wait. Once when I was pregnant." She frowned. "How did I get in here?"

"I carried you." Her pale cheeks made her blue eyes bluer and her pink lips pinker. "We need to take your hose off."

She pushed the washcloth a little higher up her forehead. "Can we wait a few more minutes to get naked?"

Behind him his brother burst into laughter.

"Stop, Beau," Stella shushed him.

Natalie turned her head and her gaze followed the sound of his brother and his brother's fiancée. Her eyes got wide and she tried to sit up.

"Not yet." He put his hand on her shoulder to keep her from rising. "Stay down for a bit more."

The washcloth slid off her head and fell on the couch. "There are two of you?"

"I told you I have an identical twin brother." He picked up the wet cloth and tossed it on an end table.

She shook her head and her gaze returned to him. "You told me you have a brother. I would have remembered if you'd mentioned a twin. Especially a twin who looks just *like* you." Her face flushed, turning her cheeks and throat from white to red. "I have to go." She pushed his hand away and struggled to sit. "I want to go home."

He helped her sit but blocked her from standing. The last thing he wanted was for her to drop again. "I'll walk you home in a few minutes." He glanced over at his brother. "What did you do?"

"I didn't *do* anything." He cleared his throat and tried to hide his shit-eating grin. "She thought I was you, and she may have said some things that, upon reflection, were private between the two of you."

It must have been something sexual. Something so embarrassing she fainted. "What things?"

"Never mind!"

He turned back to Natalie. She looked good

flushed. Much better than pale. He pushed her hair behind one ear and touched her heated cheek. "You'll tell me later," he said, low enough so that his brother couldn't hear.

"No." She shook her head, and her chin brushed his palm. "I'm never saying it again."

He'd get her to say it when they were alone. Maybe while he was pulling that dress over her head. "How do you feel?" He slid his hand to her shoulder.

"I have a little headache, but I'm okay. I can't believe I fainted."

"I brought you juice and an energy bar." Stella stepped forward and handed over a cold bottle and a PowerBar.

"Thanks." Natalie ripped off the wrapper. "I'm starving. Carla burned Thanksgiving."

Blake unscrewed the bottle cap. "Thanks, Stella." He handed the juice to Natalie and introduced the two women. Then he stood and turned to his brother. Their whole lives, people had mistaken them. Most of the time they laughed about it. This was not one of those times. "Natalie, you've met my brother, Beau. He can be a real dick."

"Karma's a bitch," Beau said through a big

grin. He stepped forward and reached for Natalie's hand.

Normally Blake would agree. When he'd first met Stella, he'd let her think he was Beau, but he hadn't made her faint.

"Hello." Natalie shook Beau's hand and swung her feet to the floor. "I'm sorry I fainted on you." She looked down at her legs. "And obviously made a mess."

"Sorry I made you faint. That's never happened before."

"I think it was seeing both you and your brother at the same time. My brain just couldn't accept two Blakes without a little forewarning." She took a bite as her gaze moved from one brother to the other. Trying to pick out the differences.

Stella laughed and folded her arms over her ULV sweatshirt. "The first time I met Blake, I thought he was Beau's clone."

Blake didn't really know Stella. He'd met her only a few times. What he did know he liked, and he hoped to get to know her better in the future. Like tomorrow. He had different plans for tonight.

"I thought you were spending Thanksgiving in San Diego."

Blake glanced at Beau, then sat on the couch next to Natalie. "That was the plan until Beau punched my dad in the head. Needless to say, that put a damper on the holiday." And with the holiday ruined, the three of them had hopped an early morning flight to Idaho.

Beau crossed his arms over his chest and rocked back on his heels. "I'm not going to apologize for that. He came on to Stella."

Stella blushed and threaded her arm through Beau's. "I could have handled it myself. I've handled a lot of drunk men in my lifetime."

"You don't have to now. That's my job."

Blake didn't know how he would have handled the old man if it had been Natalie. He would have been pissed, but he wouldn't have hit him. That's where he was different from his brother. He understood alcoholism and Beau did not. "He always comes on to women."

"Then someone should have knocked him out years ago."

Beau was also less forgiving than Blake. "Finish your orange juice." He turned to Natalie.

"Then we need to get you cleaned up. You smell like a winery and probably have glass in your stockings."

"How often do you drink with my brother?" Beau had discovered his bottle of Johnnie Walker and assumed Blake had relapsed.

"She doesn't drink with me, Beau." He stood and waited for Natalie to lower the juice before he reached for her hand. "Don't grill her. She's been through enough today."

Beau turned to him and he didn't need to say a thing. His expression told Blake that he was going to let it go—for now—but they would talk about it later.

Natalie set the half-empty bottle of juice on the end table and stood. "It was nice to meet you, Stella and Beau."

"You have glass and wine in your shoes." Blake looked down into her face and her pink mouth he'd kissed before he'd left town. He missed her mouth and the rest of her, too. He wasn't surprised that he'd missed her. Whenever he traveled to third-world countries, he missed people more than things he'd left behind. What did surprise him was how much he'd missed her. How much he'd thought about her. "You have to strip out of those hose before we go anywhere."

"Right here?"

"We'll leave," Beau volunteered, and put his hand on the small of Stella's back. "We were going to check out the lake at half-time anyway."

Blake waited until he heard the back door shut before he said, "Pull your dress up."

Natalie's gaze darted to the left where his brother and Stella had disappeared before she lowered her hands to the outsides of her hips. Her fingers gathered the sweater material, raising it up her thighs, inch by agonizing inch. She looked up into his face and tried to smile, and he went from semi-erect to full-blown. "Sorry about the broken glass on your porch." Her fingers stopped. Obviously she couldn't talk and pull her dress up at the same time. "I'll clean it up."

"I don't give a fuck about that." He reached beneath the bottom of her dress and hooked his thumbs in the waistband of her panty hose. God, he hated panty hose. They always got in his way and slowed him down. He yanked them down and took her pink panties with them. He went from full-blown to painfully hard.

"Blake!" She grabbed her underwear and pulled it up.

"Don't waste your time pulling those up," he said as he got down on one knee. "I'm just going to take them right back off." He helped her out of the hose, then balled them up and tossed them on top of her shoes. He ran his hands over her smooth shins and calves looking for small cuts. "Do you feel any slivers of glass?" When she didn't answer, he looked up at her. He looked up past her bare thighs and the pink triangle of her panties. Up her bunched dress about her waist to her face. Her lips were parted and her blue eyes were warm and wanting. Wanting what he wanted, too. He sat back on his heels and slid his hands to the backs of her thighs. "Did you behave while I was gone?" he asked.

She nodded. "I waited for you to get back to act up."

"I appreciate that." He leaned forward and kissed her flat belly just above her panties.

"We can't do this here. Your brother might come back."

She didn't step away or drop her dress and his kiss turned to a smile. He slid his face a little farther south and pressed his open mouth in the center of the pink triangle.

"Blake, we can't do this here. Take me home." She ran her fingers through his hair and held the sides of his head in her palms. "Take me to bed."

He planned on it, but first he wanted to make sure she didn't change her mind. He pulled down her panties and stuck his hand between her legs. She had a landing strip of pubic hair he hadn't noticed the other night, but he hadn't been this close to her pretty little box. She was already wet against his hand. He brushed the tips of his fingers upward and kissed next to her strip.

"I'm going to pass out again," she whispered.

He couldn't have that. He pulled her panties back up her thighs and stood. If he didn't stop he'd forget he had a bedroom upstairs. "What did you say to my brother when you thought it was me?"

She dropped the end of her dress and he thought she might balk again. "I said I want some hot monkey love." She wrapped her arms around his neck and said next to his ear, "I said I want to get you naked and eat off your menu."

"Holy Jesus." The air left his lungs like he got hit in the chest.

"Let's go, big fella."

Blake rarely had to be told twice, and this was not one of those rare occasions. He took her hand, then walked behind her as they moved toward the front of the house. He not only had a bedroom with a big bouncy bed, he had a four-person spa tub.

"I don't have shoes."

"You don't need shoes." He put his hands on her waist and steered her toward the stairs and up the first few steps.

"Where are we going?"

"Up. I'm going to put you in my tub and clean you up. Then I'm going to take advantage of you being naked." There was no way he was going to wait until they walked to her house to jump on Natalie. He didn't want to give her a chance to change her mind or decide she wanted another quickie.

Chapter Thirteen

Natalie stood on a big white throw rug and ran her hands all over Blake's arms and shoulders. Her bare breasts and stomach were glued to his chest and belly, and his hard muscles and tight skin threw off heat like he was set on simmer. His hot, wet tongue swept the inside of her mouth as his erection pressed into her through the thin fabric of his underwear and hers. Water ran full blast in the spa tub and their clothes were scattered across the bathroom and Blake's bedroom beyond.

Before today, she'd only had glimpses of Blake's body. She'd tried not to look the night she'd brought Sparky back, or the other night when she'd been preoccupied with her own pleasure. She hadn't stood back and appreciated the full impact of his beautiful body. She'd let her imagination fill in some of the blanks. Her mind had not lived up to the living flesh, and she pulled back from his kiss to slide her hands over the defined ridges and hard contours of his chest and abdomen. He reached for her, but she stepped out of his grasp. He dropped his hands to his side and looked down at her through eyes drowsy with lust.

"Come here, Natalie."

She shook her head and placed her hand over his heavy heartbeat. She watched her fingertips slip down his chest. His pecs bunched. "I like touching you," she said. "I want to touch you all over."

"God, yes." He sucked in a breath. "Please."

She touched his hard chest and the ladder of muscles on his stomach. She loved him. Loved him with her heart and body and deep down in her soul. She wasn't falling in love, she was there. Standing in the middle of a feeling so strong it made her hands shake, her chest squeeze, and her throat choke with emotion. Her fingers followed his dark blond happy trail past his navel to his lower belly.

"What's Hosea 8:7?"

"'For they have sown the wind,'" he answered, his voice tight from holding his breath. "'And they shall reap the whirlwind.'"

She reached into the pouch of Blake's boxer briefs. "Are you the whirlwind?"

"Something like that."

Blake inhaled deeply as she pulled him out of his underwear, huge and hard and hot in her palm. The other night she hadn't seen his penis, only felt it deep inside, but that was the difference between a quickie and making love. A quickie was just about getting satisfaction. Making love was more. It was giving and sharing and connecting with more than just a man's body. "Maybe I'm the whirlwind."

"You're going to reap the whirlwind in about five minutes," he said on a tortured breath as she rubbed her thumb along the corded vein just beneath the bulging head. It had been a long time since she'd stood before a man she loved and held his ridged penis in her hand. A long time since she'd felt the power of her touch over him.

She slipped her palm up and down his thick shaft and squeezed her thighs together against the heat and liquid between her legs. It had been a long time since she'd loved giving pleasure to a man. A long time since she'd loved giving pleasure to the man she loved.

She kissed his chest and stomach and slid to her knees to kiss his tattoo. Just above the line of his blond pubic hair, she sucked his skin into her mouth.

"Natalie, Jesus." He ran his fingers through her hair and held it from her face. "What are you planning down there?"

"An in-depth lesson on oral sex." She turned her mouth and licked the clear bead resting in the spongy cleft of his erection. She brushed her lips across him and he sucked in a breath between his teeth. Just because it had been a long time since she'd knelt in front of a naked man didn't mean she didn't know how to make his knees buckle and bend him to her will. She had all the power. "Tell me I'm the whirlwind."

"*I'm* the whirlwind."

She tickled the sensitive spot on his shaft with her tongue. Then she pulled back and looked up at him. "Natalie 11:28," she said, referring to the date. "She who blows a reaper shall be called the whirlwind."

His smoky eyes looked down at her, all shiny and hot with lust. "You can be called anything you want. Reaper, whirlwind, fucking Queen of England."

"Whirlwind is good." She smiled, then slid him into her mouth, taking as much as possible. His fingers tangled in her hair as she alternately sucked him hard and caressed the sensitive vein beneath the head of his penis with her tongue. She moved one hand up and down his long shaft and lightly squeezed his testicles with the other.

"That feels good, Natalie." He tilted his head back. "So fucking good."

She worked him over, loving the taste and texture of him in her mouth. Losing herself in the pleasure of his body. She loved the power of it and how much it turned her on. She took him deeper, heard his deep groan mix with the sound of water splashing in the tub. She loved how she turned him on with her mouth and hand.

"Stop."

She sucked him harder and pressed her thumb into the corded flesh beneath the head of his penis. "Stop," he repeated, but he didn't push her away. Instead, he groaned from deep in his gut and made that sound when he orgasmed. A sexy, guttural "uhhhn." She stayed with him as he locked his knees and curled his hands in her hair. When he was through, she lifted her face and looked up at him. His lips were parted as he sucked air in and out of his lungs. Without a word, she lifted her thumb, and his warm semen splashed across her breasts.

"Sweet baby Jesus." He sank to his knees in front of her.

"I'm your whirlwind." She wrapped her arms around his neck and whispered in his ear.

"You sucked the whirlwind right out of me."

"When you get your strength back, clean me up and take advantage of me." She expected it to take him a few minutes, if not a half hour, but Blake had hidden reserves. Lots of stored-up energy.

He picked her up and put her in the tub. The water lapped and swirled about the bottoms of her breast as he washed his ejaculate from her skin. He soaped her nipples and drove her crazy with the teasing touches of his hands and mouth. She sat back as he soaped up her shins and calves and slid his hands up her thighs. He pressed his thumbs into her slick crotch and touched her until she was more than ready to have him deep inside.

Blake's energy reserves lasted as she straddled his hips and placed her palms on the sides of his face. His hands grabbed her hips and she looked into his eyes as he lowered her onto his thick erection. The tips of her breasts brushed his chest and she watched the need for her flicker and shine in his eyes. With him hot and deep and filling her body, it was more than just sex. She moved, rocking her hips and kissing his neck and his throat, running her hands all over him. She made love to him with her body and every pulsing beat of her heart. His steady breath brushed her cheek as he steadily pumped into her, stroking her inside walls. She pulled back to look into his eyes, deep gray with lust and need. She placed both hands on the sides of his face. She sucked in his breath, and he sucked in hers as she stared into his soul. She shared her heart and body. Her love worked a shudder free from deep in her own soul. She hugged him tight against the almost violent orgasm spreading through her, grabbing her heart and clenching her stomach, and feeling as if she might implode. She hugged him against her heart. Against the emotion she couldn't keep inside. Against the love that changed her life and blew her world apart.

Blake couldn't recall the last time he'd spent the night in a woman's bed. Completely sober. Whether it was a few beers or a few bottles of Johnnie, he'd always had something in his hand besides a woman.

Against his throat, Natalie's soft blond hair tickled his skin. She lay butt to nuts, or as she had preferred, spooning, in her girly bed with mounds of pillows and ruffles and lace. Her soft, even breathing brushed across his biceps and gently raised her breasts. They were both worn out from a sexual trifecta that had started in his bathroom; moved to her kitchen while she cooked a meal of steak, salad, and Poppin' Fresh croissants; and ended in Natalie's bed. A woman's even breathing was usually his cue to slip from bed, grab his clothes, and head out. It was around midnight, and the only light entering the room was from a crack in the bathroom door. He could easily go. Leave without stirring a hair on her head. He was stealthy as hell, gone in a puff of smoke.

He buried his nose in the top of her blond hair. She smelled like clean sunshine, and he pulled her tighter against his chest. He didn't know if it was sobriety or the fact that he hadn't had sex for months, but the sex with Natalie was better than he'd had in a long time, if ever. She was gorgeous and hot and he'd been trying to get her naked for weeks. After the quickie in her living room, he'd definitely wanted more, but he'd never guessed that behind her beautiful face and proper facade she gave fantasy blow jobs. The kind a man dreamed about but never actually got. The kind where a woman moaned and sucked and acted like she couldn't get enough of him in her mouth.

"I'm your whirlwind," she'd said. He didn't know about that, but he did know she turned his head around. He talked to her about things he'd not even mentioned to Beau yet.

"Why did your brother want to know if I drink with you?" she'd asked as they'd sat at the kitchen table eating like they were ravenous after having ravenous sex against the refrigerator.

It wasn't a secret. He'd had a problem and dealt

with it. "Because I spent two months in a rehab last summer."

She'd slowly chewed, then swallowed. "Why were you in rehab?"

"Alcohol. I was drinking too much." Just because it wasn't a secret didn't mean he wanted to talk about it. He'd had a few white-knuckle hours at his father's house, which Blake suspected contributed to Beau punching their dad.

"How much is too much?" She gazed at him with those dark blue eyes of her. Damn, she liked to pry.

"More than was good for me and less than my dad. My old man drinks beer from noon until five, then switches to whiskey until he passes out." That had been his routine for years, and he had no interest in disrupting his routine. He said he was too old to stop, but he'd promised Beau that if "his boys" spent Thanksgiving with him, he'd stay sober. He'd even locked up his sauce in his gun safe. He'd lasted two hours before he began sneaking out to the garage. By the time the old man came on to Stella, he'd been tanked and Beau had decked him.

"That's a shame your father couldn't stay

sober for you." She reached for a glass of water. "My mom's addicted to her fifth wheel and she couldn't even make it up here for Thanksgiving. She'll probably miss Christmas, too." She raised the glass. "Granted, they aren't in the same league, but both parents miss out, I think." She took a drink and swallowed. "How many days have you been sober?"

"One hundred and nineteen," he answered without hesitation.

A wrinkle pulled at her brows as she licked a droplet of water from the bow of her top lip. "Then why do you have a bottle of Johnnie Walker in your wine cellar?"

That was the same question Beau had for him. "To remind myself that I can control it. Same reason I shoot photos of it."

She looked at him for several heartbeats. "You don't go to meetings?"

"I don't need meetings. I don't need to go to a shrink at the VA, either." He'd looked up from his salad. "I have everything under control."

She looked back at him, and he should have known she would not let it go. "What's everything?"

He was having a good time. He liked Natalie. Talking about his addiction and flashbacks wasn't a good time. "Never mind."

She put down her fork and leaned slightly toward him. Her eyes stared into his like she meant business. "Blake, my life is an open book. I don't have any secrets. Every embarrassing thing that has happened to me is out there for the world to see. Your life cannot be worse than being married to a man who embezzled half the town blind. There are those who still think I had something to do with it. Sometimes shit happens that isn't our fault." She picked up her fork and stabbed a carrot in her salad. "And sometimes it is our fault, like the time when I drove my mother's Chrysler Town and County through Howdy's Trading Post. His display of Jesus bobble heads flew everywhere."

He tried not to laugh. "Foot slip?"

"Wasp. It was buzzing around my head and I was slapping at it and screaming and I missed the turn on Shore Lane and ran into Howdy's. Thank goodness Howdy's never has much business or I could have ended up with more than a ticket, five thousand dollars in restitution, and a Buddy

Christ bobble head stuck in the grille." She raised the fork and asked one more time before she took a bite, "What is your everything?"

"I have occasional flashbacks," he confessed, because talking about those was easier than talking about booze.

She chewed. "How occasional?"

"It's only happened about four times, and it's not a big deal. Something like a noise or a smell will make me disoriented for several seconds, and I feel like I'm standing on a roof in Ramadi or crouched behind a rock in the Hindu Kush." This was the part he'd never mentioned to anyone. Not the shrink in rehab or his brother. Although he suspected Beau guessed. "For a few seconds I feel stuck between what is real and what isn't."

"And you feel helpless." It was a statement. Not a question.

He wasn't helpless. "I have it under control." Like his addiction.

"What do you do when you have a flashback?"

"Do?" He was getting annoyed and wished he wouldn't have mentioned it. Now she was going to think he had PTSD and would shoot up the joint. "You don't have to worry that I'll strip off my clothes and run down the streets, drooling, and shooting at phantom targets."

"I wasn't worried. You should give me a little more credit than that." She frowned at him. "What you describe sounds a little like the anxiety I used to have shortly after Michael was arrested. My biggest trigger was the sound of the CBS News. I'd hear that *bing-bong-bing* and my heart would start booming in my chest. My face would get really hot, and I'd pace and pace and pace, and I'd think I was having a heart attack. I really did think I was going to die." She picked up her knife and cut off a small piece of steak. "I was diagnosed with extreme anxiety due to stress, but I was pregnant and couldn't take drugs. So I went to a therapist who taught me how to talk myself out of a full-blown attack."

"Cognitive behavioral therapy." He picked up a croissant, relieved that she didn't look at him cross-ways like he might howl at the moon.

"You've heard of it."

"Of course. That's what they teach and preach in rehab." He expected her to pry or nag or press him to find a sponsor, but she didn't. They spent the rest of the meal talking about his family and hers, and he told her he'd been talking to Roy Baldridge about the vacant house down the street.

She paused as she pushed her empty plate aside. "You flip houses, too?"

"Yeah. I stared working construction with my cousin just for something to do when I wasn't deployed or training out of state. It started as a hobby, but I found I really enjoy gutting a house and rebuilding it."

"Do you ever just relax?"

"I'm not good at that. Jungers are overachievers." Which was probably an understatement.

Charlotte called while he helped Natalie with the dishes. Mostly he rinsed while she put things away and loaded the dishwasher.

"If you want me to come and get you, call me. Even if it's late." Natalie spoke into her phone as she set a plate in the sink. "Yes. Even if its three lates. Late, late, late." She talked for several more minutes about some fairy movie before she hung up and put her phone on the counter. "I'll be glad when Charlotte's home with me."

"How was Thanksgiving with the Coopers?" He'd been surprised when she'd mentioned where she'd been before she'd shown up on his porch and fainted. When she'd told him, he didn't like it. He didn't want her around her former husband when he wasn't around, but it didn't matter what he liked. It wasn't his business.

"Hell. I made everyone cry but Ron, and I think that's only because he tunes out everything around him. Carla got so upset with me, she ran into her bedroom and burned the turkey."

"Meanie." He moved behind her and massaged her shoulders. "What did you do to the poor Coopers?"

"I told them the truth. I told Carla that I wasn't going to get back together with Michael." She moved her head forward to give him better access to the base of her skull. "Charlotte cried because she was acting up at the table and spilled her milk all over. I had to take her in the kitchen and give her a good talking-to."

He chuckled. *A good talking-to.* "What about Michael?"

"I'm not sure he actually cried, but his eyes got kind of misty when I told him I don't love him."

She turned and looked up at Blake. "I felt so horrible, Blake." She frowned like *she* might cry. "I don't love him and I feel it's best to be honest right up front. I think it's kinder to rip off the Band-Aid than to give him false hope and lead him on. But it was hard and I feel horrible and mean."

He smiled. "I have something to make you feel better." He slid his hands down her sides and around her waist. "Show me your bedroom."

"You're not tired?"

"I'll sleep tomorrow after Charlotte comes home. Right now I want to play with Charlotte's mom."

She led him to her room filled with white wicker furniture and frilly stuff that was enough to make a weaker man's balls shrink. Blake had not had a problem with shrinkage, and had sex one more time before Natalie fell asleep.

The ceiling fan above his head stirred the cool night air as he turned on his back and took her with him. She curled against his side, and again he wondered if he should just grab his pants and go. Home to his own bed that didn't have a warm woman in it. Instead he fell asleep with her knee next to his groin. He woke several times during the night with her snuggled against him. She was a beautiful woman with a beautiful body, and as the rising sun leaked through the slats in the window blinds, he woke for the last time. Her back was against his chest, one of his hands cupped her breasts, and his erection rested against the crease of her behind.

"Natalie," he whispered, and lightly pressed his hard penis against her smooth butt. "Are you awake?" Her even breathing continued and he slid one of her legs on top of his. His hand moved to her crotch, and within a few short moments, she was wet against his fingers. He touched her until she arched her back and a long, sleepy moan escaped her lips. So sexy it seeped beneath his skin and tightened his chest.

"Are you awake now?"

She pressed her behind into his erection. "Is that a banana or are you happy to see me?"

"It's not a banana." He slid his hand between them and moved his erection between her legs. She was slick and hot and he slipped inside. "But I am happy to see you." He wrapped both his arms around her and held her still. Held her against his chest and closed his eyes. Her hair tickled his cheek and he rested his forehead against the back of her head. He liked this. He liked her. He'd like to wake like this every morning. With his penis in Natalie Cooper.

"You're holding me too tight. I can't breathe, Blake."

"Sorry." He didn't know he was squeezing her and loosened his hold. He slipped his hand down her belly to cup between her thighs. He adjusted her behind and legs, and positioned himself further beneath her.

"I love being inside you." He kissed her neck and bit her shoulder and drove into her until he felt the first squeeze of her orgasm. She was right. She was the whirlwind and he joined her in a wild, out-of-control climax that spun his head around and around. He squeezed her against his chest as if he wanted to absorb her into him. She called his name, a rush of pleasure ending in a wheeze from lack of oxygen.

"Blake, I can't breathe."

"Sorry," he said again, and when it was over, he lay on his back looking up at the whirling ceiling fan. He'd never given a woman a chokehold. Not once, let alone twice.

He thought about it as he dressed and she tied a silky pink robe around her waist. It didn't leave his head as he tied his shoes and she left the room to let out Sparky. He was still thinking about it when he grabbed an apple off the kitchen counter, and she passed him on her way down the hall.

"I have to get in the shower before Charlotte gets here in about an hour," she called out to him. "I'll see you later."

Blake bit into the apple and moved to the side door. He shoved the puzzle of Natalie and his sleeper hold to the back of his mind and reached for the handle. Beau and Stella had one more day in Truly. Maybe they'd want breakfast at the greasy spoon in town. He and his brother loved a greasy spoon breakfast. He shut the door behind him and stopped on the top step as Charlotte and a man with dark hair moved down the side of the house with Sparky running and jumping in circles around them. He recognized the man wearing new sneakers and jeans and a dark blue ski parka. He'd seen him in Natalie's photo store before he'd left town.

"Hi, Blake," Charlotte greeted him. She wore

her purple coat above a puffy dress, bare legs, and dress shoes. "Did you bring Spa-ky to my house?"

He took a big bite of apple and watched the man as he chewed, sizing him up in a few short seconds. Nice-looking guy. Kind of pale. Prison would do that to a man. "Yeah." He wiped the back of his shirtsleeve across the back of his mouth. "He missed you."

"Ahhh." She grabbed the dog around his neck until he yelped. "I love you, Spa-ky."

"Blake?" The man held out is hand. "I'm Charlotte's father, Michael Cooper."

Blake shook his hand and had to give the guy points for looking him in the eyes and not being a pussy. His handshake could be a little more firm, though. Blake dropped the guy's hand and moved down the steps as Charlotte moved up.

"Guess what, Blake?"

"What?"

"I watched the fairy movie four times. I ate popcorn and hu-t my tooth right here." She opened her mouth and pointed inside.

He pretended to look. "It looks okay. I don't think you'll need surgery."

"No way." She continued up the steps and turned with one hand on the door. "Bye, Blake."

"See ya, kid."

Then she looked at Michael, and Blake wondered if she was still worried that she might not like him. "Bye, Dad."

"Bye, Charlotte."

She gave a little wave and she and Sparky ran into the house, leaving Blake and Michael looking after her.

"Charlotte talks about you," Michael told him.

"Oh yeah?" Blake wasn't wearing a coat and headed down the sidewalk toward the front yard. He could cut through the trees, but he wanted to make sure Michael Cooper left the way he came.

"She says you two are friends."

"We are." It was good that Michael walked beside Blake so Blake didn't have to drag him by one leg. "She's a good kid." Blake took another bite and chewed. Charlotte was funny and smart and a drama queen, but he'd let Michael find out what a great kid she was all on his own. He didn't feel the need to help the guy out.

"What is Natalie to you?"

Michael was getting right into it. No nice,

friendly chitchat, which was fine with Blake. He didn't like nice, friendly chitchat. "That's none of your business."

"Maybe not." Michael stopped by the front of a red Jeep Cherokee. "When I was in prison, I had a lot of time to think about my family. I really fucked up a lot of lives. It will take Natalie a long time to forgive me, and I can live with that if I know she's good."

"She's good." Blake took the last bite of the apple and tossed the core into the trees. He didn't have a problem with Natalie's ex. Not unless the ex created a problem. "You don't need to concern yourself with Natalie."

"Natalie is the first woman I ever loved. I remember what she wore the first day I ever saw her in sixth grade. I remember the first time I kissed her and how she looked in her wedding dress."

Blake folded his arms against the crisp morning air and debated whether he should tell the guy that he knew five different ways to kill a man with his bare hands. "Do you have a point, or is this a pissing match?" He looked the other man directly in the eyes. "I don't do pissing matches."

"Not a pissing match." Michael held up one hand as a corner of his lips lifted like he was amused. "I would never get into a pissing match with a Navy SEAL."

"Natalie tell you that?"

"No. I did a public records search. Then I paid fifty bucks for a criminal background check on you. I trust Natalie, but I wanted to make sure for myself that you're safe around my daughter."

Blake couldn't be mad at that. Could probably respect it, even. "And safe around Natalie."

"Yes. It's hard not to think of her as my wife. I will always love her."

"She doesn't love you."

"I know." He looked down at the toes of his shoes, then looked back up into Blake's eyes. "Natalie told me she loves you."

Chapter Fourteen

"Mom, there he is."

Natalie looked up from her grocery list. "Who?"

"Mason," Charlotte said just above a whisper, and pointed to a little boy wearing a Spider-Man coat and boots. "He's in my class."

Natalie knew about Mason Hennessey. Charlotte had mentioned his freckles several times. "Is he the little boy you like?" She reached for several boxes of macaroni and cheese and put them in her cart.

"Not anymore. I had to give him up."

Natalie chuckled. "Why?"

"Amy chased him at recess and kissed his cheek." She climbed on the side of the cart. "I don't want him now."

Poor Mason, used goods before he graduated from kindergarten. She grabbed a bag of spaghetti noodles and canned vegetables, then headed for the produce aisle. She thought about last night and Blake. She'd never had so much sex in one night in her life. Not even when she'd been younger and she and Michael used to skip school and go to her house while her mother had been at work.

"Can I have fruit snacks?"

"Go grab some but come right back." Charlotte jumped off the cart and darted around the corner.

Natalie didn't remember sex being that good. If it had been, it might have been harder to go without for so long. Every time she woke last night, she'd been glued to Blake. Either she'd been on her back with his arm across her, or she'd been on her side with his hand on her breast, the other cupping her crotch like he was afraid to have her parts too far away from him.

The last time, he'd woken her from an erotic dream only to discover she hadn't been dreaming at all. "I love being inside you," he said. At the time, his whispered admission thrilled her. Now she thought she'd read too much into it. She'd thought it meant something, but it only meant that he loved sex with her. He didn't love *her*.

After years of living free of her anxiety, she felt it clog her throat and pick up her pulse. What if he never loved her? She loved him so much she'd let him into her life. She loved him so much she'd broken her rules with him. Her love for him was new and scary and made her heart all achy and wonderful.

Natalie chose a bunch of bananas and placed them in her cart. He had to feel something for her. Until last night, he'd been tight-lipped about his life. He'd kept everything close to the vest, but last night he'd told her about his flashbacks. She wasn't surprised. A person couldn't live through the things he must have seen and done and not have it imprinted on his subconscious. Thank God for the men and women who were brave and dedicated and served their country, but it had to take a toll. Even superheroes had a chink in their armor. Superman had kryptonite and Batman was only human without his tool belt.

She added oranges to her cart. Blake was an alcoholic. That had been a surprise, but it didn't make a difference to her. She loved him. All of him. Drinking or not drinking wasn't a problem for her. The only time she drank was with Lilah, and that wasn't often. The only other alcoholic that she knew was Mabel Vaughn, and she only knew about Mabel because Mabel used to talk about it with her grandmother. Mabel was a big AA supporter and it was one of the only groups or meetings or people she didn't gossip about.

After the grocery store, she and Charlotte drove to the dry cleaner's before heading back home. She'd always closed Glamour Snaps and Prints the day after Thanksgiving, and it was a rare Friday that both of them had off. They had plans to bake cookies and make Christmas cards. Later when Charlotte went to bed, Natalie had other plans. Grown-up plans with the neighbor boy.

In the backseat, Charlotte sang her ABCs, over . . . and over . . . and over, and Natalie white-knuckled the wheel.

"There's Spa-ky!" Charlotte paused at L-M-N-O-P.

Still several blocks from home, Natalie slowed the car and came to a stop in the road. If she had to chase the dog, she was going to be pissed.

What I Love About You

Charlotte pointed to the Loosey house and Blake's red Ford sitting in the driveway. Sparky was tied to the front porch, and Natalie pulled her Subaru in behind Blake's truck. As soon as she put the car in park, Charlotte unbuckled herself and opened her door.

"Blake," she called as she jumped out. "Where are you?"

Natalie got out of the car herself and stopped to study the abandoned house. The yard was nothing but frozen weeds and dirt, and the blue siding was warped in several places and some of the windows were cracked. She remembered the Looseys and their well-groomed yard and flower boxes.

Blake had talked about buying this house, but it looked like a ton of work to her. God knew how many wild animals had made the house their home in the past few years.

The front door swung open. "Who's causing such a ruckus?" Blake walked from inside the house, wearing his brown jacket and jeans. His confident and easy stride carried him across the large porch. Happy tingles rushed across Natalie's skin, and she buried the lower half of her face in the collar of her coat to hide her smile.

"It's me, Blake." Charlotte ran up the steps. "What are you doing here?"

"Just looking around." He put his big hand on Charlotte's head and messed up her hair. Then he raised his gaze to Natalie as she walked across the lawn and up the steps. Smile lines creased his warm gray eyes, and he said a low and sexy "Hello."

One word. One word that made happy tingles lift her heart like her chest was filled with carbonation. "Mr. Junger."

"What do you think of my new house?"

"You're gonna move here?"

Blake looked down at Charlotte, who stood between them. "No. I'm just going to buy it and fix it up."

Natalie guessed that meant he planned to live in Truly for a while. This time she didn't hide her smile. "Did you make an offer?"

"This morning." He looked at her as if he was remembering last night. All hot and steaming as if he was tempted to throw her down and relive it.

The door to the house opened and Beau walked out. Looking at Beau was like looking at Blake, only there was a minute difference, so slight that she really couldn't put her finger on the difference.

"Hello, Natalie. It's good to see you again."

"I don't have wine and I'm not going to faint today."

Charlotte peeked around Blake's side and looked up. For once she was speechless.

"You must be Charlotte," Beau said. "I've heard a lot about you."

Charlotte finally found her vocal cords. She opened her mouth and screamed like Natalie had never heard her child scream before. It was high and loud and filled with terror.

"It's okay, Charlotte," Blake said.

She looked from Beau to Blake and screamed again. This time she turned and ran down the steps for the car. One word, "robot," trailed behind her.

The three adults watched as she opened the car door and dived inside.

"Jesus." Beau was the first to speak. "Sorry I scared your kid."

"I've got to go," Natalie said, and moved down the steps. "Sorry she screamed when she saw you." She walked across the yard and stuck her head in the open door to the backseat. "Charlotte. Don't be scared, baby. That man isn't a robot. He's Blake's brother."

"I wanna go, Mama," she cried.

"Okay."

"Should I talk to her?" Blake asked as he moved toward the car.

"Maybe later."

He ducked his head to look inside the car, then returned his gaze to Natalie. "Hasn't she seen twins before?"

"Not like you and your brother. The Olson triplets aren't identical." She dug in her coat pocket for her keys. "Ever since she saw *I, Robot* with Will Smith, she's been terrified of robots."

"I'll come over later and see how she's doing."

"I'll talk to her and she'll be okay. We'll Google 'twins' and I'll show her Beau's not a robot." She lowered her voice a fraction. "Why don't you come over about nine? I have a surprise for you."

His smile started at one corner of his lips and spread. "What?"

She shrugged and hurriedly got in the car before he pressed and she told him. "You'll find out at nine."

What I Love About You

Blake placed a hand on the roof of the car and the other on top of the door frame and looked into Natalie's blue eyes. "I'll be there, whirlwind," he said, then shut the door and took a step back. He glanced at Charlotte's teary-eyed face and felt like a shit head. Who knew the sight of Beau would terrify her?

He watched the Subaru pull out of the driveway, then he turned back to the house. He'd walked through the house this morning with the Realtor, and despite it having been empty for so long, there were no major problems with the home. It had been gutted and most of the fixtures stolen, but those things were easily replaced. The Realtor had left him the keys and he'd brought Beau to see the house while Stella took a nap. He wondered if his brother's fiancée was pregnant or the altitude was making her sleep a lot. Blake wouldn't mind being an uncle, and a grandbaby would get his mom off his back.

"You have an interesting effect on the Cooper girls," he said as he walked back up the steps. He grabbed Sparky's leash secured to the front post and untied it.

Beau looked as baffled as Blake when he'd first met the pair. "At least the little kid didn't faint."

They moved inside and Sparky went crazy

Rachel Gibson

sniffing around. The carpet was filthy, but the hardwood floors just needed a little sanding and sealing. "The biggest problem I foresee is finding licensed subcontractors to do the work I don't want to do. Like the plumbing."

Beau looked up at the ceiling fan hanging by some wires. "Your plan is to work on this between jobs?" He returned his gaze to Blake. "When's your next security assignment?"

Blake shrugged. "Day before yesterday I got offered a lot of money to work on an oil rig in the Gulf of Oman."

"Shit job."

"That's why I said no." He looked at the staircase to his left and the iron rails. The house wasn't dialed up, but it was built solid. In a climate with such extreme temperatures, that was important.

Beau bent down and scratched Sparky's head. "What about Natalie Cooper?"

The house had nice bay windows and a big fireplace. He returned his attention to his brother. "What about her?"

"She has a kid."

"Yeah. I know. What's your point?" he asked, even though he already knew the answer.

"You're not just messing with the mama. When you walk out of Natalie's life, it's going to affect that kid."

He knew that, and it was why he'd avoided women with children in the past. "Who says I'm walking out?"

Beau crossed his arms over his thick sweatshirt. "Have your thoughts about marriage and settling down with one woman changed?" When Blake didn't answer, Beau shook his head. "I didn't think so. You can't fuck the mother and not fuck up the kid's life."

Sometimes he hated having a twin brother. Someone who knew him like he knew himself. Someone who pissed him off more than anyone else on the planet. "Watch what you say," he warned.

Beau lifted one brow. "It's like that?"

Again, he knew exactly what his brother meant. Did he love Natalie? He liked her. He liked to spend time with her in and out of the sack. He felt protective over her and he felt comfortable with her, but that wasn't love. "Ever since you decided your orgasms should mean something more than getting off, you've been a self-righteous son of a bitch. Ever since your dick had some miraculous conversion to 'meaningful sex,' you think I should convert, too." Anger lowered his brows and he pointed at his brother's face. "Natalie Cooper is none of your goddamn business!"

"You're just mad 'cause I'm right," Beau said, calm and cool. "You're already in that little girl's life. What do you think is going to happen when you walk out of it?"

"What are you? A fucking psychic?" Blake dropped his hand. "Who says I'm going to walk out?"

"Because it's what you do. Until a year ago, that's what I did, too. Because you still live for the chase. Whether it's bad guys or women. Because you don't know that loving one woman isn't weakness. You don't know that planting roots in one place, with someone you love, doesn't take away your superhero powers and make you average. It's normal, Blake, and God forbid the Junger men are normal."

Part of what his brother said was true, and that just pissed him off more. They'd been raised to be better at everything. Even better than each other.

What I Love About You

Beau dropped his hands to his sides. "From what you've told me, Natalie doesn't let a lot of men in her life. She's going to develop stronger feelings for you than you have for her. If she hasn't already."

He opened his mouth, then closed it again. He wanted to say Natalie didn't have feelings for him and Beau could shove his sanctimonious bullshit up his ass, but he couldn't exactly do that now. "Natalie told me she loves you," Michael Cooper had informed him just that morning. He hadn't thought much about it since because he hadn't been able to figure out the guy's motive. If he'd said it to see a reaction, Blake hadn't given him one. It was too soon for Natalie to mention anything about love. They'd had sex only four times, not counting the amazing blow job. They were neighbors and shared a dog. He liked Charlotte and Natalie a lot. Since he'd left for Mexico, he'd known that if he wanted more than a quickie with Natalie, and he definitely did, she would want more from him than booty calls. He was prepared to give her more. He was prepared to have a friends-with-exclusive-benefits-to-the-other's-naked-body relationship. It was the logical next step but a giant leap from the L-word. There was no way Natalie loved him any more than he loved her.

"Natalie seems like a nice woman. Smart. Beautiful."

She hated lies and was the only person he'd ever known who truly lived her life as an open book. If Natalie really had told Michael that she loved him, Blake knew her well enough to know she believed it.

"You can't treat her like you have all the other women in your past," Beau said over his shoulder as he walked toward the front door. "Shit or get off the pot, frogman."

Natalie checked on Charlotte one last time. Her daughter was curled up in her own bed asleep. She shut Charlotte's door and moved into her bathroom. She hurriedly shucked her robe and stepped into her old blue and gold cheerleader skirt. It hit her a bit above mid-thigh, and she could still zip up the side. It was tight around the waist so she left it unbuttoned. The sweater still had her name patch embroidered in a megaphone on the left breast, and her spirit ribbons were still pinned on the right. She pulled the sweater over her head to her waist. It was also tighter across her breasts and pulled when she lifted her arm to brush her hair into a high ponytail.

When she was finished, she moved from the bathroom to the kitchen. It was almost nine and she dug around in her purse sitting on the table. After she'd left Blake at the Loosey house, she'd come home and found the old box with her high school yearbooks and old cheer uniform. She grabbed a tube of lip gloss from her purse, and she had to admit that she felt a little ridiculous. She coated her lips with a thin smear of pink and took a moment to rethink her surprise. What if Blake thought it was stupid? What if . . . She made a scoffing sound and dropped the lip gloss back into her purse. Blake was a guy with cheer-leader fantasies. He'd like it, especially the part about her not wearing underwear.

A light knock drew her attention to the side door and she glanced at the clock. Blake was right on time. Natalie walked across the room, took a deep breath, and opened the door. With her arms wide, she said, "Surprise!"

He stood on the porch, half covered in darkness. The light from the house fell across his throat and chest but left his face in covered in darkness. Her heart thumped heavy in her chest but he didn't say anything, obviously stunned speechless.

"Come in and I'll show you some of my best routines." She stepped back, and the second he moved inside, she could tell he wasn't stunned speechless. Instead of lust or even a smile, he looked at her like he had the first day they met. Cold. Like stone. Like he couldn't wait to be away from her.

"What's wrong?" A panicky little flutter settled in her stomach. "What happened?"

He didn't take off his coat, and instead leaned back against the closed door. "I'm leaving in the morning."

"Oh." She might have felt a measure of relief if not for his closed face.

"I don't know when I'll be back."

She knew what he did for a living. Knew he didn't work nine to five, five days a week. "Okay."

"I don't know if I'll come back."

"If?" A little pinch grabbed a piece of her heart. She must not have heard him right. Hadn't

he just made an offer on the Loosey house? "I'm confused, Blake."

"This isn't really working out," he said, and made a motion with his hand, pointing to the both of them. "My job takes me away for weeks and maybe months at a time. You want a relationship, but that can't happen if one person is gone most of the time."

She looked into his beautiful face and eyes, reflecting nothing but a chilly indifference. "I've known that about you for a while now. We can make it work." God, did she sound as desperate as she felt? "I don't care about your job."

"You will."

She took a deep breath and said past the growing pinch in her chest and the pride jamming her throat, "I love you, Blake. I don't care about the rest."

"There is no rest. I'm not a relationship guy. I told you that from the start." He pushed away from the door and reached for the handle like he hadn't heard her confess that she loved him. Like he couldn't get away from her fast enough.

"I just told you that I love you and your response is to walk out?"

"You don't love me. Sex isn't love."

"You don't think I know the difference?"

"I think you're confused."

She folded her arms across the pain in her chest. "Then clear it up for me."

He frowned the way he always did when she forced him to say something he didn't want to talk about. "Sex with you was great. I had a good time. You had a good time, but it's time to move on."

Oh God. She dropped her head and looked at her bare toenails she'd painted red just for him. She didn't want to see his cold, closed eyes.

"I'm sorry to hurt you. You're the most honest person I know, and you deserve me to be honest with you. And the last thing I want is to lead you on and make you think there's a chance I'll return your feelings one day." He opened the door but she didn't look up. "Please tell Charlotte good-bye for me," he said, then closed the door behind him.

Then she did look up and stared at the door, unable to move. Had that just happened? Had he just said he was leaving and didn't know if he'd be back? Had she just told Blake she loved him and he'd said there wasn't a chance he'd return her feelings? He'd walked out on her? Had he just used the words she'd said about Michael on her?

The backs of her eyes stung and her chest ached like it was caving in on her and pinching her heart. She loved a man who didn't love her. A man she'd known better than to fall in love with. She'd known he couldn't be trusted with her heart, but she'd gone right ahead and handed him her heart anyway.

And now? Natalie pulled out a kitchen chair and sat. She was a fool. A tear slid down her cheek and the pain of loving Blake felt like a weight pressing in on her. He'd always said he didn't want a relationship, but that wasn't how he'd acted. He'd always acted like he wanted her. He'd pursued her, and when she'd given in to her feeling for him, he'd dumped her flat and shattered her heart.

Maybe this was the reason she'd avoided relationships. Maybe it had nothing to do with a moral dilemma and everything to do with the pain of once again loving a man. The physical pain in her chest and stomach and crawling across her skin.

Her watery gaze fell on the Christmas cards she and Charlotte had made earlier. What about her daughter? He was just going to up and leave and walk out of Charlotte's life? He was going to leave it to Natalie to say good-bye for him?

Anger bubbled in her veins like lava and threatened to explode, but this time there was no marching over to his house like when he'd stuck her with a dog.

The dog. What about Sparky? He was going to walk out on her and Charlotte and his dog? He was okay with leaving her heartbroken, Charlotte sad and confused, and Sparky abandoned?

Natalie wiped her nose and cheek with the arm of her sweater. She was angry, and heartbroken, and a fool. Such a fool. Once again she'd thought she knew a man. Thought that beneath Blake's hard, cool exterior was a man who was soft and warm inside. Once again she was clueless about the real heart and soul of the man she loved.

A clueless fool in a stupid cheerleader outfit.

Chapter Fifteen

Blake relaxed among the insertion gear in the back of a Knighthawk heading over the Indian Ocean. The same three security contractors he'd worked with in Yemen occupied the other seats while the pilot kept his eyes on the two green blips off the northeast corner of Somalia.

The four men wore black skin suits and waited for the signal to jump. It came two miles out from a cargo ship, the *Fatima*, which had been boarded and held by Somali pirates. The latest intel reported that the crew hadn't been seen. Either they were all dead or they had locked themselves in the panic rooms.

The *Fatima* operated under the Panamanian

flag and listed bulk cargo on its manifest. While it was loaded with grains, ore, and hatchets out of Hong Kong, the U.S. government had learned that deep in the cargo bay, a dozen fifty-gallon barrels of yellowcake uranium were stowed. Several hundred feet in front of the *Fatima*, an eighty-foot attack boat kept watch, waiting for the cover of darkness to unload the nuclear material. The boat had no markings, no name, and was armed with deck-mounted .50-caliber weapons. Not exactly the usual rusted-out skiff of impoverished Somali pirates.

The helo hovered forty-five feet above the surface of the ocean and the pilot flipped a switch. The light in the starboard door changed from red to green, and Fast Eddy gave the signal. The men pushed a Zodiac into the waves and fast-roped into the rolling inflatable boat. The copilot lowered their gear, and within three minutes, they had everything stowed and assembled and heading for the *Fatima*.

Blake had flown out of Boise a week ago, going to Houston and the new contract that had waited for him at the private security company he'd worked for over the past year. It was for more money and more time out of the country. More time away from Truly, Idaho, and the big house where he'd lived a different life. A life that wasn't him. A life where his best friends were a five-year-old girl and her beautiful mother.

As much as he hated Beau for being right, Blake had to leave Truly before his leaving hurt Charlotte and Natalie.

The image of Natalie's face when he'd told her he was leaving was stuck in his memory like an ax to his skull. He'd hurt her. He'd never meant to do that. She and Charlotte were the last people on the planet he wanted to cause pain. He cared about them. Cared enough that the thought of their hurt feelings churned inside him and found the weaknesses in his detached heart and soul.

She loved him.

The memory of pain in Natalie's blue eyes filled him with guilt and the overwhelming urge to take her in his arms and save her from the pain. To fold her into his chest and make love to her, but that wasn't the right thing to do for her. He was a man who had plenty of faults, but he always tried to be the man who did the right thing, and the right thing was to stay out of her life.

For right now, he needed to push those memories and guilt feelings out of his head. It was imperative that he concentrate on the mission in front of him. The other three men were depending on him to do his job. To keep his focus on the mission. Years of training enabled him to easily force the memory of Natalie and Charlotte to the back of his mind and keep the front clear and focused.

The closer the Zodiac got to the coast of Africa, the bigger the swells grew. The rubber boat crested them, then slammed to the bottom. Blake's stomach rose and dropped, and moisture fogged his night vision goggles. Each country had its own unique scent and visceral memories. Somalia smelled of decades of rot and decay mixed with the sweet smell of tropical flowers. Surrounded by flowers and decay, the streets were filled with the sound of continuous AK rounds and gangs of boys loaded with RPGs.

A hundred meters out from the *Fatima*, Fast Eddy gave the signal to cut the engines, and the men donned masks and rebreathers. They attached their gear stowed in waterproof bags to a caving ladder. Each man grabbed his section of the ladder and slid into the Indian Ocean.

What I Love About You

Poor visibility made it difficult to see the gauges and dials on their dive watches as they swam at the same speed, twenty feet beneath the surface. Each knew how many kicks it took to swim one hundred yards, and they surfaced on the starboard side near the cargo bays.

Without making a sound, Farkus attached the ladder on the side of the ship, and they shed their scuba gear and hung it on each rung. They grabbed their weapons and ammo from the waterproof bags, then boarded the *Fatima*. Their faces were painted black like super stealth ninjas. They coordinated their dive watches, and Fast Eddy tapped his helmet twice. Each moved silently into position. Blake had done dozens of board, search, and seizure missions in his career, and this time he headed toward the ship's foremast and winch platform. With his MP5 submachine gun on his back and a 9mm on his hip, he climbed the platform. Without a sound, he knelt on the damp steel and snapped the custom-made tripod on the MP5. He lay on his stomach and dialed in the night scope. Within seconds, he calculated the range and velocity using the conversion chart in his head, then took into account the humidity, drop, and full wind value.

The pirates on the smaller boat below bobbed in and out of his sight, and he estimated there were three of them on the bow, and another two in the cabin. He took his eye from the scope and looked at his watch. In two minutes each operator would be in position. Fast Eddy would transmit a signal on his watch and the games would begin.

Thirty seconds into the two minutes, gunfire erupted in the cargo bay behind Blake. "Shit," Blake whispered, and put his eye to the scope and his finger on the trigger. Short bursts of AKs smashed against steel as the smaller boat bobbed out of his crosshairs. Beyond the bow, the white-capped waves shimmered and shifted, wavered for a split second, then within the green optics turned white with snow. The wind across his face took on the cold bite and unique scent of winter in the Hindu Kush. With his heart pounding in his ears, Blake took his eye from the scope and his finger from the trigger. His vision flickered between what was real and what was an illusion. He knew he was on the *Fatima* two miles off the Somali coast. Not the caverns and crags of the Afghani mountains. He could control this. It wasn't happening. The lives of three other men depended on him. He put his forehead on the cold steel platform beneath him and took deep breaths, trying to control his breathing and the vision that wasn't real. The harder he tried to control it, the more it would not be controlled. The more it couldn't be controlled, the more panic grabbed his gut. He let out a shaky breath and gave in to it, looking directly at the granite rock and snow peaks, and just as quickly as it came on, it wavered and flickered and melted away. He lifted his head and put his eye to his scope. His heartbeat pounded in his chest and thumped the hollow of his throat. Nausea rolled in his belly but he didn't have time to get sick. The smaller boat rose in his crosshairs but the pirates were no longer standing at the bow.

Shit. Damn. Mother-goddamn-fuckers. He swung the barrel to the left and caught sight of a pirate running toward a .50-caliber deck-mounted weapon. His body memory took over and he squeezed the trigger and put three rounds center mass. The man fell, and he turned the barrel to the other .50-caliber mounted on the foredeck. Bullets hit the deck around Blake in tight bursts, *whack-a whack-a whack-a*. Hot metal shards flew through the air as he put his crosshairs on a second man in a black and white keffiyeh. The smaller boat bobbed out of sight and rose again. The guy got off several rounds, but Blake was a better shot and took him out. He spotted three bad guys boarding the ship to his left. Bullets furrowed and dented the steel around him as he sent lead down his sights and took them out, too.

Within minutes it was over, and Blake took a deep breath of salty air and let it out. He rose to his knees and looked for the men on his team. He spotted them in the lighted cargo hold and wiped away a bead of sweat sliding down his temple. He'd been on missions that were textbook and missions that got ugly real fast. He'd seen his friends and fellow servicemen blown apart by roadside bombs and RPGs. He'd stood next to men who were practically cut in half by AK rounds, but he'd never been on a mission where he hadn't been able to do his job. None of the men he'd see die lost their lives because he couldn't pull the trigger.

"Are you okay, Junger?" Fast Eddy called up to him.

"I'm good." But he wasn't. His hands shook and sweat poured down his face and pooled on his chest. He needed a drink and he needed it bad. Nausea rolled in his gut and had a firm grip on his throat. The kind of nausea that had nothing to do with the pitch and roll of the ocean and everything to do with his addiction.

Why was he putting himself through this? Abstaining from alcohol was bullshit. Where had it gotten him? He had been better off before rehab. One shot of Johnnie Walker would cure his flashback and shakes and white-knuckling his way through life. It would cure guilt and his desire to find Natalie Cooper and bury his face in her neck.

Blake rose to his feet and joined his team. He learned that three members of the *Fatima* crew had been killed by the pirates and the other had made it to the panic room. Twenty minutes after the last of the *Fatima* crew was loaded into the medevac helicopter, and the U.S. Navy was ready to board and take over, Blake and the other contractors slipped back into the Indian Ocean.

He needed a drink, and as soon as he hit dry land, he was putting an end to his dry spell. He was going to kick back with a glass of Johnnie Walker over ice. Guaran-fucking-teed. He could practically hear the rattle of ice cubes and taste the first splash in his mouth.

He couldn't control his flashbacks. He couldn't control his cravings for alcohol. He couldn't control Natalie Cooper from crowding his head. Booze would take care of that. It would take care of it all. It would dull it all and make him feel back in control.

Blake and the other four operators landed at the Air Force base in Durban and hopped a flight out of Africa. He knew that once he started drinking he would not stop. He was looking forward to it, but there was something important he had to take care of in Houston, and he respected the men who employed him too much to walk in shit-faced. He alternately slept and white-knuckled his way through the next twenty-two hours until his flight landed in Houston. He caught a cab to the steel and glass skyscraper downtown. The Texas sun bounced off the blue glass and he rode the elevator to the twenty-first floor. He sat in a white chair across from James Crocker, the current president and CEO of Trident Security Worldwide. James Crocker was a former national security advisor and now head of the most powerful private military company in the world. Blake respected the man greatly, but it would have been easy to lie about why he needed to resign after he'd just signed a new contract. So much easier to lie than confess that he could not control his flashbacks and was a danger to the men around him.

James offered him a job at their training facility in North Carolina, but Blake declined. He didn't know what he wanted to do for a job now. He didn't know what he wanted to do with his life beyond heading home and drinking until he passed out. Then getting up and doing it all over again. He didn't want to drink in a bar. He didn't want to drive. He didn't want to see anyone. He just wanted to drink alone, George Thorogood–style.

From Houston, he flew to Denver, then Boise. It was just afternoon when he landed, and he hopped into his truck in long-term parking. A brilliant sun shone in the valley, but the closer he got to Truly, the colder and snowier it got.

He didn't care. He was going to start a big roaring fire and tip back a bottle. Before Beau had left town, he'd replaced Blake's three-hundred-dollar bottle of Johnnie Walker with a local Alcoholics Anonymous pamphlet. Like that would keep Blake from drinking. He'd never been to the liquor store in Truly, but he knew it was located on the corner of Third and Pine, just down the street from Hennessey's Saloon.

Almost home, his addiction whispered in his ear as he passed the "Welcome to Truly" sign. It was two in the afternoon. Plenty of time to buy a few bottles and maybe a couple of cases of beer.

I'll make you feel good, his addiction whispered in case he hadn't heard it the first time. *No one will know.* He pulled the truck to a stop at the only traffic light. He was tired. Tired of trying to control his life that had spun out of control. Sitting there at the red light, he thought of Natalie and her face when she smiled at him. The sunshine in her hair and the deep, beautiful blue of her eyes. He remembered the touch of her hands and mouth and breath against his neck.

Like his addiction, she was a constant craving,

and he reminded himself that he got out of her life because it was the right thing to do. He got out because leaving sooner would cause her and Charlotte less pain than leaving later. He got out because she loved him. She loved him, but she deserved a man who could love her in return. Beau was right, loving one woman felt like a weakness. Weakness was not an option.

A horn honked behind him and he looked up at the green light. He took a right on Pine and pulled to a stop in front of the liquor store advertising the Christmas specials in the window. He wasn't interested in peppermint vodka or rum eggnog. He got out of the truck and zipped his coat against the howling wind. He stood on the curb and looked through the plate glass windows at the rows of booze. Walls lined with clear and amber bottles, each row more tempting than the last. Tubes of neon advertised different brands of alcohol, and on the door hung a green sign advertising the Winter Festival.

He took a step forward and stopped. His heart pounded *boom-boom-boom* in his chest, and sweat broke out across his skin.

Take me. Grab me. Don't be weak.

Blake's hands shook, and he ducked his head and turned to the right. He moved down the sidewalk away from the liquor store and past Annie's Attic antiques. He kept walking, past Hennessey's Saloon and Helen's Hair Hut. His addiction alternately promised salvation and called him a weak pussy. A thousand times he fought the powerful urge to turn around, retrace his steps, and go grab his lover and friend. With his fists shoved in his pockets, he walked along the side of Grace Episcopal and moved down the steps to the basement. He paused with his palm on the handle. *I'm not your enemy. I'm not your weakness. I'm the only thing you've ever loved.*

His addiction was a skilled liar. He'd told himself that he'd left Natalie because it was the right thing to do. His leaving would cause her and Charlotte less pain than his staying. But that wasn't true. He'd left because he'd lost control. Loss of control was a weakness. He was a Junger. A man. He kicked ass and took names. He was the whirlwind, and he'd lost control of his feelings over a woman.

He pulled open the old wood door and stepped inside the stone building. To his left,

What I Love About You

Mabel Vaughn stood at a podium. She hit the wooden stand with a gavel and Blake slid along the wall to the back of the room. He found a seat and sank down in it as everyone around him said the serenity prayer. Designated people read from the big book, and everything in him, every fiber in his body, told him to leave. Just pick his ass up and get the hell out. He didn't need this. He could control his life. This was weakness.

"Do we have any new members today?" Mabel asked.

Blake looked up at Mabel's eyes staring right back at him. He'd faced bands of Taliban. Towns filled with terrorists. At the moment, he'd rather face an army of Islamic jihadists than stand.

He glanced around to see if anyone else was jumping to his feet. It wasn't a rule. He didn't have to stand up. It would be easy just to sit there and listen to other people, but if he wanted his life, he had to do the hard thing. The right thing. He had to admit that he was powerless. He was powerless over alcohol and flashbacks. He was powerless over loving Natalie Cooper. She was his weakness. There was no other option.

He stood. "My name is Blake Junger and I'm an alcoholic."

"I saw your boyfriend at AA."

Natalie looked from the top of her Christmas tree to Michael's legs and black hiking boot sticking out from beneath the bottom. *Her boyfriend?* "Who?"

"The Navy SEAL," he answered as he screwed the tree stand into the trunk.

"Blake?" Her heart fell to her stomach like a lump of lead. Blake was back in town?

"Yeah." Michael backed out and rose to his knees. "Didn't you know he's an alcoholic?"

"Yes. I know." She hadn't told Michael that he wasn't her boyfriend though. It was easier if he didn't know.

"You sounded surprised."

"No." She'd let Michael carry her tree in the house because that was easier, too. "I just thought the second A in AA stood for anonymous."

Michael stood and shrugged. "If you already know he goes to meetings, it's not a big deal."

If Blake was back, it was a big deal. If he was going to AA meetings, it was a very big deal. A part of the lead lump of her heart worried about him. Had something bad happened? Another part of her lead heart that wasn't totally hurt and angry swelled a little bit at the thought of him next door. That same small part wanted to desperately ask Michael when he'd seen Blake at AA. Today? Yesterday? It had been a week since he'd left town. When had he returned? Not that it mattered. Not after she'd dressed up for him in her stupid cheerleading outfit and he'd told her it wasn't working out for him and he'd never return her feelings. He'd just wanted to be *honest*. Well, good for him. Honestly, he was raging asshole.

"What are you and Charlotte doing tomorrow?"

"I'm closing the shop and we're going to the festival." The first Saturday of December always kicked off the Truly Winter Festival.

"We should all go together." He brushed a few pine needles from his jeans. "Unless you're going with your boyfriend."

Charlotte walked into the living room with an ornament she'd made out of construction paper and glitter. "Ooh. I love the tree!" She held the glitter snowflake toward Michael. "I made this for you." Before he could take it from her, Sparky tried to rip it from her hand. "No, Spa-ky." She held it up over her head. "This is for my dad. Not you."

"Thanks, Charlotte." He took it from her hand as if it was delicate.

"Where are all the ornaments, Mama? I want to get out the angel."

Natalie had drawers full of Charlotte's drawing and art projects. This was Michael's first, and despite her personal feelings, she felt bad for him. "I carried the boxes as far as the kitchen." Each year she stored them in the attic, and the kitchen was as far as she'd gotten so far this year.

"Can I go look for it?"

"If you're careful. I think it's in a blue tote."

Charlotte clapped her hands in excitement and ran down the hall. Sparky charging after her. At least one of them was excited about Christmas this year.

"Is that a yes or are you going to the carnival with Blake?"

She returned her gaze to her former husband. "I haven't talked to Blake about it yet." Which was the truth.

"Then come with me. We'll have fun. Like old times."

She sat on her couch and shook her head. "Not like old times. We're not kids and we're not married."

"I know." He sat next to her and placed the snowflake on the table. "But we have a kid and I'd rather go with the two of you than my mom and dad." He looked across his shoulder at her. "My mom is driving me nuts."

Natalie almost laughed. "Is she ironing your jeans again?"

"She's trying." He glanced about her living room before he returned his gaze to hers. "I gotta get a job and get out of there. I applied at a couple of places, so hopefully I'll get hired soon." He glanced back at the snowflake. "Then Charlotte can come over and hang her drawings on my own refrigerator."

"That's not going to happen, Blake." The thought made her heart a bit panicky. What if he took off with Charlotte?

"We have to work something out, Nat. I know you don't love me anymore, but I want us to have a good relationship."

"A good relationship?" It was a little soon for that. He'd been out of prison only two weeks. "I don't trust you, Michael. I don't trust that you aren't going to get bored and take off again. This time, I'm not the one you'll hurt. You'll hurt Charlotte."

"I told you I'm not going anywhere."

"I know that's what you say, but I don't believe you. I believed you once before and I paid a big price."

He stood and walked to the mantel, picking up the same photo of Charlotte that Blake had held just a few short weeks ago. "I'm not the person I was before," he said, and put the photo back. "I'm not that Michael. That Michael wasn't content with life. I'm a different man now." He turned and looked at her. "Growing up in Truly, I was a star. I loved the way people treated me. The way they treated us. Do you remember?"

"Yes."

"I was a big man around here, and when we moved to Boise, I missed it, as pathetic as that sounds." He laughed without humor. "For a while, the poor college student life was kind of cool, but by the time I graduated, I was tired of feeling like a nobody. When I was hired at Langtree Capital, I had to start out on the third string. I'd never been third string in my life and I hated that." He paused for several heartbeats as if reliving a painful memory. "I wanted to be a star again, Nat. I wanted it so bad. I worked hard but things weren't happening fast enough for me. I decided to accelerate the timeline. I decided to go out and drink with clients and brokers and other investors. I started to feel like a big man again. The bigger I felt, the more I wanted to get even bigger. The more I thought I deserved. Drugs made it all okay. That's how it started." He swallowed and cleared his throat. "We know where it ended."

Yes. She knew about Michael's drive to be the best. She hadn't known about the drugs though. She should have known. Looking back, it made sense.

"A felon and a drug addict who lost everything." He gave her a tired smile. "Charlotte is the only good thing to come out of that time. I'm glad I got caught. I thank God I didn't get away. Now I have a chance to be a father. There was a time in my life when I wanted it as much as you did."

He looked so much like the man she used to know that she believed him. Or rather, she believed that he believed it right now.

"I want for us to be friends, because I want to be in her life as much as possible. I want to be at Christmas programs and birthday parties. I want stick figure drawings with *me* in them. I want glitter snowflakes." He lifted a hand and dropped it to his side "Do you think we can be friends?"

"Yes," she said, because if they could really be friends, it was best for Charlotte.

He smiled. That charming Michael Cooper smile that used to make her brain all fuzzy. "Does that mean you're ready to forgive me?"

Her brain remained real clear. "Don't push it."

Chapter Sixteen

The town of Truly kicked off the Christmas season with the annual Winter Festival. It started with the parade down Main, and anyone with a business, social club, or enough money to pay an entry fee could participate in the parade. Booze was strictly forbidden and had been since 1990 when Marty Wheeler took a tumble out of Santa's sleigh and cracked his head on the street. And while that had been shocking enough, the pink corset he wore beneath his Santa suit had caused quite the scandal and the alcohol ban. Not that anyone paid attention to it.

Natalie and Charlotte stood in the crowd as three police cars and McGruff the Crime Dog made their way down Main. The two of them were bundled up for the chilly weather and had feet warmers in the soles of their snow boots. Last year, Natalie had participated in the parade by decorating her Subaru with funny photos and streamers while Charlotte waved out the window. It had been a lot of work and she just wanted to relax and enjoy the festival this year.

Michael and his parents were somewhere in the crowd and she was supposed to call to meet up with them. She'd accidentally left her phone charging in her car and had to scan the crowd looking for them, but it wasn't Michael's dark hair that Natalie searched for as she surreptitiously glanced about the packed street. If Blake was back in town, it was best if she saw him first. Forewarned was forearmed; at least that's what she told herself. She thought she spotted the back of his head on the corner of Main, and again across from Mort's, and once more by Bernard's Deli, but each time he turned, it wasn't him. Each time, for one brief moment, her heart slammed against her ribs. And each time she felt stupid that just the sight of blond hair in a crowd could make her heart react. A goofy, small-town parade probably wasn't the sort of thing to attract a man like him anyway.

After the parade, she and Charlotte bought hot cocoa and wandered to Larkspur Park to see the town's ice sculptures. They passed Paul's Market's sculpture of a big fish in a Santa hat. Frankie stood by its glassy tail, all bundled up and giving out Christmas ham coupons. The fire department had sculpted a full-size replica of a fire truck, and the members of Buy Idaho had made an attempt at an icy sleigh filled with potatoes. But the sleigh was too small and the potatoes too big, and if not for the sign, Natalie wouldn't have known the big lumps were Idaho's most famous veggie.

The park was packed with locals and tourists, and she hadn't been able to spot Michael or the Coopers. Nor had she spotted a certain blond head in the crowd, and she started to think that Michael had been wrong about Blake being back in town.

The most spectacular sculpture every year belonged to Allegrezza Construction. This year they had made a gingerbread house big enough to walk through, complete with a big table and eight chairs. Nick Allegrezza and his wife, Delaney, stood at the entrance, chatting with friends. Nick stood behind his wife, his arms looped around her waist as she leaned back into his chest. He whispered something in her ear, and she dipped her head and smiled as if they shared a private, intimate secret. A tiny stab of envy settled next to Natalie's heart. She wanted that. She wanted a man to whisper something in her ear that only the two of them shared. Something that came from years of knowing and loving one person. She'd been a neighbor of the Allegrezzas for years. She'd always noticed the way they looked at and touched each other, but she'd never felt one way or another about it.

She blamed Blake. Until he'd smashed into her life like a wrecking ball, she hadn't thought about feeling the comfort of a man's arms around her. Until Blake, she'd forgotten.

Charlotte laughed, and Natalie glanced at her daughter, then at the six Allegrezza children dressed as elves and giving out candy canes. The five dark-haired girls smiled and giggled while their lone brother scowled from beneath his elf hat. She guessed him to be about three, and her laughter joined Charlotte's as he stuck his tongue out at the Olson triplets. She thought she should say hello to Shanna and Nick and Delaney, but a hand on her arm stopped her.

"Natalie." Her back stiffened. She knew that voice. Knew the sound when he whispered her name. She turned and came face to thick throat with the man who'd crushed her heart and made her look at happy couples with envy.

"Blake!" Charlotte said, and wrapped her arms around his waist, giving Natalie a few precious seconds to paste a fake smile on her lips. "I missed you, Blake."

His eyes looked into her, open and unguarded, so unlike the last time she'd seen him, and for one split second she thought that might mean something, but this was Blake. The man who'd pursued her until they'd slept together. Then he'd dumped her flat.

His gaze lingered a second longer before he got down on one knee and Charlotte wrapped her arms around his neck. "I missed you, too."

Liar. He'd planned on leaving town for good and without even saying good-bye. She'd planned to wait until Charlotte noticed that he was no longer around before she'd tell her he was moving, but he'd only been gone a week. Natalie looked down at his familiar blond hair and wide shoulders in his familiar brown coat. She knew how his hair felt between her fingers, and she curled her hands inside her mittens. She turned her face away before she did something she'd regret. Like fall on top of him like a hungry monkey or kick him in the leg like she was on the playground.

"Guess what, Blake?"

"What?"

"Mom showed me twins like you and your brother on the Internet. I don't think you're a robot now."

His deep laughter bubbled up from him and felt like it settled in her stomach.

"Guess what else?"

"Your mom found you a unicorn."

"No! I got a Christmas tree."

"Is it big?"

"Yeah. Weally big. You can come see it."

Natalie glanced back down at the top of his head and Charlotte's hat. "I'm positive Mr. Junger has better things to do than see our Christmas tree."

He looked up at her, and once more his familiar gray eyes locked with hers as he stood. "There is nothing Mr. Junger would rather do than see Charlotte's Christmas tree."

Two steps. Two little steps and she could press her face into the side of his neck and breathe him in. Breathe the scent of his skin deep into her lungs and hold it there forever.

"I need to talk to you," he said.

"There is nothing left to say." And what good would come of breathing him deep in her lungs? He didn't love her. He was never going to love her. He'd made that clear. So clear, she was still bleeding inside from the jagged edges of her broken heart.

"You're wrong, Sweet Cheeks. There's a lot to say."

The backs of her eyes stung. Right there in Larkspur Park. Surrounded by people looking at the gingerbread house sculpture. She didn't want to cry. Not here. Not now. Not in front of the town. Not in front of him. He'd hurt her enough. She would not cry in public over him. "Let me put it a different way," she said, letting her anger take over because it was better than falling apart in the middle of the Winter Festival. "You don't have anything to say that I want to hear."

"I can appreciate that you are pissed off at me, but we're going to talk. Right here, right now, or later at your house. You choose."

It was just so typical of him that he thought he could order her around. So typical that he made his orders sound like a choice. She covered Charlotte's ear in preparation to call him a really bad name when Michael's parents found her. She'd never been so glad to see Carla and Ron in her life. She introduced them to Blake because not introducing them would have been even more awkward.

"Michael's waiting for us at the snowmobile jumps," Carla said. "Do you all want to go together?"

She'd included Blake. As if they were a couple. "Charlotte and I will go with you," she answered. "Blake was just leaving."

His gaze zeroed in on her as if he was sighting in one of his scopes. Letting her know the conversation wasn't over. He was wrong, though. He couldn't just come back into her life and boss her around. As she walked away, she hardened her heart by replaying in her mind the night she'd dressed up in her old uniform and had been prepared to give him a B and a J followed by a split jump on his lap.

She told herself not to look back, but of course she did. He stood where she'd left him, only now he was surrounded by several women she didn't recognize.

Jerk.

After the park, she and Charlotte went home instead of the snowmobile jumping ramps. She was cold and Charlotte wanted to finish decorating the Christmas tree. As she'd pulled her car into her driveway, she might have glanced next door a little longer than necessary to see if Blake's red truck sat in his drive. It wasn't there and she felt silly.

She and Charlotte shucked their coats and boots and got busy with the tree. Charlotte hung the low ornaments, Natalie hung the others. She dragged the ladder next to the tree and put the angel on top. With each sound she heard, each brush of a tree against her house, her pulse jumped. Blake said he was coming over tonight, whether she wanted him to come over or not.

After dinner, she and Charlotte sat at the kitchen table to make snowflakes to hang on the mantel. It had been six hours since she'd looked into Blake's gray eyes, and she was jumpy and feeling neurotic. A part of her hoped he didn't show up, while another part longed to see his face. One part of her hoped he'd hurry and move away, while another part felt sick at the idea. She was just so confused by today. Confused and angry that he thought he could show up and she'd just naturally want to talk to him.

She didn't want to see him at all. The pain of loving him was still raw and real and hadn't begun to heal yet. Seeing him today proved it was going to take time and distance.

"Mom, do we eat meat?" Charlotte asked as she glued some silver glitter on a paper snowflake.

"Yes." Natalie cut out the intricate patterns and almost stuck the scissors through her hand when she heard a car door shut down the street.

"Is meat from animals?"

"Yes." She carefully poked a hole in the top and threaded a piece of yarn through it. "The hot dogs you love are made from pork."

"What's pork?"

"Pork is a pig." She stuck the end of yarn in her mouth to wet it.

"We eat a pig?" Charlotte gasped.

"Yes." Natalie twisted the frayed end and poked it through the paper.

"I don't want to eat a pig. I don't want to eat animals. Animals are nice."

Natalie put down the snowflake. If she'd been paying more attention, if she hadn't been distracted by thoughts of Blake, she would have answered more delicately.

Charlotte's eyes got a little teary with real sorrow. "Animals are my friends, Mama."

Natalie didn't want to change her child's diet, but she didn't want Charlotte to think she was eating her "friends," either. "We only eat the mean animals." Charlotte frowned and brushed at her eyes. Natalie saw the wheels turning in her child's brain and she headed off further "tears." "Mean and old animals. Really old." Yes, it was perhaps a bit of lie, but if it made Charlotte feel better about eating her animal friends, then Natalie was okay with it. Especially tonight when her nerves were fraying faster than the yarn she held in her fingers.

"Like Grandma?"

"Older."

"Oh." Charlotte nodded and squirted a glob of glue.

The doorbell rang and Natalie dropped the end of the yarn. She slid out of her chair. "I'll be right back. Keep the glue on the newspaper." Her heart pounded in her ears as she moved to the front of the house. She looked through the peephole even though she expected Blake, and even though she expected him, her heart still slammed into her ribs. Blake's cheeks were red from the cold and his eyes stared back at her. He smiled, all charming and handsome, and rage bubbled in her blood just as hot as the night he'd left. He rang the bell again and she yanked the door open.

"Hi, Natalie. Do you have a minute?"

"Not for you." She slammed the door in his face and told herself not to look through the peephole. Of course she didn't listen and rose to the balls of her feet and peeked out at him. Peeked at him still standing there staring at the closed door with that bewildered look on his face she recognized. She expected an angry frown to chase away the straight line of his lips. Instead he smiled and waved good-bye.

The next night he rang her doorbell again and asked if he could have Sparky.

Natalie folded her arms over her chest as if that could protect her heart. *Now* he remembered he had half a dog? He'd abandoned Sparky. And unlike Charlotte, she didn't think it was in Sparky's best interest to see his "father." She was the one who fed the dog and took him for walks and had taken him to the vet to get neutered. Blake couldn't just come and go in the dog's life.

"He isn't your dog anymore."

"He's half my dog."

"You can't just come and go and see him when you please. You can't confuse him that way."

"He's a dog, Natalie." He rocked back on the heels of his boots. "He doesn't get confused."

He was right. Sparky was too dumb to be confused over anything. "He got his balls whacked. You should try it," she said, and once again shut the door in his face. This time he did frown and must have forgotten to wave when he walked away.

For the next few days, she half expected him to show up at work and cause a new round of gossip like the last time he'd entered her business. She was glad he'd given up trying to talk to her. It was for the best. He was an emotionally stunted jerk with commitment issues, and the only reason she knew he was still in town was that when she came home from work Wednesday, he and Charlotte and Tilda were building a snowman in her front yard. She pulled into the garage and shut the door behind her car. The nice thing to do would be to make cocoa and take it to the three of them. Instead she watched from behind her bedroom curtains as Blake lifted two big balls of snow and stacked them one on top of the other. Then he picked up some snow and lightly packing it in his gloved hands. He dumped it on Charlotte's head and the fight was on.

Natalie felt a tear slide down her cheek and she turned away. Watching him with Charlotte was like poking an open wound. She refused to watch, but she could hear Charlotte's happy screams mixed with Blake's deep laughter, filtering through the house.

She didn't see or hear anything from him Thursday, but Friday afternoon he sent in an order of photos for her to print.

There were just two, and Natalie stared down at them sitting on the front counter of Glamour Snaps and Prints as Brandy placed other orders in photo envelopes. The first of Blake's pictures was a ransom note that read:

This is not a joke. Your dog Sparky is being held at 315 Red Fox Road. Bring one pork chop in an unmarked bag to the above address to secure his release.

The kidnapper

The second was of poor Sparky. His legs tied together with white rope and a red bandana tied around his eyes.

"Ridiculous." She frowned so she wouldn't laugh. She glanced at the clock. It was three hours before closing and she debated with herself for ten minutes—okay, maybe five—before she handed the keys to Brandy. She was fairly sure she'd be back before closing, but just in case, she trusted her employee with the responsibility. She drove to Paul's Market to buy the ransom, then headed toward home.

Her nerves were shaky and jumpy and she folded her arms across her chest as she walked up the steps to his porch. The same porch where she'd once demanded that he take his dog back. The same porch where she'd fainted and he'd carried her inside.

She rang the bell and waited. When he didn't appear fast enough, she rang again.

His big blur appeared a moment before the door swung open. He had a satisfied grin on his face when he said, "Hello, Ms. Cooper." He was so big and so handsome and her heart ached so much, she wanted to punch him even as she wanted to throw herself against his chest.

"Where's Sparky?"

"Did you bring the pork chop?"

She handed over the grocery bag with a dog bone inside. "A pork chop will give him the runs."

Blake opened the door wider and she walked in. She followed him through the entry, her gaze taking in his brown T-shirt and his wide shoulders and back. She didn't want to look at his butt, but she did.

She followed him into the living room, where Sparky lay in front of the fireplace on a cozy dog bed. The mutt was no long tied up or blindfolded and barely lifted his head to look at her before he went back to sleep.

Traitor. "He looks scared."

"Can I take your coat?"

"I won't be staying that long." Sparky was a

traitor. Her heart was a traitor. The little flutter in her stomach was a traitor.

Blake simply looked at her and held out his hand.

"Fine." She slipped her arms out of the sleeves and handed it to him. He took it and tossed it toward the sofa. It totally missed and fell on the floor. She moved to pick it up but his hands on her arm stopped her. "Blake, what do you think you're doing?" She looked at his hands and then up into his face. "You can't just—" she got out before he wrapped his arms around her waist and hauled her against his chest, squeezing her until she couldn't breathe. "Stop," she gasped. "I can't breathe."

"You can breathe later. Just let me hold you for a minute," he said, and buried his face in her neck. "I missed you."

She'd missed him. So much it tore at her heart. So much it stung the backs of her eyes. "This isn't fair."

"Fuck fair," he said against the side of her throat. "You slammed your door in my face."

"You smiled about it."

"I knew you were watching." He chuckled, and his breath tickled her skin just below her ear.

"And I knew if you didn't feel anything for me you wouldn't be so damn mean."

"Mean!" She pushed him away, and his arms fell to his sides. "I'm not the mean one."

"You let me freeze my nuts off waiting for you to come outside Wednesday." He shook his head. "You're brutal, Ms. Cooper."

"Me?" She pointed at herself and took a step back. "I told you I love you and you couldn't get away from me fast enough!" Her bottom lip threatened to quiver and she took a deep breath. "I dressed up in my stupid cheerleading uniform with nothing on underneath. While you said I confused sex for love, I was commando!"

"Wait." He held up one hand like a traffic cop. "You were naked beneath that skirt?"

She ignored his question. "You said you would never love me."

He reached for her but she took another step back. "I didn't say I would never love you."

"Maybe not those words, but you said you couldn't return my feelings." She swallowed hard. "I think that was your way of *trying* to let me down gently."

He shook his head. "No, Sweet Cheeks. That was me lying. That was me trying to do the right thing."

"You were running away." She folded her arms across her heart.

"I'm not running now. I'm standing here." He pointed to the floor beneath his feet. "I'm standing here, a man in love with a woman. A woman I want to spend the rest of my life loving."

Her hands fell to her sides.

"And believe me, I never thought I would be this man. I never thought I'd be strong enough to embrace my weakness for one woman." He cleared his throat and swallowed. "A wise man once told me, 'Shit or get off the pot.'"

"Gross."

He laughed and closed the distance she'd placed between them. "So that's what I'm doing. I love you, Natalie. I love Charlotte and Sparky and I want to be worthy of you and Charlotte. I've been going to AA meetings. I gave up and gave in and gave it to a higher power." Smile lines creased the corners of his eyes. "Mabel Vaughn wants to be my sponsor." He took her hand, and his smile disappeared. "I love you and I'm kind of hoping you still love me."

She nodded as his touch and the emotion in his eyes soothed the cracks in her broken heart. "I do love you, Blake. I tried not to love you, but I just couldn't help myself." She wrapped her arms around his neck. "I'm still a little mad at you, though. You really broke my heart."

"I'm a handy man to have around if you need anything fixed. Like broken doors, wiring, and especially broken hearts." He put his hand on her waist and pressed his forehead to hers. "I love you, Natalie. I love everything about you." He kissed her lips, soft and sweet and filled with the same longing that filled her heart. "I love when you look at me like you are right now," he said. "I love that you make me want to look at a future and not my past." His soft, smoky eyes looked into hers. "You're my here and now and my future. You're my life and my love and my woman."

She grinned. "I'm your whirlwind."

"Yes, and I get to reap you forever." His smile matched hers. "That's what I love about you."

Don't miss the new
wedding novella from
New York Times bestselling author
RACHEL GIBSON

I DO!

Available October 14
from Avon Impulse

Read on for an excerpt!

At the age of twenty-three, Rebecca Ramsey found her artistic passion. While some artists worked in oil or fabrics or clay, Becca worked in hair. Since graduating from the Milan Institute of Cosmetology, she'd worked diligently at perfecting her art. Becca was good at cuts and blowouts, fabulous with highlights, ombres, peekaboos, and dip-dyes, but when it came to the up-do, she was a true master. She exceled at creating everything from simple French knots to complicated runway hair, complete with twigs and birds and working fountains.

Of course, there wasn't a lot of demand for runway hair in Lovett, Texas, the small town where she lived. Or even sixty miles south in Amarillo, where she worked at Lily Belle's Salon and Day Spa. But this *was* Texas, where special-occasion hair was in high demand. Proms, graduations, and her favorite, bridal hair.

Becca pulled her Volkswagen Beetle out of her apartment complex and headed across town to pick up the latest photographs of her work before driving to meet with her client, Sadie Hollowell.

I Do!

Sadie was more than Becca's latest bride client. She was engaged to Becca's good friend, Vince Haven, and had become Becca's friend, too. So much so, that Sadie had not only hired Becca to do her wedding hair, she'd included Becca in some of the planning. She'd sought her advice on flowers, the arbor, and the maid of honor dress. Vince had been no help at all. His favorite colors were brown and dark brown and talk of flowers made him fold his arms over his big chest and scowl. Sadie's sister Stella wasn't much help either. Stella was busy with school and her own fiancé, and frankly, Stella wasn't a Texan. Like Vince, she didn't understand that a simple wedding was never simple, and Stella's taste ran more toward leather and combat boots than lace and satin pumps.

Bless her heart.

Becca had offered her help with the wedding, and Sadie had jumped on the invitation. It was a good thing, too, because even though Becca would never say it out loud, Sadie wasn't very good at special-occasion planning, and neither was the event planner she'd hired. Which was ironic, given that Vince's sister, Autumn, was a wedding planner. Too bad Autumn lived in Seattle.

Becca pulled her car into Parrish American Classics and parked in the empty lot. Several weeks ago, local photographer Daisy Parrish had taken promotional photos at the day spa where Becca worked, and she'd hired Daisy to take extra up-do photographs for her portfolio. There were several she thought Sadie would like, and she wanted to pick them up before heading out to the JH.

It was Saturday and Parrish American Classics was closed, but Daisy had offered to leave the photographs at her husband's auto restoration shop rather than have Becca drive to Daisy's home ten miles in the opposite direction.

The afternoon sun glinted off the gold frames of Becca's sunglasses as she got out of the car. Sadie had just received the final RSVP for her wedding, and the guest list had risen to seventy-five. Most of those guests were Sadie's family, but several were Vince's military buddies. Big guys with big arms and egos, and Becca had briefly met two of those big guys last summer, twin brothers Blake and Beau Junger. The brothers were so identical it was freaky, but evidently not all women were freaked out by the big, muscular twins with cold gray eyes. Both men were engaged, and Beau's fiancé had had to have her maid of honor dress let out due to her pregnant belly.

The front doors of the restoration business were locked, and Becca followed the sound of heavy metal music around the side of the building. The heels of her wedge sandals tapped across the concrete. She'd paid seventy bucks for the crochet-straps in scarlet tango. A big splurge for a girl on a tight budget, but she just hadn't been able to resist.

Her last boyfriend liked to say that women who wore red didn't wear panties, but Toby Ray had said a lot of things like they were facts instead of something he'd made up in his own dumb head. No one had ever confused Toby Ray with a deep thinker, but then again, no girl dated that boy for this mind.

Bless his heart.

Becca's shadow followed her as she rounded the building and a warm May breeze ruffled the bottom of her white and red sundress. The slight wind tossed a few strands of her medium-blond hair, brightened with perfectly placed level-nine highlights. The heavy beat of music and screeching vocals assaulted her ears, and behind the lenses of her sunglasses, her gaze landed on a faded orange truck parked at an angle behind the garage. It had a blue door and fender and the hood was up, the Chevy emblem pointed toward the sky. A Beats speaker and iPod rested on the ground by the left front tire, and a pair of legs stuck out from beneath the old truck. Presumably the legs belonged to a man who wore faded jeans and gray Vans on his feet.

Skater shoes? In Lovett, Texas, where men wore Justin boots? She continued past the patch-work truck and the skater shoes toward the two-story house several hundred feet behind the garage. She knocked on the front door several times, and when no one answered, she retraced her steps to the truck.

"Hello?" she called out over the horrible music.

Instead of an answer, the man beneath the truck sang along with the screeching. His deep voice was even worse than the lead singer/ screecher, which Becca would have thought impossible. She bent down, unplugged the iPod, and yelled, "Hello!"

A painful thud was followed by a loud "shit" and the sound of tools hitting concrete. "God-dammit," then squeaky little wheels rolled the rest of him from beneath the engine. Long legs led to a spiky belt and white t-shirt over a flat belly. A blue work shirt fell open across the t-shirt and two greasy hands grabbed the old bumper. Wide shoulders appeared just before his chin and strong jaw, covered in dark stubble.

Becca stared down into blue eyes the color of the Texas sky. Angry blue eyes beneath dark slashes of brows surrounded by dark lashes. An even angrier red mark on his forehead seemed to turn even redder by the second.

Despite the scowl and welt and spiky belt, he was quite possibly the hottest guy she'd seen in a very long time. "Hello," she managed past her suddenly dry throat. He was the kind of guy who looked good in tight t-shirts and jeans. Good-looking, like the kind of guy she usually fell for and handed her heart. Hot guys with names like Tucker or Slade or Toby Ray. Guys who cheated and lied and were nothing but a heartbreak waiting to happen.